'JOY is what happens to us when we allow ourselves to recognize how good things really are.'

UPON ENTERING MAJOR CITY, one is greeted by a large, weathered sign that reads: *Welcome to Major City*. Beneath, spray-painted in black letters, are the words, GOOD LUCK!

The rising sun over the city announces the beginning of a new day. Eyes pop open to the sound of dogs barking, police sirens and the smell of garbage trucks.

People slow-drag themselves off the morning train, beat from working the graveyard shift at jobs they detest. Walking down creaking flights of stairs, they pass familiar faces, equally exhausted, that will replace them on the day shift.

Both groups are greeted by crackheads who are willing to sing, dance, and straight up beg for a quarter, nickel, dime, or penny to support their daily habit.

On the corner of Struggle Street, forty-something-year-old men drink 40s of malt liquor for breakfast, whistle at the women walking by, and reminisce about the good ol' days when they were Macks.

In a filthy, roach-infested apartment, a single mother who was voted, Most Likely to Succeed, prepares for a day of prostitution down by the docks with a pint of vodka.

Under a dark project stairwell, a drug dealer enlists another junkie into his army of zombies.

Meanwhile, members of rival gang's stagger in from a night of *havoc* and *mayhem* so that they can be well rested for another night of sin.

Like the sign says, GOOD LUCK!

Chapter 1

THE RISING SUN PEEPED THROUGH THE SKYLIGHT as the nude black man tore the sheets from the mattress right in the middle of an orgasm, with the beautiful black woman who was riding him like a stallion. Their sweaty bodies were intertwined like climbing vines as they simultaneously moaned with ecstasy. Then, out of breath and energy, he rolled onto his side grinning at her with a wide Kool-Aid smile.

"Damn, baby-shit! That was so good, I feel like having a cigarette. And a brotha' don't even smoke, you know what I'm sayin'? Can I be Frank?"

"You can be whomever you want to be. But I would think under the circumstances, you'd chose John." She replied rolling her eyes, like she didn't really want to hear what he had to say.

"Normally I don't do stuff like this. It's just that, when I saw you sitting at the bar looking so damn fine, something came over me, and I just had to have you," he explained, like a scared schoolboy revealing his first crush.

She smirked. "Um, sweetie what's your name again?"

"It's Bryann." He replied.

"Well, Bryann if I had a dime for every time some trick told me that I was the first piece of ass he picked up at a bar, I could retire and do this strictly for pleasure—not profit—know what I'm sayin'?"

From the embarrassed look on his face, Bryann had momentarily forgotten there was a fee for his pleasure. Realizing his flattery was getting him nowhere he scanned the room, nervously scratching his head. "What's your name again, Miss um?

"It's Rita. And for the record, I never told you."

"Miss Rita, I'm not altogether sure about the payment procedure. Do you take cash, check or credit cards?" he asked meekly.

"Credit cards?" Rita repeated, with her faced all screwed up like she bit into something that tasted way past the expiration date. "Now what chu' think you gonna do, slide your Visa card between my cheeks? And my ass'll wind up on the back of a milk carton if I go back to Violent Vaughn with some damn bouncing check!"

"Violent Vaughn?"

"My pimp! And he's big and got scars and he's—"

"Violent, I got it! Your pimp is a very scary man. So how much do I owe you?" Bryann asked, reaching for the balled-up pants on the floor.

"Well, judging by the goofy look on your face I'd say you were one hundred and one percent completely satisfied. So, how's about an even thou and that's including tip?" she said, as if she were in a generous mood and used to receiving far more for her services.

Bryann choked. "Forgive me, but I've been playing my iPod way too loud, and I think it's finally affected my hearing. Did you say a 'thou'—as in one thousand dollars?"

"Umm-hmm," she answered, sucking her teeth.

"American?" he double-checked, looking at her like she was insane.

"No fool, pesos! Of course American! What's the problem? Hold up! A minute ago, you were ready to take up smoking because my stuff was so good. What, were you lying?" She leaned forward, daring him to say yes.

"No-no-no! Of course not!" Bryann's head shook against his will. In his haste to peel off her painted-on dress and get to the treat underneath, it never occurred to him that it might cost more than he could afford.

"Exactly as I thought," Rita said, with a stylishly manicured hand extended for payment.

Beads of sweat began to form at Bryann's hairline from worry. He had no idea how he was going to come up with that kind of money when he had less than a hundred in his wallet, and even less than that in the bank. He could say that he didn't have that much on him and had to run to the ATM, then keep on running. But Rita didn't strike him as the gullible type. And what if Violent Vaughn was waiting outside? GULP!

Bryann slowly turned to Rita to explain he was broke as a joke. Nervous he'd have to deal with the consequences for thinking with the head in his pants instead of the one on his shoulders. But when he opened his mouth, all that came out was gobbledygook. The panic-stricken black man suddenly turned three shades lighter.

Rita's eyes tightened into angry slits and she hissed. "Vaughn! Get in here! Dis fool ain't trying to pay!" She shouted at the door.

Bryann turned to the door with fear in his eyes. He was already picturing what his tombstone would read, 'Here lies Horny & Stupid!' A moment passed and nothing happened. "Hmm, so I guess he's not so violent after all." He said smugly. Then unable to hold her scowl any longer, an infectious grin formed at the corner of Rita's lips stretching across her face. Bryann, also unable to continue the charade snorted and the attractive pair burst into laughter at their role-playing. After being together for so long they welcomed different methods of play in the bedroom to keep their sex life fresh and healthy. From pretending to be a John who was low on funds, to Rita showing up at her husband's job wearing nothing but a raincoat and a smile, then taking him straight to a hotel without a word uttered. But none of these methods could have ever worked, were it not for the fact that in all their years of marriage the thought of an affair never crossed either of their minds.

"Violent Vaughn? That's a new touch. I almost believed he was coming through the door." Bryann chuckled.

"And I almost believed that you're broke." Rita said.

"I am." Her husband winked and squeezed her tight sharing a laugh. As the happy couple snuggled beneath their warm comforter, ravishing swirls of pink, yellow, and blue augmented the skylight over their canopy bed.

"Isn't it beautiful? Everything's so quiet and peaceful. This is my favorite time of the day. It's like the sky belongs to just us." she whispered.

Bryann sniffed the air then frowned.

"What?" Rita asked.

"How can such a beautiful woman, have such bad morning breath? Oh, wait a sec. That's my breath. Whoa! My breath smells **this** bad?" he asked holding his hand to his mouth and blowing.

"Every morning." she grinned. "That's nothing compared to when you blow up the bathroom."

"And you haven't asked for a divorce?"

"What can I say. I love your stinky butt." She said and kissed him.

"I'm a lucky man." Bryann admitted causing his wife to blush. At an hour when most women needed to apply blush and mascara before facing the world, Rita's natural beauty blossomed. Her dark-skinned complexion and exotic-looking features were flawless. Whatever it was she was thinking about caused her to smile, revealing lovely white teeth and deep dimples in her cheeks. "Hey!" he called, feeling left out of her thoughts. "What's got you thinking so hard?"

Rita turned over on her side to face Bryann and pulled her long, curly jet-black hair out of her face. "I was thinking about my Great Grandmother Lottie May."

"So, you were thinking about your Great Grandmother after we just made love? Gross!"

"No silly. I was thinking how it's too bad you never got to meet her. And how she didn't live to see us get married, because she definitely would have been there. And given us her blessing. There was something she told me right before she passed away."

"Which was?"

"True love transcends and has no boundaries. It can rewrite history. Erase rules written in stone. Defy all logic without a reasonable explanation. And if you are blessed enough to find a love that strong at a young age, grab onto it for dear life regardless of what others might say. Because those same people when they're older, will be searching for the love you have that they foolishly rejected when they were young. I remember she had this saying, 'love is not possible without sacrifice and sacrifice is not possible without love.'"

"Sounds like us. And she sounds like a really awesome lady." Bryann complimented.

"She really was."

"But I'm confused. Was she saying that our kind of love is like a superpower?"

"Well kind of since true love conquers all. Remember when we first started dating?"

"Remember? How could I forget? Your family hated me big time!" he said in a sour tone.

"Oh, stop exaggerating. My parents did not hate you." She waved at him.

"Babe, you can't be serious. They could not stand me! Whenever I called your house, your moms would be like, 'Rita can't come to the phone right now, she's, um, doing homework.'" Rita laughed at Bryann's spot on imitation of her mother's habit of saying 'um', a dead giveaway when she wasn't being honest. "No matter when I called, you were 'um,' doing homework. Saturday night: 'Rita's, um, doing homework.' One in the morning: 'Rita's, um, doing homework.' Your birthday: 'Rita's … um … doing homework!' And I'm not even going there with your dad. To this day, I swear the man had us followed every time I took you out."

"Aw, come on, sweetie. My parents weren't that bad. Okay, maybe they were. But you've gotta' admit, back in the day, you and your cousin did have bad reputations. They didn't want their daughter dating a roughneck."

"And *your* friends," Bryann said, ignoring the roughneck comment or mentioning of his cousin. "They were worse than your parents! Trying to hook you up with that cornball with the dry-ass Jheri Curl. What was his name again? Mervin? Myron?"

"You know it was Marvin. And you didn't have to treat him like that."

"You damn skippy I did!" Bryann said with a Cheshire Cat grin as he reminisced about stepping to the drippy-headed boy from Rita's church who tried to get too close to his soulmate. "But it doesn't matter cause all these years later we're still together." He said holding out his hand.

She locked fingers and kissed him passionately, then whispered in his ear, "Sacrificing, for true love."

Suddenly, the radio alarm clock began singing, 'Stairway to Heaven' by The O'Jay's.

"Ok did you call the radio station and request that?" Rita

asked.

"No. But what are the odds?" Bryann asked and the happy couple gazed at each other with love in their eyes, proving eye contact is far more intimate than words could ever be. Most mornings, the sudden burst of music meant it was six o'clock, time to get up for work. But today it meant something different. Twelve years ago, at the exact hour, two eighteen-year-olds who had been dating exclusively for two years felt in their hearts and minds that they were ready to make a commitment to each other for the rest of their lives. So, on a bright and early Monday morning, the two lovebirds met and took the subway downtown to stand in line with other nervous couples to exchange wedding vows at City Hall. They had no choice but to settle for a no-frills marriage since they had little money and everyone they knew—with the exception of Bryann's older sister, Dee-Dee and her boyfriend Gainer—was against their getting married, insisting they were too young. But everyone's opinion, and their own lack of money, seemed irrelevant as soon as his best man, Gainer reminded him, *'Son, you got a woman that everybody wants, but she only wants you. The only people who truly matter are here.'* then the judge pronounced them, *'man and wife.'*

To celebrate their nuptials, Dee-Dee and Gainer treated them to dinner at a fancy restaurant. And upon finding out there were newly weds in the house, the piano player serenaded them by playing, Stairway to Heaven by the O'Jays which became their song.

The couple climbed out of bed and slow danced body to body, in the nude. "This takes me back to that day in the hallway at school. You smiled at me and I felt it all the way down to my toes." Rita said in a giddy voice.

"Then I asked you out." Bryann nodded.

"And here we are still dancing all these years later, on our wedding anniversary."

Bryann sported a confused look. "Hold up! Oh, snap! Is that today?" he asked, smiling, then backing it with a kiss. When he pulled away, Rita looked unamused.

"Boy, don't play. I will hurt you!" she warned with a balled fist.

"Aw, baby, you know I was just playin'. Besides, I could never forget….Dang, remind me. What's today again?"

"Bryann!" Rita yelled, swatting his arm, then folding her own arms across her chest, pouting. She knew he was playing, but it was a sensitive topic for her.

"Okay! Okay! Sorry. Listen to me." Bryann sidled up to his wife, took her hand, and replaced the smirk on his face with a look of seriousness. Rita stared straight ahead, still pouting. He gently turned her head in his direction, inhaled deeply, and cleared his throat. "Twelve years ago, you made me the happiest man alive by saying, 'I do.' I swear I've never been so scared in all my life. I remember thinking, maybe your father was right—maybe we were just a couple of silly kids with our heads in the clouds. That with no money or definite plans it would not last. But you knew even when I was beginning to have doubts that we were making the right decision.

"Over the past years, Lord knows, we've had our share of good times and twice as many bad times. But through it all you were right by my side. Remember our first place?"

"The tiny loft over the subway, that had a toilet in the kitchen. We had to snuggle in the nude for body heat because we didn't have any." Rita sighed.

"I kinda' liked that part. But what about surviving paycheck to no check, because often the paychecks were spent before they were received? Bumming meals at my sister's two, sometimes three times a week, because there was no money left for groceries after scraping together the rent and paying tuition."

"Oh, I remember. We were so broke we had to save up to be poor." Rita said with a smile, recalling how the young college students were barely making ends meet while stacks of bills piled to the ceiling.

"No matter what we've been through, I know one thing for sure and two things for certain, being your husband has been the greatest joy of my life. You are my heart. My everything. And I will protect you with every bit of my faith and strength. When I was down and out on my luck, you were there. Always there for me mentally and emotionally. Always giving of yourself. When I went through my trials and tribulations, you were there. When I was the target of people's ridicule and bullshit over past mistakes, you were there. My world. My light. My better half. I'm so grateful, thankful and blessed to have you in my life Rita. I worship the rain that waters the grass, that grows on the ground you walk on. You're my best friend, my lover, the mother of my child and the number one reason I am who I am today. Happy anniversary baby. I love you, my Bella." he said, squeezing her tightly.

"Damnnn!" Rita whispered. She felt the tears swelling as she fell in love all over again then she shot him a side eye and pulled away. "Hearing you say that was better than any gift you could ever buy me."

"Gift?" Bryann asked, looking slyly down at Rita. "Whoa! I thought I just gave you your gift."

"Quit playin', Bryann. You really drive me crazy sometimes!"

"Then go see a doctor," Bryann teased then reached halfway underneath the bed, leaving his bare butt sticking up in the air. He started digging like a dog burying a bone. He pulled out an old sneaker, a dirty bowl, an orphan sock, and other items that had been under there almost as long as they were married.

"What are you doing?" Rita asked Bryann's butt.

"Just a minute," his butt responded. "I know it's here. Ah-ha—found it!

Bryann said and crawled back out and turned to his wife holding a yellow envelope in his mouth.

"What's that, silly?" she asked, pointing and giggling.

Bryann shrugged cluelessly. Rita took the envelope out of his mouth and opened it with hasty fingers. Inside was the personalized greeting card he made on the computer at the Hallmark store. On the cover was a picture of Garfield the cat standing on a boat in a sailor suit. Over Garfield was a bubble with words inside. Rita read them aloud:

"Roses are red, violets are blue…." She paused and glanced curiously at Bryann, who still looked clueless, then opened the card to read the rest. Two movie ticket–sized strips of paper fell out onto her lap. She continued reading, "Pack yo bags, baby, cause you're going on … a cruise?"

Rita snatched up the tickets and upon inspection, got excited. Her arms flailed about like an infant wanting to be picked up. Her bottom lip dropped, and she gasped for air. Her eyes opened so wide they were about to leap out of the sockets. Off to the side Bryann watched, beaming with pride over her reaction. Then, unable to contain herself any longer, she threw her arms around him tightly and began pecking like a chicken all over his face, shouting, "I love you!" in between kisses.

"Sooo, it's safe to say you like your gift?" Bryann asked.

"Like my gift? Iz ya crazy, mon?" she asked in a credible Jamaican accent. "Me goin' on a cruise to Jah-mai-ca! Now who in der right mind wouldn't like dis?"

"I figured we could get the captain to renew our wedding vows while we're there. What do you think?" He asked.

"I think I'm the luckiest woman on the planet cause you're my baby?" she reached out to him.

"Forever, Angel." He said and kissed her hand.

Rita smiled then suddenly realized she hadn't given Bryann his gift yet. With a surge of energy, she sprang over a pile of dirty laundry, then disappeared inside her walk-in closet. When she came out she was holding a huge gift box wrapped in a red bow that partially covered her body. She began dancing seductively behind the box like a feather dancer, giving Bryann a peek here and there. He cheered her on as she climbed back into bed and presented the box to him. "I hope you like it."

Bryann slipped off the bow and opened the box, and his bottom jaw dropped. "Baby, no you didn't!" he shouted, holding up the stylish vintage black butter leather trench coat he'd fallen in love with at the mall. He wanted to get it the moment he laid eyes on it but he could not afford it with his anniversary right around the corner. "I've had my eye on this bad boy since—"

"The middle of august." Rita finished his sentence.

"But how'd you know? I never even mentioned it."

"You didn't have to. The way your eyes lit up whenever we passed it in the window said it all. Well, are you gonna stare at it or try it on?"

Bryann nodded then slipped into the coat. He buttoned the big black buttons down his chest and flexed. It fit him like a second skin, and the swank, sharp collar revealed his broad shoulders and hid his slight gut.

"Aw sookie-sookie now! Check me out," he said, posing in front of a full-length mirror with his arms extended and turning around so Rita could appreciate it from all angles.

"Ooh, baby! It looks nice. Especially that part," she complimented, pointing at his dangling sex organ peeking out, her turn to beam with pride. "Too nice actually. You know, on second thought, you can't wear it because I hear a lot of single women go on these cruises just to meet men, and, once they see you in your coat, I may have to act ghetto." She was joking but not above taking off her earrings, slathering her face with Vaseline, and lacing up her Reeboks to fight tooth and nail for her man if need be.

"Act?" Bryann teased. "Well, then we don't have anything to worry about now, do we? Cause I ain't single," he reminded her with a kiss.

The ding of an automatic timer erased the smile on her face, and she got up and promptly went into the bathroom.

"Baby, I'm really feelin' this coat," Bryann said, carefully placing it back into its box like a baby in its crib.

"Look inside, I had something stitched."

Bryann opened up the jacket and there was a message sewn over the inside pocket he read aloud. "I met you. I liked you. I love you. I'm keeping you."

"This is beautiful babe. It's perfect."

"I'm glad you like it," Rita replied, sounding preoccupied from the small room. After a minute she walked out hiding something behind her back and sat on the edge of the bed. "I have something else for you."

"Is that right?" Bryann smiled, like a kid on Christmas morning, assuming that they were about to make love again. He plopped down on the bed beside her, shaking the bed with his weight. "So, darling? What else am I getting? Is it butt sex?" he asked, rubbing his hands together.

"No."

"But it's our anniversary. And you said once a year we could."

"This is better."

"Better than butt sex?"

"I think so. Here." she said, quickly handing him a small plastic tube with a blue strip down the middle.

"What's this?" he asked.

"Either a boy or a girl."

Bryann held up the tube with a confused look. Rita stared wide-eyed at her man, biting down on her bottom lip, awaiting a reaction. Then slowly the bewildered expression dripped from his face, leaving behind a fresh coat of comprehension. He turned to Rita in slow motion, eyes open wide, mouth hanging open, and pointing a finger like he was about to tattle on her.

"Is this?…Are you?… Are we?…"

"Pregnant," Rita completed his sentence, again proving her theory about being soul mates. "Yes, my love, we're pregnant. You're going to be a daddy, again."

Bryann didn't reply, he sat staring off into space.

"Bryann? Bryann?" Rita called.

Five years ago, Bryann and Rita became the proud parents of a beautiful, healthy baby girl. Bria was definitely unplanned. All those years of trying to make ends meet were finally behind them, and they were at last making good salaries from their chosen careers. With their combined incomes they were able to move out of their tiny, cramped apartment and into a nice, spacious two-bedroom condo with no responsibilities. Or so they thought. When the nurse asked for a name to put on the birth certificate, Rita looked at her husband, then at their daughter, only minutes old, and it came to her. "Bria. Because she's a part of us, her name should be, too."

Although he never said anything to his wife, Bryann felt slightly disappointed. How could he say anything? She was so excited. She had already read books by experts on how to care for the baby while still in the womb. It was all those years of sacrifice to make a decent life for them as a couple….and then, along comes Bria. He would have preferred it if they had waited until they had done some traveling together. Gone on a real honeymoon. Put some money away for the baby's future. But after he was handed his daughter and she looked up at her daddy with those big bright eyes, all the worry and logic went out the window, and he wondered why they waited so long to have her.

"Bryann?" Rita called for the third time. She was starting to worry he wasn't thrilled about the news. After all, it was only a month ago he was saying how glad he was that Bria was no longer in diapers and that, although he loved having a baby, he didn't miss waking up for four A.M. feedings.

Bryann looked at his wife through foggy eyes and parted his lips. She braced herself for whatever he was about to say. He smiled. "You're right. It is better than butt sex. Woman, just when I thought you couldn't make me any happier than I already am, you go and pull a stunt like this. C'mere, you," he said as he grabbed Rita and pulled her close, smothering her with tender kisses.

"Oh, God—what a relief!" Rita said exhaling. "For a minute there I thought you weren't too happy about the news."

"Of course, I'm happy," he said with the utmost confidence. "It's just that you caught me by surprise, that's all. So, how far are we?" he asked, placing an ear on her flat stomach.

"I can't say for sure, I just found out a minute ago myself. That ding you heard from the bathroom was a timer. I took this home-pregnancy test this morning after my boss insisted I take it because she had a dream about fishes. So, I'll have to make an appointment with my doctor since these things are seldom wrong. And then we will find out how far long."

"Sounds good! So, I guess the next question would be… is it mines?" Bryann asked playfully.

"I'm not sure exactly. You know with all the men I sleep with it could be anybody's. The grocery boy, the cable man…."

"Markeith's? I see the way you check him out." Bryann said with a smirk, as the two laughed together.

"Yeah right. I'd sooner get with Mister Marin. At least he knows how to treat women." She laughed.

"I knew there was something going on between you and Ed. But seriously, how are we going to tell Bria? You know she's not used to sharing us with anyone."

"Yeah. I thought about that, too," Rita said, covering a slight yawn and leaning into her pillow, wishing she didn't have to get out of bed. "But I think we're underestimating our daughter, Bryann. I think she'll be thrilled to have a little brother or sister and she'd be very helpful."

"I hope you're right. So, when do you want to tell her and the family?"

"Not yet. I thought we could enjoy the news ourselves first because when they find out everyone's going to make a big fuss over me."

Bryann threw his arms around his wife and nibbled on the back of her neck, knowing that drove her crazy as he slowly made circles with his finger on her inner thigh. "That's because you're worth fussing over, Mrs. Bonner," he whispered in her ear as she moaned, responding to his touching. "Do me a favor?"

"For you, anything."

"Say something else in that Jamaican accent again. It was starting to turn me on."

Rita giggled with a sexy smile then cleared her throat, and said, "Why Mista Bonna, you're a very naughty bwoy. If me didn't know any betta me'd swear you was tryin' ta get a second helpin' of lovin'." She then positioned herself beneath her husband, parted her thighs and arched herself into him. Things were beginning to heat up beneath the sheets when Rita noticed the time on the cable box.

"Ooh shoot, Bryann. Get up, baby, it's six-forty. We're gonna be late!" she said, smacking him on his rear to get him moving.

"Shit!" Bryann twisted his face at the clock. "But, babe, I'm right there."

"Later, Mr. Energizer Bunny." Rita said.

"But…but…I'm there. All I gotta do is stick it—"

"Mmm mmm … stop," she moaned, biting her bottom lip. "We will continue later," she promised and gave him a kiss on his pouted lips, then crawled out from under his torso. She got up and removed her housecoat off the exercise bike that was used more for resting clothes on than working out.

"I'll get Bria dressed," Bryann volunteered while sliding into a pair of old sweatpants as Rita rummaged through her closet for something to wear.

"You?"

"Yes me. I am capable of dressing our child."

"Well, let me see what you pick out first. Because you're not gonna have my child looking like no box of crayons," Rita said, teasing Bryann about his color blindness that was so bad at times she had to stop him at the door to make him change into something that matched.

"Whatevs," Bryann sucked his teeth as he pulled the drawstring dangling over the bed to close the blinds over the skylight.

"Oh, don't be so sensitive, Mr. Magoo," Rita teased, opening the bedroom door. She paused wishing she could hit the rewind button on life and replay the beautiful moment that just transpired. "Life would be so simpler if you could live it backwards."

"Is that right?" he said frowning at his reflection in the standing full-length mirror with his bottom lip poked out.

"What's that look about?"

He sucked in his gut. "You're pregnant. But I look pregnant."

"Watch it. That's my gorgeous husband who just rocked my world, you're talking about." She said with a contagious smile that spread to her husband's lips.

"You're so, choco-lishously beautiful." Bryann said with love in his eyes.

"I know." She smiled and rose on her toes executing a perfect pirouette, then floated out of the room like she was about to go on stage and perform Swan Lake.

An orange-and-white striped tabby cat strutted in, rubbing Rita's leg, then hopped up on the bed next to Bryann. "Hey, what's up, Princess?" Bryann said, scratching the family pet behind the ears and holding out his hand. "Gimme five!" Princess placed her paw in the center of Bryann's wide palm. He grinned at the cat, then rolled over and picked up the plastic tube. He smiled at the object that represented the arrival of his unborn child. Maybe it would be a boy. Someone to carry on his name. That would be nice. He already pictured father and son on the couch screaming at Roy Jones Junior to show no mercy as he pummeled his opponents in the boxing ring. Then a look of concern came over his face, as if something had just occurred to him.

"Hey! Rita, don't you have to pee on this thing in order for it to work?"

"Baby, after all the bodily fluids we've exchanged for the past zillion years and a few minutes ago, a little pee won't kill ya." Rita laughed, disappearing down the hall to take a shower in the larger bathroom.

"Eww!" Bryann grimaced, placing the tube down, then headed into the smaller bathroom.

Bryann's philosophy on life was simple: If it ain't broke, don't fix it. This theory had been proven time and again over the years through his appearance. Ever since he was old enough to go to the neighborhood barber shop on his own, Bryann got the same short haircut, always leaving the sharp widow's peak in the middle of his forehead. He even remained faithful to the same brand of pomade—Murray's—that caused his hair to form those neat rows of S-shaped patterns on his head that looked like breakers in the ocean. Occasionally women would flirt with lines like, "Excuse me, but I'm *hot,* could I skinny-dip in your waves?" or "How much *motion* you got in that ocean?" Flattered he still had it, Bryann would blush politely and explain that there was only one woman who could swim in his waves. Some women didn't care, but he did, and would never do anything to jeopardize his foundation at home.

At age thirty, Bryann possessed rugged good looks. He was

caramel brown with a neat mustache, and beard with flecks of gray that covered a three-inch scar on his neck which he referred to as a souvenir from his misspent youth. Traces of a once rock-hard body were still evident in his slightly flabby physique, which came about from a combination of a perfect marriage and delicious home-cooked meals.

After his shower, Bryann used the sleeve of his robe to wipe the layer of steam off of the mirror over the medicine cabinet. He then scooped up an adequate amount of Murray's from the half-empty jar on the sink and massaged it into his scalp. Afterward, he brushed his waves into place with the care of a micro surgeon, then opened the clothes hamper and thrust his hand into it up to the elbow. After a minute of fishing past jeans and shirts, he pulled out his reward, a long, juicy stocking. With a toothy grin he rolled up Rita's stocking to the foot and squeezed his head into it. This was so that the tight-fitting garment could hold his wavy locks into place as they set. When he was a child, his mother and sister constantly fussed at him about stretching their stockings out of shape. Now decades later, history repeated itself as his wife voiced the same complaint.

After slipping into a crisp yellow shirt, a blue-and-yellow pinstriped tie and a pair of dark blue khakis with creases so sharp they looked like they could slice cold cuts, Bryann stepped into his shiny blue wingtips and checked himself out in the mirror. Trusting his wife's taste in dress since he couldn't trust his own eyes, Bryann headed out of the bedroom and down the hall. He stopped at the first door and opened it. The room was empty, with toys all over the floor and a tiny unmade bed with Lion King prints on the sheets. He made a mental note to get on his daughter about picking up her toys so in the future she'd keep a tidy home, unlike her parents. He opened the miniature dresser drawer and took out a skirt that looked brown and a beige top. With Bria's clothes picked out, he continued down the hall stopping at the door of the larger bathroom. He pushed open the door and was hit with a blast of humidity and steam.

"Hey!" he yelled over the running water.

"Hay's for horses," Rita yelled back.

Fearing Rita would stick her head out from behind the shower curtain and see he'd stolen another of her stockings, he stepped back into the hall. "Bria took her shower yet?" he asked from a safe distance.

"Yeah. She took one with me. She's in the kitchen waiting for you to make her breakfast."

"Okay. I'll get her dressed. You want me to make you some coffee?"

"No thanks. Your coffee is basically a milk shake with all

the sugar and flavored creamer you add to it. Before our child gets dressed, let me see what you picked out. Bryann?" Rita stuck her head out the shower, calling out to him.

Bryann was long gone before she could catch him. Not watching where he was going, he failed to notice Princess and stepped on her tail. She let out a loud, Meow!

"Oh, shoot. Sorry, girl," Bryann apologized. Princess rubbed his leg to inform him he was already forgiven, then continued down the hall.

***

If Bria Lark Bonner were any cuter Disney would own the rights to her likeness. Sitting at the kitchen table with one arm buried to the shoulder in a box of Lucky Charms while kicking her little legs wildly, she crammed handfuls of dry cereal into her mouth as she loudly sang, "Eep-op-ork-aha and that means I love you!" along with the animated cast on the Jetsons cartoon show she was watching on the small television in front of her.

"Busted!" Bryann said, waving a long finger at his daughter. Startled, Bria snapped her head in his direction and dropped her jaw. "Just what are you doing, young lady?" he asked.

"Huh?" Bria uttered the common response all children used when buying time to come up with a good answer.

"Young lady, if you can 'huh' then you can hear."

"I'm sorry, Daddy. I wanted the toy," Bria answered in the cute, innocent voice she knew her father couldn't resist. She pulled her arm out of the cereal box clutching a small plastic case and wiped the crumbs on her robe.

The pressure of the tight stocking on his forehead reminded Bryann that only minutes ago he was being sneaky himself, and he smiled because there was no denying she was Daddy's little girl.

Bria was definitely her parents' child. From her mother she inherited her long, curly black hair. Her dark green eyes sparkled like emeralds, a combination of Daddy's brown and Mommy's hazel. Her skin was a smooth golden brown, the result of having parents with gorgeous bright clear complexions. When it came to looks, she was a tiny replica of her beautiful mother. But when it came to characteristics and mannerisms, it was her father's genes that were dominant. Bryann couldn't hold the stern look on his face as Bria flashed her pitiful, *'I'm sorry Daddy'* look at him. He smirked and said, "Come here, Ladybug," with outstretched hands. Realizing her father wasn't upset since he called her by her pet name, Bria sprang out of her chair and into his arms.

"Whoa!" Bryann said, catching her. "Now, what am I going to do with you?"

"I dunno." Bria held her father's rough face grinning and

18

hunching her shoulders like a baby bird flapping its wings. "Happy annie-verseree!" she said, planting a kiss on his nose and wrapped her arms around him then hugged.

"Thank you," Bryann replied. His sister always said the man upstairs never gives you more than you can handle, but he questioned that as he wiped crumbs from his daughter's face and wondered would he be able to handle both her and a newborn.

"So, do you know your colors, sweetie?"

"Of course, Daddy," Bria replied confidently as she bit open the plastic wrapper containing a small rubber ball and jacks. "Play with me Daddy."

"Honey we don't really have… okay fine, one game." He gave in.

"Yay!" she said and placed the jacks on the table, bounced the ball and scooped up three out of five. "Threesies. Your turn."

"Darn it!" Bryan huffed when he was unable to grab more than two of the spiked pieces.

"Try again."

Bryann bounced the ball and this time he was only able to grab one jack and almost missed that. "You kidding me?"

"You're slow daddy." His daughter teased.

"So, it would seem."

"Wanna play some more?"

"Later Ladybug. Hey, let's see if you're Spellman material. What color is this?" Bryann asked, holding up the skirt. He felt guilty about deceiving his daughter, but he couldn't bring himself to tell her Daddy's not perfect.

"Yuck! Orange. I like oranges, but I hate the color," Bria said, grimacing like she just swallowed a mouthful of cod liver oil. "Darn eyesight. Could've sworn that was brown," Bryann mumbled. "I've got an idea. Why don't you pick out something to wear to school yourself?" he asked her.

The thought of picking out her own clothes like grown-ups excited Bria. "Yes!" she said in a thrilled voice.

"Well, you've had your breakfast … sort of, so go on. I'll clean up. Just don't tell Mommy, okay?"

"Okay, Daddy." Bria scurried out the kitchen and down the hall. Bryann heard Princess yelp again.

"Sowy, Princess," Bria said.

Shaking his head with a slight chuckle, Bryann closed the box of cereal and wiped off the table before heading to the opposite side of the kitchen and through a narrow hall. He walked past the wall unit—which housed a personal library of encyclopedias, a gigantic Random House Dictionary, history books, and paperback best sellers—into the living room.

Their six-room condo was comfortably furnished with

many accommodations for gracious living. Sitting in the corner was a 42-inch, high-definition television, flanked by four surround-sound speakers. Directly beneath the television was an oak entertainment cabinet with glass doors. Inside the cabinet sat a DVD player, and along the sides were compartments stacked with movies—some classics, others recently released. The next shelf housed a PlayStation with some video game discs. The last shelf was filled with CDs organized by genres along with a CD player with countless features that Bryann enjoyed, being a man who found greater enjoyment at home with his family than in the streets.

After cleaning up a few toys Bria left around the living room, Bryann paused before the large heart-shaped mirror over the tan pullout sofa. Carefully, he removed Rita's stocking from his head as if he were peeling a Band-Aid from a hairy wound. He was pleased with the results until he noticed the deep red wrinkles embedded in his forehead from the elastic band. With no other choice, he began wiggling his eyebrows up and down vigorously, smiling and frowning, snaring and glaring in an attempt to stretch the wrinkles out of his skin.

"What are we doing—deciding on today's mood?"

Bryann spun around to see his family dressed in their coats standing in the archway and inconspicuously dropped Rita's stocking on the coffee table without her noticing.

"Excuse me, but can a brother do his daily facial exercises without a hassle? It takes work to look this good you know," he said, slipping into the camel hair overcoat he got for Father's Day. Bria struggled to hand him his leather briefcase.

The two turned to Rita, who opened the front door and stepped aside. "Okay, you two: On your mark, get set, go!"

Father and daughter bolted out the front door as they did every morning, leaving mother to lock up. As she smiled at the two most important people in her life then rubbed her stomach over her unborn child, she turned to lock the door and saw something on the coffee table.

"Bryann Anthony Bonner!" Rita's voice carried down the hall. As soon as Bryann heard his wife call him by his entire name he knew he was in for it. "You stretched another pair of my stockings with your big head?"

Bria looked up at her father grinning. "Oooh, Daddy. You in trouble."

Cornered in the elevator, Bryann had no choice but to listen to Rita rant and rave about yet another good pair of stockings he ruined. He always wondered what made a good stocking anyway? To him, a stocking's a stocking.

"I don't ask for much do I? Just an empty seat on my

commute to work and a husband who doesn't ruin my good stockings." She griped. Bryann winked at his daughter who giggled back. When Rita noticed she was being made fun off, she eyed her husband. "Boy are you lucky I'm not a hoarder, cause I would have kept the receipt when I got you, then I'd be able to take you back to the store."

"Nooo! Mommy don't take my Daddy back to the store." Bria protested grabbing his leg, taking her mother seriously.

"Don't worry Ladybug. Mommy's just teasing. She would never send your dad back. Especially after this morning." Bryann said wiggling his eyebrows and reminding his wife of the three orgasms she had.

"Does what you gave Mommy have to do with why she was singing this morning?" Bria asked.

Bryann and Rita exchanged knowing glances and laughed. "Yeah, something like that."

"Well, at least Bria looks nice," Rita said, with forgiveness in her voice. For the first time Bryann noticed the matching brown sweater and tan jeans Bria was wearing and how they complemented her little brown boots. He smiled at her as she kept their secret and played with her toy. He wanted to tell Rita that it was their little lady who had picked out the ensemble, but after the tongue-lashing he'd just gotten he decided against it. Besides, as bright and gifted as Bria was, there would be plenty of other accomplishments to brag about. Maybe Rita was right, perhaps she will be helpful when the baby arrives.

The building's super, Mr. Marin, was mopping the floor of the lobby when the Bonners got off the elevator.

"Buenos dias," the short, balding Dominican man dressed in denim overalls perked up upon seeing his favorite tenants.

"Ed, what's going on?" Bryann nodded.

"Senor and Senorita Bonner." The super greeted.

"Hi, Mista Marin. Bendos cheetos," Bria said shyly.

Mr. Marin smiled at her. "My and aren't we pretty this morning!" he winked over the oval frames perched on his nose.

"T'ank you." Bria blushed, then whispered, "Mista Marin."

"Yes?"

"Know what today is?"

"No, I do not. What is today?" Mr. Marin asked in a child-like voice.

"It's my Mommy and Daddy's annie-verseree."

"Why, you don't say!"

Bria nodded proudly as Mr. Marin turned to her parents. "Congratulations. So, how many years?"

"Thanks. Twelve. Yep, count 'em. Twelve looong years attached to the hip with this one." Bryann said, jutting a thumb at

Rita with a sly grin.

"That's right, buster. And prepare for another sixty cause you're mines," Rita said, wrapping her arms about his waist and kissing his cheek.

"Mines too! Mines too!" Bria said, following her mother's lead and wrapped her arms around her father's leg with a joyful squeal.

Mr. Marin chuckled at the loving family. "It does my heart good to see a young, beautiful couple like you two in love so," he said, as Bryann and Rita blushed. He sighed, then shook his head. "My beautiful Lucinda, God bless her soul. She and I were just like you two. Always happy, always in love. We were the first person on each other's minds when the sun rose and the last when it set." He paused, tugging at his chest as if he wanted to pull the memory of his wife right out of his heart, then continued. "Bria's very fortunate to be raised in such a loving household. Most couples your age would never entertain the notion of a commitment, much less marriage. They'd much rather"—he glanced down at the wide-eyed child hanging onto his every word and decided to rephrase what he was about to say "—well, you know what *they* do." He winked.

"No, I don't. What do they do?" Bria asked, unsatisfied with Mr. Marin's shrouded message.

"You don't need to know, young lady, because you will never do that," Bryann said, causing Rita and Mr. Marin to laugh while Bria stood clueless. As far as Bryann was concerned, no smooth-talking roughneck was going to take away his princess, even though he did it to Rita's parents.

After some more chatting, Bryann, Rita, and Bria headed outside. The early-morning chill turned Bria's golden cheeks apple red and forced her to clutch at her jacket collar. As they walked talking and laughing, they looked like they were on their way to receive an award for *Ebony* magazine's picture-perfect family of the year.

Bryann scanned the neighborhood he grew up in and where he was now raising his own family. Being born twelve blocks away, on Quincy Street, afforded him the opportunity of noticing just how much the times had changed. The dilapidated tenements that lined the crumbling blocks in the neighborhood reminded him of how lucky he was to have a super like Mr. Marin who still took pride in the appearance of their building.

A thin, pretty hooker stood on the corner pulling her daisy dukes out of her crack with no shame and scanned the vicinity for an early john so she could score some breakfast. Breakfast, being crack. Her huge almond eyes, intent and piercing, widened at the sight of the handsome young man in his suit and she began to daydream that it was she he was proudly walking down the street with. That is, until Rita woke her up with a pensive glare that snapped her back to reality.

This was not how Bryann remembered the place where he grew up. It was now a neighborhood where boys learned to be tough according to the unforgiving rules of the street. Where beautiful brownstones were transformed into eyesores by graffiti. Bodega owners barely made a living, and customers paid with food stamps. Where the streets were lined with victory gardens that once boasted beautiful flowers were now flanked by weeds. Where most mothers would not let their children play outside, and the elderly were too fearful to leave home, even to attend Sunday mass.

Back in Bryann's day, Major City was a place where a man could slow down for a walk and live life to a measure. The district took pride in its appearance, and you couldn't find a gum wrapper on the streets of any district. But, as time went by, the city fell victim to the corrupt and self-serving leadership of city officials who put more emphasis on fattening their pockets than serving those who placed their faith in them. Ultimately, jobs became scarce. Without opportunity, and with corruption on the rise, Major City slid into poverty and decay from which it never recovered. For the hundreds of forsaken youth, gangs became the last resort. As a result, crime escalated to an all-time high, and for many, drugs became a way of life. Either selling, using, or both. All this affected the quality of life, transforming Major City into one long stretch of graffiti-covered gas stations, liquor stores, and abandoned buildings that outsiders passing through nicknamed the Land of the Lost.

"Daddy!" Bria called for the third time.

"Bryann, do you hear your daughter calling you?" Rita asked, tired of hearing Bria call her father over and over.

"Huh?" Bryann said, snapping out of his trance then turning to Rita.

"Your daughter's been trying to get your attention for the last two miles," Rita overexaggerated.

"Is that right?" Bryann said, glancing down at Bria. "I'm so sorry, Ladybug. Daddy was wrapped up in his own thoughts. What did you say again?"

"Put me on your shoulders!" the child demanded. Her father shot her a familiar look, and she knew what it meant.

"Please?" she asked, sounding less pushy.

"That's better," Bryann nodded with a smile. Then he got down on one knee and leaned forward like knight about to be dubbed. "Climb aboard!"

Bria squealed with delight as she climbed onto her father's

back and let her short legs dangle over his shoulders as if she were mounting a carousel horse.

"Careful now—hold on," Bryann cautioned, as he handed his briefcase to Rita, then got a firm grip of both Bria's legs before slowly rising to his feet.

Balancing herself forward, she giggled and yelled, "Whoa!" as Bryann continued down the sidewalk, speaking to his wife.

Rita half-heard what Bryann was saying and interrupted twice to make sure Bria had a secure grip. "Relax, I'm not gonna drop my kid," he replied.

After walking three more short blocks, Bryann put his daughter down and the three waited inside the Plexiglas bus shelter. He glanced at his watch. It said eight-thirty.

"You can go on to work. We'll be fine, honey," Rita said after observing Bryann look down the street for the bus, then sighing impatiently and loudly.

"Nah, it's cool. I've got some time," he said, running a finger along the bus schedule. "Besides, I don't meet with my first case until nine."

"Oh," Rita said with raised eyebrows. "Cause the way you were looking for the bus I thought you may be running late."

"No, it's not that, but don't you have to drop Bria off at pre-K and be at work by nine yourself?"

"Oh, um, yeah, true," Rita replied, avoiding eye contact and nodding feverishly as if she had something on her mind and tardiness wasn't it.

Bryann found her nonchalant attitude odd, expecting her to be pissed off about the lateness of the bus. In all her eight years as a court reporter, Rita took pride in that she was never late. He was about to make a comment, but his thoughts were ambushed by the sudden appearance of four hoodlums. The three young men and young woman were all dressed the same, in dark green Army fatigues, dark green leather jackets, and dark green Timberland boots.

The four stopped on the corner, tossing profanity openly in the chilly air in what appeared to be a debate. The only girl in the group removed a slightly bent Newport from behind her ear, lit it, and took a long drag before continuing.

"I wanna know who the fuck's keeping root beer in business. That shit tastes like transmission fluid." She frowned as a bus rolled by with an advertisement for A&W on the side.

"Ma, you tripping, root beer is good. I love me some A&W and Barqs." One of the men replied.

"So, you're the one person who says, I'm thirsty. I need a cold root beer." She chuckled then eyed him like she had something else on her mind and smiled, "So Bama speaking of root beer, my sister's baby's daddy's next-door neighbor's cousin, Taffy, told me that she saw you and Tyeisha creeping into your apartment late last night. What's up with that?" she asked, and the other two men turned to him for an explanation.

"Number one what the fuck do that got to do with root beer? And number two, your sista's baby's daddy's next-doe' neigh-buh's cuzin, Taffy, need to stop spreading rumors! Nobody was creeping. We was kicking it outside my building and she asked to use my bathroom. She wasn't there for no more than a hot minute," Bama said, annoyed at the girl's prying. He was short and thick, like a fire hydrant, and spoke in a deep Southern accent which is why people called him Bama.

"Oh really? Funny…that's not how I heard it!" Krystal said with a smirk. She was attractive, with a copper brown complexion and full lips. After glancing over her shoulder to make sure she had the attention of her friends, she continued. "Tyeisha is going around the PJs, telling everybody that you laid her carpet."

"I laid … her carpet?" Bama.

"Yo man, I think what she's trying to say is, your definition of eating out means not having any dishes to wash," the tall black man said, tossing an arm around Bama's shoulders.

"Huh?" Bama scratched his head even more confused.

"Nigga she's saying that you ate the pussy!"

"What?! Yo, she a goddamn liar!" Bama protested as his face turned red from embarrassment. "…Okay-okay, I hit it. I-ight? But I swear that was it!"

"Pussy and pork, two things niggas lie about eating." Big Ant, the biggest man in the group and usually in most rooms, clowned and hi-fived Krystal.

"Y'all got jokes." Bama hissed.

"I'm just sayin'. A minute ago, you was like she stopped by to use the bathroom then left. Now you tapped dat ass. See now, if it was me. And I boned Tyeisha's freaky ass, I would've wrapped duct tape around my Johnson, two times—fuck a Jimmy! But personally, I'd be more worried about knocking that skeezer up. She already got what, three kids?"

"At least pregnancy is easy to fix." A guy in the group with a thick gold chain and giant letter E covered in diamonds dangling on the end reasoned.

"True dat. I hear she got a buy two get one free punch card at the abortion clinic." Krystal snickered.

"Hey, don't listen to them. I totally get it. Tyeisha has no looks, no talent, obviously not much for brains. So I'd take it to the grave too. Know what I'm sayin', E-Murda?" Big Ant laughed, bumping fists with the tall black man nicknamed E-Murda. "But one thing's for certain, unlike this fool I wouldn't be laying no carpet… I'd strictly be laying pipe!"

Big Ant and E-Murda erupted into uncontrollable laughter as Bama made a weak attempt at a comeback by mumbling: "Fuck y'all niggas." Then laughed at himself as he twisted the cap off his 40-ounce of Olde English. "Crazy part is she had the ill na-na. Crazier part is I'm hooking up with her again tonight for another session." He admitted and his friends cracked up.

Rita glared at the four, struck at what passed for entertainment these days and how none of these young people had no qualms about foisting it on the public. Whatever happened to civility?

Big Ant passed a blunt to Bama, and his glassy eyes caught Rita's stare, and he licked his lips perversely. Rita cringed from the combination of sticky lips and gold teeth, then pulled her daughter close. Bryann was too busy looking out for the bus to notice.

"Yo, I think I'm in love." Big Ant confessed to his friends.

"Who is it this time, nigga'?" Bama asked, removing the 40 from his lips with a deafening belch.

"Honey dip over there at the bus stop. She's so fine she got my dick harder than ten Jaguar payments!"

Krystal took a long toke on the blunt. "Man, is you high already? That classy looking lady is over there with her husband and daughter literally looks like her shit don't stink. She ain't hardly thinking about your big spooky ass!" she said, getting laughs and pounds from her friends.

"Whatchu fools know? I bet that corny dude in the suit ain't hitting that right, else why would she be staring at me?" Before one of his friends could answer with a snide remark, Rita nervously glanced over in their direction and looked away when she saw they were all looking at her. "See, what'd I tell you? She wants some of this," Big Ant bragged, grabbing his crotch.

"Then call her over, playa," E-Murda instigated.

Big Ant smiled devilishly, then called to Rita. "Sup, Ma! Can I talk to you for a minute?"

Bryann heard Big Ant, then looked around to see who he was talking to and saw his wife looking uncomfortable. "Um, Rita. Do you know this guy?"

"No." She shook her head with wide eyes.

"Don't be that way, sweetheart. Come here. Lemme holler at you for a minute." Big Ant asked as if Bryann was invisible.

The punk's boldness left Bryann slack-jawed. "No, this clown ain't trying to mack you while I'm standing here!" he said to Rita, and then turned in Big Ant's direction. "Excuse me. I don't know if you are aware of this or not, but this woman standing here is my *wife*."

Big Ant twisted his face at Bryann as if noticing him for the first time. "And clearly, you do not understand the degree of a fuck that I don't give, Gramps!"

"Gramps? Oh, I gots your, Gramps!" Bryann glared at Big Ant so hard his eyes became slits and he could feel the blood boiling in his veins. Rita placed a gentle hand on his shoulder.

"Hey sweetie, you're right—this bus is taking forever. Since I'm already late, why don't we walk down to St. James Place and catch the bus there. That way you won't have far to walk to work, okay?" she said, knowing what her husband's intentions were and hoping to prevent an altercation.

Her words fell upon deaf ears as Bryann said, "Stay here. I'll be right back."

"No, Bryann! Let it go. He's not worth it!" Rita pleaded.

Bryann was beginning to listen to reason, then Big Ant blew a kiss in his direction and laughed. He wasn't certain whether the kiss was for his wife or him, either way it meant he had no respect for him or his family. And that didn't set well. He was about to go over and demand respect when he felt a tug at his sleeve. He looked down at his daughter.

"Daddy, where are you going?" Bria asked.

Bryann shook his head and blew steam for almost losing his cool and getting into a fight in front of his child. He smiled warmly at her for making him realize what he was about to do. "Well, first Daddy's going to walk you and Mommy over to St. James to catch the bus, and then I'm going to work." he said, smiling at his wife.

Rita exhaled. She knew her man was bigger than those punks on the corner, he just needed a little reminding. Then suddenly her smile dropped. Bryann could tell something was wrong. It was times like this he regretted not knowing how to drive.

"So, baby, what's up? Didn't you hear me call you?" Big Ant asked, blowing smoke, flanked by his crew.

Bryann spun around to catch a face of smoke and stared directly into his dark eyes. "Look, I don't know what you're trying to prove, but I am not stooping to your level with my family here. So I'm only going to ask you once, and I'm not going to let you waste my time by thinking it over. Apologize to my wife and daughter, then haul your hoodlum asses out of here!"

Big Ant did a Robert De Niro impression, looking around smug-faced like he didn't know who he was talking to. "And what if we don't?"

Bryann stepped in close enough to smell his rancid breath which was hot enough to strip paint. With a stare he said through clenched teeth, "Then I will stoop to your level."

For a moment, the only sounds were the rustling of the brown and orange leaves dancing in the autumn wind and a car or two traveling up and down the street. Then over Bryann's shoulder Big Ant recognized a black Escalade sitting half a block away. While everyone waited for his next move his eyes remained locked on the SUV. A hand with diamond rings on every finger reached out the passenger window and waved for him to rethink his next move. The thug huffed like he was defeated, then without saying a word, he bumped past Bryann's shoulder, stopping before Rita.

"Pardon me, Miss," he said in a polite voice that betrayed his looks. "I, uh, just wanted to say sorry about all that back there. We was just playing around. No disrespect to you or your daughter."

Rita replied with a nervous nod. Grateful for the change of events and pulled her daughter close.

Krystal, Bama, and E-Murda could not believe their ears and stood there with their mouths hanging open. Big Ant looked back at Bryann and nodded, "My bad."

Bryann nodded with tight eyes. The Escalade seemed to be pleased with Big Ant's choice and made a U-turn and disappeared with no one the wiser. Big Ant turned to his crew. "A-yo, we out!" The three slithered past Bryann, shooting sinister glares at him. They caught up to Big Ant and headed down the block, promptly being told to "Shut up!" when they asked what was that all about.

"No good punks. They're the reason why the city is falling apart!" Bryann said as he watched them round the corner. "Are you two all right?" he asked his wife and child.

"Yes, Daddy," Bria said, already over it.

Rita rested against the bus shelter, still trembling, and her husband took her hand and rubbed it. "I'm just a little shaken up, no problem," she said with a forced smile.

"It is a problem! And it's not just them but the rest of society as well. Tell me, at what point did parents stop teaching their children how to act in public? At what point did adults stop objecting when exposed to unacceptable conduct? And when did things like this become the norm? When I was a kid all my mom had to do was look at me a certain way and I'd get my act together! It's getting to be ri-goddamn-diculous!" Bryann vented. It upset him how each generation of kids was becoming less and less respectful, and he worried about what was in store for his daughter.

"I know what you're thinking. And, trust me, neither our daughter nor this one in here will ever act like that," Rita said, reading her husband's mind and pointing at her stomach.

"The bus!" Bria said pointing as the number six bus pulled up to the shelter.

"Are you sure you—"

"I'm fine, baby. Really. I'll call you later," Rita said cutting him off with a kiss in mid-sentence, before boarding the bus.

Bryann was determined not to let her go upset. "Hey!" With a foot on the first bus step, she looked back. "Eep op ork aha!" he said goofily.

Rita looked confused and Bria tugged at her coat. "That means I love you, Mommy," the child explained, grinning.

Rita blushed at her husband, and her frown evaporated. He always knew the right things to say or do to make everything all right. "Oh, I almost forgot. Check your coat pocket for your other gift." Bryann said.

Rita fumbled in her pocket and pulled out a cassette. "Baybee, you made me a mix tape?" she cooed.

"Yup." He smiled and she blew him a kiss he pretended to grab it out of the air and place it over his heart.

With his wife and daughter safely on the bus, Bryann headed to work. In the back of his mind, he hoped this wasn't an indication of what his day would be like.

Chapter 2

"YOU'RE LATE! Here. Deliver this package to Slam," the fat man said, reaching through the open window to mute Dr Dre rapping, 'Nuthin' But A 'G' Thang' on his truck's stereo, then handing a brown duffle bag over to the outstretched hands of a tall, lanky teenager strolling up in a baggy shirt and falling-down pants. "And don't be stopping to see none of dem skeezers you be messin' wit. Slam's waiting on that fresh supply of stuff," he added, tearing himself away from the half gallon container of chocolate milk he was gulping.

The young man peeked inside the bag full of tragedy. Dizam! There was crack and cocaine and heroin and marijuana, plus some pills he wasn't even familiar with. Each drug was separated from the others and neatly packaged in small plastic bags and vials. As he closed the bag, he wondered just how much he would be transporting today. Fifty, sixty thousand worth?

"Hey! Is you listening to me?" the fat one asked, wheezing as he stood up from the black Escalade he was leaning against, causing it to rock.

"Yeah, I hear ya, Pig. Just wait a damn second!" the young man replied with attitude as he used the tinted backseat window of the truck as a mirror to groom himself and pat the knotty braids that spiraled around his head like a winding road.

Pig exhaled loudly. "Everything with you is wait. You know weight is what broke down the bridge," the big man said, attempting to drop some knowledge.

"Oh, really? And here I thought it was your fat ass," the young man snickered. "But hold up, hold up! I gotta ask. What the fuck won't you do for a Klondike bar?"

"What a funny guy you are, Darrius. I wonder if Trig were here would you give him the same back talk." Pig, a born hustler who had his pudgy hands in everything from drug trafficking to black market videos, scoffed at the blatant disrespect he felt he was receiving from the young boy still wet behind the ears who hadn't been through half the things he had. He sported a navy-blue Le Coq Sportif velour tracksuit that seemed too small even though it was size triple X. His features were nasty and thick, mainly endorsed by the full lips of a true food lover. He had a head like a giant boiled egg, evil-looking squinty dark eyes, a pug nose that resembled the snout of a pig, and teeth covered in so much plaque they looked like he was always eating cottage cheese. Standing in the neighborhood of around five feet ten, he weighed three hundred and thirty pounds, with bumpy skin the color of wet mud and a close-cropped haircut that showed off the thick wrinkles in his scalp and back of his neck. As he struggled to suck oxygen,

Darrius frowned at him like he was nauseous, trying to figure out why the obese man would eat to the point where breathing was a difficult task

"Hell yeah, I would! Shit, y'all kill me. Acting like Trig is the mother fucking Messiah or something," Darrius snickered and continued to pet himself. "And I don't know why I gotta deliver this shit on a whack ass Mongoose BMX bike when you got this big-ass whip."

"Don't question why. Just do! Now let's go. The early bird catches the worm" Pig said.

"If good things come to those who wait why do they say the early bird catches the worm?"

"Nigga I don't know. They just do! Now trust me you don't want to still be here when Trig shows up."

"Trust you…nigga I can't trust you to go to McDonald's and not go in my fries. And you can tell Trig what I said."

Suddenly, the window rolled down with a slight hum, and a figure, adorned in Gucci Stunnas, barely visible in the Escalade's interior, save for the orange glow of a blunt, was revealed. Darrius's arrogance quickly abandoned him. "

"Fuck!" the boy said under his breath. "Heyyy Trig. Wassup brother. I, uh, didn't know you was in there." he said with a nervous smile and cut his eyes at Pig for not warning him. Pig grinned back with a dingy smile.

"Obviously." A raspy voice said from the darkness. "So, please enlighten me. What was, it you wanted to tell me?"

Darrius stood there frozen. "Me? Nothing man. I was just…"

The same hand that only minutes ago melted Big Ant's heart now silenced Darrius's groveling. "Darrius, why are you giving Pig a hard time?"

"Come on Trig, everybody knows I play too much."

"And that's the problem." Trig hissed, shooting a demonic stare over his designer frames. "Because nobody is playing with you. We're not kids. We're all grown ass men! In a grown ass business!" Darrius opened his mouth not even sure what he was about to say, and Trig cut him off. "Save it! All I want to hear from you is, 'Yes, sir.' Do I make myself clear?"

"Yes, sir," Darrius lowered his head like a child being scolded.

"Very good. Now, deliver *my* product to Slam at *my* spot so *my* pockets can get fatter," he said. Trig took another pull of his blunt, then blew a cloud of smoke out of the window into Darrius's face.

"Yes, sir." Darrius answered, coughing and fanning.

"Good. And one more thing." Trig's hand reached out of

the window holding a loaded nickel-plated .38 automatic pointed at the young man. "Disrespect me again and you'll be on the ground doing the murda man dance. Understood?"

Darrius was terrified. He knew the man in the car killed more people than cancer and had no problem adding another notch on the butt of his gun. "Yes, sir," he whispered.

"Good boy," Trig said, as the gun disappeared, and the window rolled up.

"Murda man dance. Where does he come up with this shit?" Pig laughed at Darrius and then tossed the empty milk container into the street before climbing into the front seat of the truck. He sucked in his huge gut, then slowly wedged himself between the seat and the steering wheel. Once he was snugly in place, he exhaled like he just completed six miles on the treadmill.

"The little idiot makes a good point though, if good things come to those who wait why do they say the early bird catches the worm." Trig pondered.

"Say, boss man, you mind if we stop by Abraham's Fried Chicken right quick?" Pig asked, hoping his boss was in the mood for 24-hour greasy fried chicken, too.

"Sure, I'll have a triple bypass and a diet stroke. What the fuck, are you kidding me?" Trig said in a disgusted voice from the back seat.

"Aw, come on. They the only ones I know who give away free samples of that delicious spicy red pudding," Pig whined, licking his chops.

"What spicy pudding?"

"In those tiny little packets. See, I got one right here," he said and reached in his pocket and pulled out a small white container with a tin foil lid. "My last one, too. I need to re-up."

Trig strained at what Pig showed him and couldn't believe what he was seeing. "You idiot! That's not pudding. It's barbecue sauce for the chicken nuggets. Spicy red pudding! Damn nigga—eat to live. Don't live to eat."

The fat man chuckled from embarrassment. "Yeah, maybe you're right. Actually, I could stand to lose a few pounds," he said, patting his large belly while uncomfortably clenching back a fart screaming to be released. Last time he slipped up and broke wind in Trig's escalade, his boss made him get out and walk the rest of the way home. In the rain. At night. For six miles.

"You could stand to lose a few tons. Let's roll. And I don't mean biscuits." Trig replied, cold and sarcastic. Pig obediently twisted the key in the ignition. The engine roared to life, and they pulled away.

When he was sure they were out of sight, Darrius transformed into a tough guy. "What? You don't know me, son!

Ask about me! I'm a beast!"

"Psst, hey Beast." a hushed voice chuckled.

Darrius yelped like a little girl and twisted around. "Over here," the voice called again.

Darrius trailed the voice to a dark green parked van. A young woman popped up from behind the van and waved for Darrius to come over. As he came closer, he recognized her. It was Sugar, the neighborhood junkie prostitute.

"What's going on, baby?" she asked.

"Ain't nothing. Just trying to make my outcome affect my income," Darrius replied. He glanced down at Sugar's shapely golden thighs peeking out from under the ultra-tight miniskirt painted on her curvy hips. Sugar caught him staring, and the wheels began turning. Before she was introduced to crack by her boyfriend Buster, Sugar was a very popular young lady named Alexis Ross who got her nickname for looking so sweet. Back then, she would have never been caught socializing with a sixteen-year-old that was on the bottom of the status totem pole. But times had changed, and so had she. Now she was a different woman, albeit a desperate woman out in these streets doing things for five dollars she once would not have done for five hundred dollars.

"So, what can I do for you?" Darrius asked, dividing his attention between Sugar's huge breasts smothered under a spaghetti-string tank top and her long golden legs.

"The question is, *What can I do for you?*" she asked back in a sexy voice.

Sugar's question made both of Darrius's heads snap erect.

"Look, let's not play games," Sugar said, sounding less sexy and more businesslike with one hand on her hip. "Do you wanna fuck me or what?" she asked and began violently coughing as if she had choked on her words.

The bluntness from the woman Darrius had his first wet dream about left him speechless. He was so nervous he couldn't bring himself to answer and nodded goofily. "How much?" he managed with a cracked voice.

"Twenty for a half-and-half," she said, sniffling and rubbing her hands together for friction.

"A half-and-half?" he asked.

"Duh! Ten for head plus ten for sex equals twenty," she said nonchalantly with the prowess of a schoolteacher, applying her past profession to her present one.

"So, where we gonna go?" Darrius asked, with the hook in his nose.

"I got a place. Follow me," Sugar replied. Reeling him in she spun on her heels. As she walked, her tall spike heels forced her to walk in a careful mincing manner that only added to her jiggle.

With a lick of the lips, Darrius started to follow, but the bag in his hand reminded him he had a prior commitment. Sugar sensed Darrius wasn't with her and turned to find him still rooted in the same spot.

"What's up, Boo! You coming or what?" she asked, worried she would have to continue walking the cold streets if he changed his mind.

"I want to, but I just remembered there's something I really gotta do," he said disappointedly.

"So you're telling me you don't wanna stir my sugar bowl?" she asked as her head tilted forward, allowing her long straight brown weave to fall over one eye. She was like a piece of rare black fruit, forbidden to eat and too tempting not to.

"You talked me into it," he said grinning.

"For real?" Sugar asked, pretending to be surprised, knowing there was no way a weak-minded simpleton like Darrius could refuse her charms. Junkie or not, she still had it going on.

Darrius followed Sugar with his eyes magnetized by her voluptuous ass as it bounced like twin molds of taffy down the street into a dingy narrow alley between two abandoned buildings.

"Back here, baby," she instructed behind a huge green Dumpster.

"I don't know about this." he said, darting his eyes around.

"Don't worry 'bout it baby. This is where I take all my tricks—you're safe," she assured him.

Grabbing her soft bosom and squeezing like they were rolls of Charmin he quickly forgot about the voices of reason in his head. "Take it easy! Dead presidents first," Sugar snapped, as she held up a hand rubbing her thumb against her fingers.

"Right, my bad," Darrius giggled as he withdrew a large bankroll from his pocket.

Sugar almost had an orgasm at the sight of all the money, but played it calm and shoved the twenty it into her tiny black leather purse. "Thank you, sweetie. Now lean back and let me take care of you," she said, motioning the boy against the cold steel of the Dumpster.

The prostitute kneeled before him and unzipped his fly then put her hand inside and fumbled around until she found what she was looking for. Darrius closed his eyes and smiled as Sugar kept her word about taking care of him suddenly, he looked down at her.

"I hate a bitch who try to suck dick all cute. Bitch if you don't start foaming at the mouth like a pit bull, I'm leaving!" he promised. Sugar obeyed his request and sloppily went to work. "Now that's what I'm talking bout'!" he said and closed his eyes and bit his bottom lip. When she glanced up and saw his eyes were tightly shut, she lightly tapped twice on the Dumpster. Suddenly Sugar became suspiciously nervous and accidentally nicked Darrius with a sharp tooth. "Ow! Dammit! Sucking dick is a talent and not every bitch got it!" Darrius said angrily, looking down. At that moment the sun peeked out from behind a patch of clouds to expose the shadow of a figure holding a long narrow object slowly rising out of the Dumpster behind Darrius. "What the—?" he said as his eyes shot up at the wall and discovered they weren't alone. Pushing Sugar away, he spun around reaching inside his jacket just in time to see the words Louisville Slugger on the end of a bat kiss him in the face. With a dull thud Darrius was face down in soiled discards and rotten garbage, unconscious on the alley's floor.

"Oh, I gots your bitch, BITCH!" Sugar said viciously, then hacked up a wad of phlegm and spit on the ground next to Darrius.

"So, how much did we get this time, baby?" Buster asked as he climbed out of the Dumpster. He was in his late twenties with the appearance of a man in his early forties. The whites in his eyes looked like the faded pages of a book and his cheeks were drawn inward, thanks to his constant sucking of the crack pipe. His hair was thinning badly, he had a scrawny physique and was wearing a filthy sheepskin lined denim jacket and pants so dirty they could stand by themselves.

"Gimme me a sec, baby, I'm not sure. But I know it's enough to rent a room and get our groove on all week," she replied, checking the pockets of the limp young man. Digging into the inside jacket pocket Darrius was reaching for before he was knocked out, she discovered a 9-millimeter that Buster snatched from her hands. Upon further searching, she located the huge bankroll from his pants and smiled, revealing evenly spaced white teeth.

"What's that?" Buster asked, using a dingy white sneaker to point at the bag Darrius still clutched onto.

Sugar hunched her shoulders, too preoccupied with counting money to respond she was up to six hundred and eighty and still counting. "Oh, that," she finally said, glancing over. "I dunno. But it must be important cause at first he didn't want to…come with me." As she spoke she began to realize what she was saying and it dawned on her, *Whatever was in the bag was important to a drug dealer!* The same thought hit Buster as well and he swooped down on the bag like an eagle. He tore into the bag and, upon sight of the contents, was speechless.

"What? What?" Sugar demanded.

Buster dug his hand into the bag and came out with a fist full of drugs spilling through his fingers. "Look! Look!" he shouted.

After calming down, Sugar hugged and kissed Buster, then said, "And to think my Momma said you'd never take care of me."

The two roared with laughter between the walls of the condemned buildings, king and queen of a crumbled castle.

Chapter 3

"HOME SWEET HOME, please hold. Home Sweet Home, please hold. Good morning. Home Sweet Home. How may I help you...Marisol, is that you? *Que pasa, mommy?* Hold on for a sec. I'll be right back!" the doe-eyed receptionist said once she recognized her girlfriend's voice. Connected to her face by way of headphones was a thin plastic receiver that resembled a bent drinking straw. Every time she spoke, she looked as if she were holding a conversation with herself.

After connecting the flashing buttons of the holding parties to the desired extensions on her switchboard, the receptionist switched back to Marisol for an earful of the latest gossip. After fifteen minutes of who was dating who, who was breaking up, and who was pregnant on her block, plus the latest on 90210 Beverly Hills and, *'why ain't no black and brown people on Friends?'*, she saw Bryann enter the building through the end of the long glossy white hall, then cut the conversation short.

"Yo, Mari. I gots ta cruise like Tom. Dat chocolate cutie at my job that I was telling you about just walked in, and he is looking extra Denzel this morning! I'ma call you later. Hasta luego."

After hanging up, the receptionist pulled out the bottom draw of her desk and checked her makeup in the small mirror she had propped up against a stack of textbooks. She applied a fresh coat of red lipstick and ran her hand through her long blonde hair. Satisfied with the attractive nineteen-year-old Latina staring back at her, she closed the drawer with her foot, grabbed a stack of mail, and pretended to be busy.

"Good morning, Mista Bonna. How ju doin'?" she asked, with a type Rosie Perez twang, while batting her eyelashes.

"Good morning, Miss Delgado. Fine, thanks," Bryann responded in a friendly tone. "Busy this morning?"

"Nah, ju know—a few calls here, a few calls dere. Oh, and them two is waiting on Miss Crawford to arrive."

Bryann smiled at the two young women waiting for their caseworker as they rocked their dingy baby carriages passed down from relatives. One had a bad weave the other an even worse wig, and both looked like red Kool-Aid was an acceptable substitute for breast milk.

"Ladies," he nodded with a warm smile then at their children who were consumed by their electronic Giga-pets.

When the handsome young social worker acknowledged them, they both blushed and hid behind their VIBE hip-hop magazines. It wasn't every day such a classy-looking man called them "ladies." Bryann glanced at the clock on the wall behind

Roxanne's desk. It read 8:55AM.

"Any word from Mr. Banks?" he asked with a sigh thinking he was supposed to be waiting for him, not the other way around.

Roxanne shook her head. "Nope, not yet, and Mista Bonna, I told ju before, we past formalities just call me Roxy. All my peeps do," Roxanne said, doing a bad job of hiding her infatuation. The young mothers exchanged knowing glances at her expense.

"I'm honored that you consider me a, um, peep," Bryann chuckled, feeling his age when he heard himself use the latest slang.

"Oh, jes," Roxy replied, burning a hole in his jacket with her staring.

Bryann could read the flirting loud and clear, and while he was flattered, he didn't want to lead her on. Nor start any rumors. "Well, I'll try to remember."

"Oh, here's your mail," she said, handing him a stack of envelopes.

He scanned through the pile and stopped at this month's issue of Black Enterprise Magazine with a picture of Russell Simmons on the front cover and a caption that read, 'How This 35-year-old CEO built a $34 million dollar Rap empire.'

"So, how's college going?" he asked.

Her energetic face twisted. "*Ay, Dios mio!* Crazy hard! If I'm not studying for an exam, I'm writing a ten-page paper on some old dead dude. And math! God! I don't even wanna go dere. My major is psychology, so I don't see why I gots ta' study anything that don't got nothing to do with what my major is. Ju know what I'm sayin'?"

"Well, it's because they want you to be well-rounded. But hang in there," Bryann said encouragingly, while secretly hoping she was also being force-fed English literature. "You know, when I was in college, I was the same age as you, plus married with a full-time job and loads of responsibilities. You're lucky you only work here part-time and still live at home. If I did it with more on my plate, you can with less on yours."

"Yeah, but dem was different times."

"If anything, with technology being as advanced as it is today, you have it much easier. I didn't have the Internet to help me research term papers. I had to go to the library. So what seems to be giving you the most trouble anyways?"

Roxy opened a notebook covered with scribble. "Dis problem for instance. I'm supposed to find the area of a pentagon."

Bryann studied her notes for a minute, as college freshman algebra came back to him, then he picked up a pencil and went to work. "Okay this is not so hard. All you have to do is break the pentagon into a triangle and trapezoid like so. Then figure out the area of both, add them together…and presto, that's the pentagon's area." Roxy looked at the magic he just performed; unsure she could do the same. "Look, what time do you take lunch?" he asked.

"One-thirty, why?"

"Come up to my office on your lunch hour and I'll show you a few tricks that got me an A minus in algebra."

"Really? Thank you!"

"You're welcome. Well, time to begin another fun-filled day at Home Sweet Home. I'll see you later, Roxanne." He snapped his finger abruptly. "I mean, Roxy."

Roxanne smiled as if she had just won the lottery. As Bryann walked toward the elevator down the hall, she thought to herself, *'Damn, not only is the brotha fine, he's mad smart too! Too bad dating me goes against his moral code.'* She removed her psychology book from the drawer. "Hmm, I wonder if I could hypnotize him into wanting me."

When the elevator door opened, Bryann heard a crowd laughing. Further down the hall a group of his coworkers were gathered around a slim, handsome young fair-skinned black man telling jokes by the water cooler.

"So, a guy walks into a bar on the top floor of a skyscraper and orders a drink. At the end of the bar a drunken guy says to him, 'Hey, buddy! Wanna make a wager?' 'On what?' the first guy asks. 'I bet you a shot of top-shelf scotch that if I jump outta the window I won't be hurt.' The first guy looks at the drunk like he's crazy, and the drunk guy says, 'I'm serious. It's a known fact that the wind current surrounding this building is so powerful that if you were to jump out the window, just before you hit the ground it would catch you, spin you around three times and deliver you back up here safe as a newborn baby.' The first guy looks at the drunk guy suspiciously and says, 'Whatever, dude.' 'So then we have a bet?' the drunk asks. 'Uh-huh. Sure whatever you say pal.' the first guy answers, humoring him. The drunk guy staggers off his stool and over to the window, opens it, and climbs out onto the ledge. 'Hey, what're you doing? Stop!' the first guy yells running over. 'No way. A deal is a deal!' the drunk says, and before the first guy can reach him he dives over the ledge. The first guy watches in horror as the drunk free-falls fifty stories. Then just before he hits the cement he stops in mid-air, spins around three times, and floats back up safely and through the window! 'Ta-da! Not a scratch on me.' The first guy is dumbfounded and can't believe his eyes. 'Wanna try it? It's a rush.' The drunk smiles. 'I dunno,' the first guy says nervously. 'Don't be such a pussy. You see I'm okay.' After careful consideration the first guy says, 'Sure, I'll try.' 'Go right ahead, but first my drink,' the drunk says. The first guy signals to the bartender to buy him his shot, then climbs onto the ledge, gives the drunk a nervous thumbs-up, and drops off the ledge all the way down and splat—hits the street like a safe! Afterward the drunk guy moseys over to the bar, and the bartender comes over to pour him his shot, shaking his head and says: 'You know something, Superman? You're a real asshole when you're drunk!'"

The hall echoed with laughter as Bryann made his way through the crowd toward the comedian.

"What up, Home-skillet?" the funny guy loudly greeted.

"Markeith you're still telling that same old joke from college?" Bryann laughed, bumping fists with his best friend.

"Hey if I can make at least one person smile or pee their pants or maybe spit out a drink, then my day was not wasted." Markeith said, grinning as he gripped Bryann's palm, pulled him close, and embraced him with a pat on the back. As the hall cleared, Markeith walked Bryann to his office, reached into his breast pocket, removed a small stick then offered it to him. "Peppermint chewstick my brother?"

Bryann frowned. "Nah I'm good. And to be honest, I don't know how you can stick that in your mouth. You don't even know where it's been."

"First of all, I don't 'stick' anything in my mouth. That sounds gay. And second, bruh, these chew sticks are like catnip for the patchouli smelling, dirty backpack sporting, Native Tongues playing, earring in the nose wearing, sea shell jewelry having, earthy chicks." Markeith insisted.

"So, am I to believe that you're willing to chew on a dirty tree branch just to impress women heavily into the culture?"

"No diggity. No doubt. In fact, this dirty tree branch is the reason I bagged this bad little Nigerian shorty named ZaZee I happened upon sipping herbal tea and reading the Isis papers at a poetry slam last week."

"But you're not even into poetry."

"True dat. But I sho' got into ZaZee, up top." Markeith snickered and held up his hand for Bryann to hi-five but was left hanging. "Whatever man but yo check this out. On the way in to work this morning, I'm walking up the block and this white lady with crazy zits is walking in my direction. She is literally an ad for Clearasil. We make eye contact and I smile. Cause hey, chicks' wit zits need love too, am I right? But then she eyes me up and down and clutches her knock off Gucci bag. And I'm like how in the hell, you gonna be racist **and** have acne? Bitch, worry about yo' skin! But I really wanted to ask her old Estelle Getty mixed with Bea Arthur looking ass, why do white people wear shorts in the winter? Cause it's like 30 degrees outside and she walking around out here like it's in the middle of the got-damn summer." He said.

"Stop. Not everyone white does that. That's like saying all black people drink grape soda, eat hot links and put hot sauce on everything." Bryann shook his head.

Markeith reached into his backpack and pulled out a can of Welch's grape soda and a small bottle of Frank's hot sauce then held up the items like Vanna White. "For my hot links, for later." Markeith got no reaction then quickly noticed his friend was unusually quiet this morning, like he had something on his mind. "Soooo, you gonna tell me what happened?" he asked.

"What do you mean?"

"My Dude, we go back like car seats. You can't fool me Bee. Something's up. I'm sensing darkness in your lightness."

Bryann sighed. Markeith was right. Next to his wife, no one knew him so well. The two met freshman year in college. They both majored in social science and shared classes that Bryann seemed to take more seriously due to the fact that Markeith was a party animal who went through women like condoms in a free clinic. While Bryann seldom partied and preferred spending quiet evenings at home with his wife. Aside from their different lifestyles, their common interest in their career goals turned them into fast friends.

Well aware Markeith would not rest until he told him what happened, Bryann replayed his manic Monday morning run-in with Big Ant and his crew.

"Man, I should've been there. I would've bitched-smacked them punks!" Markeith said, swinging his fists in the air.

"Is that right?" Bryann asked twitching his face in disbelief.

"If I'm lying then I'm flying, and you see I'm still on the ground, right?"

"Unless a strong wind comes along, skinny."

"That's all right. Your wife likes it skinny."

"Ay, watch it!"

"So does your sister. In fact next time you see Dee-Dee do me a solid and ask her about my silk boxers I left on her floor."

"Keep on talking, and I'm going to grab those sticks you call legs and make a wish," Bryann said as he hung up his coat and slid behind his desk.

"You gotta work on your jokes." Markeith said as he plopped down on the old, worn sofa in the corner across from Bryann's desk.

"Hey, I'm funny."

"As funny as a colonoscopy from Shaquille O'Neal. See it's funny cause Shaq's got like real big fingers."

"You stupid." Bryann snickered.

"So, how's it feel?" Markeith asked.

"How's what feel?" Bryann asked wondering if he was still cracking colonoscopy jokes.

"You know, celebrating twelve years on lockdown? The old ball and chain. Ka-clink!" Markeith said, holding out his wrists like he was handcuffed.

"If you are referring to my marriage, it feels great."

"Great enough to go out with me tonight and hit up a couple of spots and celebrate?"

"You do realize that I'm supposed to celebrate with my wife? Kinda' the rule."

"Aw c'mon. You said twelve years. What are you gonna do different this year? Play Luther before Freddy?"

"Sorry I'm not really a fan of letting my wife get upset. But while we are on the topic of my anniversary, I need to ask you a huge favor."

"Axe away."

"The word is ask. It's a verb not a hatchet."

"So, in the sentence, 'you are boring,' boring would be the adjective, which describes you?"

"Touché. So Rita and I are going on a cruise to Jamaica during the first week of November, and I need you to check on a few cases for me while I'm gone."

"Not a problem. You know I got your back. Now don't take this the wrong way Bee. I love Rita like a sister. But I personally could never bring a woman along on a cruise to Jamaica."

"You couldn't bring a woman along to the grocery store. See, I can be funny."

"You're wrong about being funny. But right about the single honeys shopping at Pathmark early Saturday mornings. But my dude, bringing your lady to a Caribbean Island teaming with baddies, is blasphemous. It's literally taking sand to the beach. Literally!"

"See, that's where you're wrong, my canine friend. If you had a good woman like I do, then you would have no problem taking her anywhere with you."

"Says the guy who's been with the same woman forever. What would you know?"

"I know that looks attract, personality keeps, and actions maintain."

"Whatever that means. And don't bother explaining it. We both know it'll go in one ear and out the other." Markeith said cynically. "I'm just saying don't you ever wish you would have waited before getting married? Maybe sowed your royal oats?"

"You're asking me if I regret not sleeping with a bunch of random women before marrying the woman who saved me from myself? Helped get me back on the right path? Has my back? And gave me a beautiful daughter? The same daughter who for some reason thinks the world of her Uncle Markeith?"

"I mean, I suppose when you put it like that it sounds like a dumb ass question."

"Ya' think?"

"Ok my bad. Yes Rita is a phenomenal Sista. And if they ever make a sequel to Love Jones, it should be based on ya'll. So, moving on. You gotta hear what happened to me this weekend."

"You finally let your mom set you up with a nice, decent girl from her church?"

"Yeah right. Man I'd sooner braid water. Besides she's still pissed with me for that time I replaced a can of air freshener in the Church bathroom with an air horn. But do you remember Tabitha?" Markeith asked enthusiastically.

"Dude, you have so many women coming and going I can't keep tabs on 'em all."

"C'mon, you remember Tabitha—cute in the face, thick in the waist." Markeith smiled but Bryann still drew a blank. "Ass so fat it takes her a week to wash each cheek. Breasts so big she gotta put her bra on backwards and spin it around. C'mon, you remember the one I brought when I doubled with you and Rita a few of months back. We had drinks at that after-work lounge that had a jungle gym in the middle of the dance floor…um," Markeith snapped his fingers trying to remember the name of the spot.

"Monkey Bar. Yeah, now I remember. The yoga instructor whose every other word was ekspecially and irregardless."

"Yeah, her downward dog is no joke."

"So what about her?" Bryann asked rolling his eyes.

"Well, Saturday night I was chilling in the crib waiting on my latest victim, this cutie named Angie, to page me after she got off of work when Tabitha called me out the clear blue. At first, she caught me off guard cause I hadn't heard from her since that night we all went out, and to be quite honest, I wasn't really sweating it because she has a son."

"So?"

"So, from past experiences with single mothers I've learned that KIDS stands for Keep Interrupting Da Sex. So anyway, she was like, 'What's up? You can't call nobody?' So, you know, I had to sweet-talk her and be like, 'Well, I wanted to, baby, but I wrote your number on my chest and when I looked in the mirror it was backwards so I couldn't read it.' Then she wanted to know what I was doing, so I told her I was lying in bed watching a porno. Give her something to think about, know what I'm sayin'? Then she asks me, 'So, what are you doing when it goes off?' Now, I knew she was making a booty call. But if she knew the rules, she would not have gone about it so amateurish."

"Oh, so there are rules," Bryann smirked.

"Of course there are rules. Hey—Biggie has the 10 Crack commandments, and I have the 4 Steps for fornication. Rule number one: no sleeping over, no explanation needed. Rule number two: no kissing cause it's too intimate. Rule number three: The preferred position is doggie style because the less eye contact the better. And rule number 4: none of that lovemaking shit! It only complicates things. So I played her little game and said, 'Well, it's kinda late, so I'll probably just go to bed…unless, you know of something *else* we could do.'" Markeith paused briefly to let what he was saying sink in. Bryann shook his head, unimpressed.

"So then she says in a sexy voice, 'Well, if you want, you could come over here and we could watch a movie together.' A movie? At two in the morning? Come on! The only thing open after two in the morning is a pair of legs! But I continued to play dumb and said, 'Sounds like a plan.' So I hit the 24-hour bodega on the corner, grabbed me a king-size Guinness Stout for a quick buzz, and floored it across town. I'm not even tryin' to stop for lights. I'm a man on a mission, know what I'm sayin'?

"When I get there, she opens the door dressed like Winnie the Pooh. Short t-shirt no panties. The tits is like, BAM! Ass is like, KA-POW! The next thing I know, I'm working shorty like a 9-to-5! But wait, it gets better! In mid-stroke my phone vibrates. It's Angie texting me to pick her up from work! Now I'm trippin' cause I don't know how the hell I'm gonna get out of this one. But then I caught a stroke of luck because her kid starts crying, and she had to get up and check on him. And that's when it hit me. I snuck over to the window and poured out my beer. By the time she came back in the room I was dressed and before she could ask any questions I told her I was going to the corner store for another forty and asked if she wanted anything. She smiled and said, 'Some watermelon Jolly Ranchers, a Zima and for me to hurry up and bring my fine ass back.' Seriously who the hell drinks Zima? It tastes like citrus flavored horse piss." Markeith cringed.

"I'm going to take a wild stab in the dark and guess that you never went back," Bryann said dryly.

"Dude, weren't you listening to the booty call rules? Number one: no sleeping over!"

"So, you're telling me that you left this poor woman sitting up waiting for you to come back and you went to see another woman?"

"Why would I come back? I already closed that deal, know what I'm sayin'?" Markeith said proudly, with a toothy grin holding up his fist to bump. "So, you just gonna leave a black man hanging, twice?"

Bryann looked at his friend's fist like it was contaminated. "Worst thing you can do to a girl is convince her you like her then disappear and not tell her why you left. I'm surprised she didn't call you to curse you out."

Markeith covered a yawn, "Oh, she most definitely did. At five this morning. She knew she'd eventually catch me home— that's why she waited. I tried to front like I told her that I wasn't coming back, but she said she didn't hear me say that. So I asked her, 'Who you gonna believe, me or your lying-ass ears?' That's when she told me I'm black history and slammed down the phone. Pissed me off!"

"Why? Because you realized you blew your chances of ever sleeping with her again?" Bryann asked, while searching for a pen that didn't skip.

"No, cause I was dead-ass tired and had to get up for work in less than an hour! Blew my chances? Get serious! I can sweet-talk my way back into them panties just like that if I wanted to." Markeith said, snapping his fingers.

"Well, I hope you have enough sense to wear protection when you sleep with all these different women."

"Aw, man! You sound like one of those AIDS-awareness tapes we show to the kids," Markeith giggled.

"That information applies to adults too, you know." Bryann said very seriously.

Markeith straightened his posture when he realized his friend was as serious as the diseases he was talking about. "Of course, Bee. I always wear a jimmy hat. Hell, I'm wearing one right now."

Bryann sighed but knew there was much more to his best friend than the countless one-night stands he had with women whose names he had already forgotten by the time he climaxed. He knew how dedicated and compassionate a social worker he was. How he fought to get his clients the help they needed to repair their lives. How he was highly respected at his job by everyone, including Bryann. And even though he lived a fast life in college, it was Markeith who got higher grades than Bryann due to Bryann's hectic work schedule. Markeith would selflessly cancel dates to study with him until they were on the same level. But Bryann still couldn't get the picture of Tabitha sitting up waiting for him to come back while he was off to see another woman out of his mind. "See, it's guys like you who give men like me a bad name because you try and juggle too much at once. Now what you need to do is find yourself one good woman and settle down with her."

"Oh Lawd, here we go. Not this again!" Markeith rolled his eyes.

Bryann ignored him and continued. "I don't know how you

do it anyway. You've got to remember so many lies. You're standing there sweating and fighting while they're screaming and crying. See, that's why I have my wife and my peace of mind."

"Brother, the only piece you have is the same one you've had for the last twelve years. And to be honest I've come to the realization that I ain't meant for nobody. My soulmate prolly a piece of chicken."

"That's not true. There's somebody for everyone." Bryann reasoned.

"With all due respect, marriage is good for you Bee. But all I know is if I tried to settle down, within a week I'd change my mind then within a couple months I'd be on Maury's show talking 'bout 'When it comes to six-week-old Jaquan, Markeith, you are the baby's daddy!' Then what?"

"Duh! You assume your responsibilities and raise your kid, who, by the way, never asked to be born." Bryann reasoned.

"That is so you of you! Look before you can make that kinda' commitment you gotta discuss bills, parenting styles, credit, debt, religion, how to deal with family, what beliefs will be instilled in your child, childhood traumas, sexual expectations, if she likes Marvel or DC, cause that's important you know,"

"Oh yes, I know."

"Financial expectations, bucket lists, dream homes, careers, education, political views and whatever else comes to mind." Markeith ran down.

"So what's your point?"

"My point is love alone is not enough."

"It was for Rita and me. And we discussed maybe two things on your list. She's team Marvel by the way."

"Yeah because you have the last good woman on Earth. The rest of these women make street walkers look like Nuns."

"What about your cousin Terrence who recently got married? He's happy right?"

"I wouldn't know. We haven't spoken since he got hitched."

"Remind me again what happened."

"At his bachelor party when I was giving a speech, I may have said that every dude's woman at some point had sex with another guy and when the dick slipped out, she put it back in. He got all in his feelings. Said I put an image in bis head he couldn't erase." Markeith said.

Bryann shook his head disapprovingly. "What the hell…why would you tell him that the night before he gets married?"

"Number one I was just clowning. And number two, it's true."

"But is it?" Bryann said.

"Oh yeah, I forgot, the only sex faces you and Rita have ever seen, are each other's."

"Like the song goes, she's my first, my last my everything."

"And the rest are headaches. Which is why whenever I see things getting too serious with a chick, I whip this little lifesaver out." Markeith said opening his wallet then removed and unfolded a piece of paper before handing it to Bryann.

Bryann skimmed it over then looked up at his grinning friend and shook his head before reading it aloud. "*Insert name, (or if you forgot it, use Ma if she's black, Mamacita if she boriqua), you're an amazing, phenomenal woman. So, believe me when I say, it ain't you, it's me. And I need to work on myself. So that I can only hope to one day be good enough for you. But sadly, that day isn't today. And right now, it seems that we're on two different paths....* okay exactly what the hell am I reading here?"

"My face-to-face script for breaking up with da honeys. Duh!" Markeith shrugged then shouted, "Hey I haven't memorized that yet!" when his best friend balled it up and threw it in the trash can.

"You haven't even memorized their names." Bryann pointed out as Markeith fished the script out, smoothed it and returned it back in his wallet.

"Look, all jokes aside I was once convinced that I'd found my 'Make it Last Forever' partner but I guess life had other plans for me." Markeith admitted.

"Meaning?"

"Meaning play me once, shame on you. Play me twice, shame on me."

"I get it. Kayla fooled you. Hell she fooled me and I'm a pretty good judge of character."

"She did more than that Bryann! Thank God she couldn't fool my sister from another mister, Rita. If she hadn't insisted I get a DNA test I'd be raising another man's child."

"But you're not. And you can't possibly believe that you're meant to bounce from one meaningless fling to the next. So how long you gonna make every woman suffer for the mistakes of one?"

"Dunno. How long is forevuary?"

With a sigh Bryann turned his attention to some documents on his desk as Markeith watched him unbutton his sleeves and neatly roll them up to the elbow. He shook his head perplexed.

"I don't get you brotherman. Just about everyone I know complains that they have to dress up to go to work, and here we can dress any way we like, and what do you wear? Corporate gear." Markeith complained. Cloaked in a Pelle Pelle leather jacket, Air Force Ones, baggy Rocawear jeans that hung low, exposing his Sean John boxers and a black oversized AACA African, American College, Alliance hoodie. The walking billboard's style of dress made him appear to be at Home Sweet Home to receive help rather than offer it.

"This is exactly why the kids we counsel don't take pride in their appearance. And it gets worse every day. Now they're walking around the streets in their pajamas. It's pathetic! I want to inspire kids and let them know that they can rise above their own challenges." Bryann said, pounding his fist into his palm in frustration.

Markeith sighed, "Anybody ever tell you that you move different?"

"I move different because I want different. Old keys can't unlock new doors."

"Meaning?"

"Meaning whether you realize it or not Markeith, we're role models. We're also therapists, second parents. And sometimes… first. I mean, it's not like they have a whole lot to choose from. Politicians are greedy, athletes act like spoiled children, recording artists and actors are either in jail or rehab, and the Reverend Smalls…hell, he drives a Lexus! And don't get me started on them attending underfunded, poorly managed schools. So, yes on casual Fridays I still wear a blazer because the last thing they need is a social worker who's a walking contradiction. Then they think it's okay to walk around with their pants hanging halfway off of their butts, just not giving a damn. Not that I'm justifying her racist prejudgment, but it's probably why that woman with the bad skin held onto her purse tightly."

"Ah, so you were listening." Markeith smirked, stroking the few hairs sticking out his chin. Then with a sincere look, he leaned forward, "Bee, I'm a college grad and fraternity brother who reads *Black Tail magazine,* eats Popeye's fried chicken, blasts hip hop at the highest volume and is addicted to Grey Goose. I contradict myself every day regardless of how I dress. But when you put it like that. I hear you loud and clear, my dude. I know I don't always act like it but I also took this job to make a difference. I was gonna tell you when I get all the particulars hashed out, but I'm looking into starting an afterschool program to keep these kids off the street. Something I wish I had coming up."

"You and me both. But that's what's up." Bryann said holding up his fist to bump.

"And I hear you. In fact I'll start wearing clothes that fit—" he stood up and hiked up his pants and tightened his belt. An instant later they fell back down. He looked up at Bryann.

"Starting on Monday."

Bryann shook his head, smiling. Hey, at least his boy was making an effort.

***

Darrius slowly opened his eyes and rose to his feet. Instantly pain filled his head as he staggered against the rusty green dumpster for support. Grabbing his face, he felt a large lump over his right eye, a stabbing pain followed. He looked around; Sugar was gone. He dug in his pockets, so was his money. He checked his inside jacket pocket, so was his gun.

"I don't believe this shit! That junkie bitch set me up!" he said aloud, angry for allowing himself to be played for a chump. Then it occurred to him something was missing. He looked around nervously. "Wait just a damn minute!" he said, patting himself down when realizing Trig's drugs were gone, too. Frantically, he began rummaging through the smelly piles of trash, praying it was overlooked in their haste to get the money.

"No! Oh, God, no!" Darrius yelled when he couldn't find the bag.

He slumped to the ground on the verge of crying then checked his watch. It was ten-forty. He closed his eyes and admitted the inevitable.

"I'm a dead man."

***

"What the hell do you mean Darrius never showed up?" Trig screamed at the muscular man who had the unfortunate task of delivering the news. "Have you called him?"

"I've been calling him for the last hour, Trig. His phone keeps going to voice mail." the muscular man answered timidly.

More pretty than handsome with olive skin and perfect hair, the muscular Dominican man, dubbed Slam, short for Sexy Like A Motherfucker, was two times Trig's size, maybe three, but that was irrelevant to the smaller man, whose angry voice caused the bigger man to nervously fidget.

Beneath a hooded sweatshirt and dark shades, Trig paced the black and white-tiled floor of the candy storefront he used to run his operation from, as the two gold "Jesus" pieces around his neck jingled like cowbells. "That little punk should've been here hours ago! If he thinks for one minute he can play me for a sucker because of who his brother is, he's even dumber than I thought!" Trig threw on his jacket and stormed outside. Slam followed behind him and lit a cigarette to keep warm. Pig waddled out third,

49

biting off the wrapper from a pack of Twinkies. "I'm going to see my girl," he snapped taking his anger out on Slam, as Pig opened the car door for him to get in.

"And if Darrius shows up?" Slam asked.

"Hold him here and call me immediately! I don't care if you gotta lock his ass in the goddamn freezer. I want to deal with him personally!" Trig said, then peeled away from the curb.

Slam took one last drag on his cigarette then flicked it into a dumpster and went back inside. Once the coast was clear, Darrius popped his head out of the garbage dumpster frantically patting the burning hole on his jacket that Slam's cigarette started then nervously looked around. After overhearing how angry Trig was about his being a no-show, he knew it would be suicide to go to him now and explain what happened.

Going to his brother could prove to be even more fatal than what Trig had planned, and home wasn't an option after the last argument he had with his mother. He needed a place to lay low and somebody he could trust. His big brother, Moola, always said the three quickest ways to spread your business was telephone, television, and tell-a-woman, so he knew going to his girlfriend, Laquita, was out of the question. And Pig would gladly hand him over to Trig. Then, spotting a billboard across the street advertising Home Sweet Home, it became crystal clear who the only person was that could save his miserable hide.

Chapter 4

WHEN BRYANN WAS YOUNG, his dad would read to him in silly voices, and his mother's kisses made everything better. It was from them he learned how to someday treat the woman he'd marry as well as how to be kind considerate and caring. Then one day they were gone.

He was scared, hurt and mostly angry over the death of his parents and gave in to negative peer pressure, thus making a lot of bad choices that almost cost him his future. With the help and guidance from his older sister's boyfriend Gainer, he eventually was able to put it behind him. Bryann felt that by choosing a career that called for him to give back to his community, he could make up for his past mistakes. And no job seemed more appropriate than social work. Sometimes he'd see people from his childhood sitting on the opposite side of his desk who had fallen on hard times and become maladjusted. And it felt good when he could help them get back on track.

Then there were the flip-side days. Days when Home Sweet Home was not so sweet. When his job had him so stressed out, he felt like he was pushing a boulder uphill. Days when he came home sick from the poverty, child abuse, domestic abuse, rape, incest, murder. And it was on these days he questioned his faith in God.

"Veronica, look at me," Bryann said softly.

The young woman seated before Bryann's desk looked up with a nervous smirk. Both of her eyes were bloodshot and swollen. Her arms and neck were covered in purple bruises. Her dainty frame was so thin she appeared malnourished, but she still retained a small amount of attractiveness.

"Tell me what happened," Bryann said.

"I told you before Mr. Bonner, it was an accident. Danny and I were play-wrestling the other day and it got out of hand," Veronica answered unconvincingly.

"Both eyes?" Bryann let out a frustrated sigh at the obvious lie and checked her folder. "It says here that on June 5 of this year you were coming in with the groceries, lost your balance, and fell down a flight of steps, which resulted in two teeth getting knocked out. Two months prior you had to be rushed to the hospital because of a ruptured spleen, which you also claimed happened accidentally. So, what's next? You're going to lean up against a loose windowpane and fall twelve stories? And God forbid, but what if these accidents start happening to Steven—then what?" Bryann asked, referring to the infant sleeping peacefully in Veronica's arms.

"My son's fine, thank you very much!" Veronica snapped

becoming incensed at the mention of her baby.

"For now. But tonight, next week, in an hour, who knows?"

"Look, are you gonna hook me up with that job you promised me, or not?"

"Veronica, it's a hostess position for a restaurant."

"And?"

"I'm sorry, but I don't think it would be a good idea for you to work there. At least not now, anyway."

"So, it's like that? I need that job! I thought you said you help people." Veronica snarled. But they both knew that her anger was not directed at not getting the job, but why she could not get it.

"Veronica, be reasonable. The deal I have with the people I send potential employees to is that they are hard-working, professionable and presentable. You would be the first-person people see when they walked into this woman's restaurant. She can't have you standing there looking like, you just went twelve rounds with Mike Tyson!"

Veronica dropped her head, ashamed, and began to cry. She didn't need Bryann to remind her about how bad she looked—the mirror and the stares she got standing on line at the welfare office were more than enough. Bryann cursed himself for being insensitive and offered her a box of Kleenex. He felt bad about making her cry, but he wanted her to realize how dangerous her situation was before it was too late. Veronica thanked him for the tissue over a sniffle, then took one and dried her eyes.

"Veronica, I apologize for that, it was very unprofessional of me," he said.

"No, it's all right. You're a good man, I know you wouldn't say those things if you didn't care. Besides, I've heard worse from my sister. But, believe me, Danny wasn't always like this," she said.

"Is that right?" Bryann said, finding that hard to believe. His experience and training with domestic violence taught him that men who hit their wives started when their wives used to be their girlfriends.

"No, not at first, but when he got laid off from his job and couldn't find anything, he started drinking and feeling sorry for himself and that's when he—" As she relived the first blow, she began to cry harder. Steven stirred, and she rocked him until he was asleep again.

"If memory serves me correctly Veronica, Danny has serious anger issues. He's an ex-boxer, who was fired for brutally beating up a coworker. And come to think of it, didn't he serve time?"

"Yes, but it wasn't Danny's fault. The guy he beat up complained to his boss that he wasn't a good worker. They had it in for him. And he was only in jail for a few months until I could get up his bail." she said, still defending her husband to the bitter end. Bryann knew it was time to throw in the towel and follow job procedure. It was difficult, but he had to distance himself from his clients and not get personally involved or it would affect his job.

"There's someone I'd like you to meet," he said while pressing numbers on his phone. "Hi! Are you busy?... Could you come down to my office for a sec?"

Minutes later, a middle-aged white woman with silver hair, wide lensed-glasses and a gracious smile, walked through the door.

"Veronica, I'd like you to meet our resident den mother, Miss Lyla Crawford." The two women graciously exchanged pleasantries, as Bryann continued. "Miss Crawford specializes in mother and children's cases like yours."

"And who is this cutie pie?" Miss Crawford asked.

"My son, Steven," Veronica replied, her dreary mood lifting as she spoke about the only person in the world who mattered to her.

"He's a beautiful baby. You must be so proud. So, Veronica, before we get started, are you hungry?"

Veronica felt a little embarrassed. She hoped Miss Crawford was just being nice and did not hear her stomach growling. "A little," she said meekly.

"Me, too. How about I treat you and Steven to brunch before we tackle your situation? I always work better on a full stomach. How about you?"

Veronica nodded and smiled. She already trusted the lady who reminded her of Paula from the Magic Garden television show, more than most people she knew all her life.

As they were leaving, Bryann called to Miss Crawford. She spun on her heels. "She's a good person, just a little misguided." he said.

"Aren't we all?" Miss Crawford winked and closed the door behind her.

After they were gone, Bryann leaned all the way back in his chair until his head touched the wall behind him. "Better relax, there shouldn't be another crisis for at least…" The ringing of the phone cut him off. He laughed to himself as he hit the speaker button. "Yes, Roxy."

"Mista Bonna? Your nine o'clock is here," she said with a trace of disgust in her voice.

Bryann glanced at his watch. "And only three and a half hours late."

"Oh, Mista Bonna?"

"Yes?"

"Don't forget about my tutoring."

"One-thirty, right?"

"Yup! See you in a hour."

A few minutes later there was a knock on Bryann's door.

"It's open," Bryann said sternly.

The door opened and Darrius strolled in with a backwards baseball cap on. Bryann glanced up from the files he was going through. "Close the door behind you, take a seat and remove your hat." Bryann instructed, visibly annoyed.

Darrius plopped down in a chair, took off his cap and began fidgeting with the zipper on his blue, purple and white Charlotte Hornets pullover jacket. "I know what that look is for," he began.

"Is that right?" Bryann asked without looking up.

"Yeah, it's about my being late, and my bad, but something important came up."

"Where'd you get the shiner from, Darrius?" Bryann asked. It had been a long morning, and he was not up to the bogus excuse the young man had for his lateness.

"Oh, this?" Darrius asked with a nervous smirk, pointing at the knot over his eye. "My girl has anger issues. And I have commitment issues. Match made in ghetto heaven."

Bryann let out another long, frustrated sigh and shook his head as he jotted something down on a yellow pad. "Darrius, were you aware that prisons are being built based on third-grade test results in certain neighborhoods?"

"What's that got to do with me?" Darrius asked.

"Nothing, I hope. So, how's the job coming along?" Bryann sighed changing the topic. Darrius' eyes riveted to the floor. "The answer isn't on your shoes." The social worker said.

"It's, uh, coming along just fine," he said out the side of his mouth.

"So, it's safe to say you like it?" Bryann asked drumming his fingers on the table with a disappointed stare.

"It's ok, I guess. I got no complaints." Darrius said and Bryann's fingers stopped drumming.

"Well how could you, since you've never even worked there?" Bryann looked up with disgust.

"What?"

"You pride yourself in keeping it real, yet you stroll in here late for our appointment and tell me one boldfaced lie after the next! You looked me square in the eye and said you'd show up and show out. And you never even showed up."

Darrius glanced down at the crisp pair of Air Jordan's he never could have afforded working as a foot messenger. "I was gonna go, but what had happened was—"

"Spare me the bs, okay? So I guess this means you're back on the streets selling drugs with those same lowlifes you got arrested with, right?”

Darrius’s cell phone rang for the tenth time that morning. He sucked his teeth at the timing and checked it. It was Slam…Again. He wasn’t ready to talk to him yet and shut it off. “Huh?”

“Nothing. I just got my answer. I don’t understand why you would trust anyone who invests more in your failure than your success.” Bryann let out another long, disappointed sigh. He once had high hopes for the young man, but now he accepted him for what he was, just another statistic in the ghetto. “Well, it’s a waste of breath to ask about school?”

“Why, so I can one day get a job like regular folks? I mean no disrespect, Mr. Bonner, but regular nig-” he paused remembering his social worker detested the word and would remind him that he nor his people are the N word. “People, work all week for chump change to get to work, plus a beer to forget about how hard they worked.”

“So, this is why you sell drugs? Because you’re afraid of hard work?” Bryann asked shaking his head. The clueless young man shrugged. “Typical. You kids today are such cowards. Scared to put in the work. Scared of failure. And scared of success. So instead, you take the easy way out. But what you fail to realize is that you are busting your tail just as hard to get over, if not twice as hard. And for what? Materialistic objects and materialistic women? Meanwhile, both will abandon you when the well runs dry.” Darrius raised his eyebrows when his social worker hit home. He knew his girlfriend would not be with him right now if he could not afford to get her hair and nails done weekly and lavish her with expensive gifts. “You know, if you and all your little friends put half that energy into something positive, you would have all that your heart desires.”

“I’m just trying to double my money,” Darrius said.

“Let me tell you something, youngster. The smartest, safest quickest way to double your money is to fold it in half and put it back in your pocket.”

“Okay, I admit it. I screwed up! Is that what you wanna hear?” Darrius snapped. He respected his social worker, but he was not about to sit and be lectured to.

“No, it’s not. What I want to hear is, ‘The job is going great, Mister Bonner. I’m going back to school working on getting my high school diploma so I can go on to college and make something of myself.’”

“Class is always in session with you.” Darrius rolled his eyes.

“And cutting class, with you.”

Darrius sucked his teeth and frowned. “You just don’t get

it, do you? I'm from the gutter. Ghetto-made and ghetto-raised. As far as I'm concerned, there are only three ways out of the hood. Rap, excel in sports, or sell drugs. Guess which one I'm good at?"

"How can you even fix your lips and say that when you're such a talented artist?" said referring to the life like drawing he doodled on a pad of Bria.

Darrius rolled his eyes. "When people see me they see a born loser from Major City."

"You should never let someone else's opinion of you become your opinion of yourself. And for what it's worth when I see you, I see a young man with a bright future."

"Whatever."

"Seriously stop allowing your insecurities to cripple you. You should be in somebody's art school honing your God given skills and talents."

"That may be, but one thing's for sure, if you don't help me, you won't have to worry about how my life's gonna turn out cause I'll be dead within a week."

"Dead?"

Darrius stood up and paced a couple of times, then turned to Bryann and said, "Keep it one hundred with me, Mr. Bonner. Are the rumors true?"

"I don't know. What rumors?" Bryann asked confused.

Darrius paused for a minute, trying to find the best way to put it, then he just blurted out "The rumors about you and Trig being cousins. Are they true?"

The question made Bryann's knees buckle. "Why do you want to know?" he asked uncomfortably.

"Because he's gonna kill me, and you may be the only person who can stop him."

Bryann flashed back to the middle of July 1984. A scorching one hundred and six degrees. Summer in the city. The slow-spinning ceiling fans did little to cool the stifling, crowded 3rd precinct. Notorious-looking men were being led in with their hands bound behind their backs as prostitutes swore 'on a six-foot stack of Bibles' that if their arresting officers let them go 'this one last time', they would never work the streets again. In the middle of all the craziness, two boys, fifteen and seventeen, sweating. One from worry, the other from heat. Both were handcuffed to a wooden bench. A tall, black police officer with hard eyes and stern features walked up and began to unlock the cuffs.

One of the boys with a permanent scowl, wiped his brow and pondered. "Yo Bee, you ever stop to think sweat and pee are cousins?" he asked the younger scared kid beside him who kept his head down.

The nervous looking young man who was the diametrical

opposite of his delinquent accomplice, ignored the ridiculous question and glanced up at the tall black police officer eyeing his ID badge. "So, are we going to jail, Officer Monroe sir?"

"Well, that all depends." the beat cop said.

"Depends on what?" the older, bald teen demanded. Unlike his partner in crime, he seemed unconcerned about what may or may not happen to him.

"If you two are dumb enough to come back. I pulled some favors and got you both off."

"Oh yeah, well thanks."

"Trust me I didn't do it for you. And it wasn't easy especially with *your* record Mordecai," the cop said, eyeballing the older teen who smiled proudly.

"I go by Trig!" he replied defiantly.

"Tell me something, Trig how do you intend to find a job in the future with a tattoo of a bullet on your neck?"

"I don't plan to have the type of job that wouldn't hire me because of it." he explained like he had it all figured out.

Officer Monroe didn't even bother to respond to the ignorance and sheer audacity of the man child who was too young to vote, and already had a long rap sheet that labeled him a delinquent prone to violence, mischief and sticky fingers. He instead turned to the younger seemingly level-headed kid then to his beautiful teary-eyed older sister,

"Luckily for you Bryann the kid you pummeled, doesn't want to press charges. Well, not after he admitted it was he who started it, when his girlfriend smiled at you in the park and he jealously shoved you. Then made a disrespectful remark about your parents and you were the one who finished it."

"I didn't mean to. I just blacked out after he disrespected my folks…they're dead." Bryann whispered softly then dropped his head in shame, almost as if he felt bad for making the wise guy pick up his teeth with broken fingers.

"My cousin, straight beat the black offa' Chico's ass!" Trig snickered. Bryann stared at his shoes.

The cop sighed. Unbeknownst to Bryann they met once before. He was one of the rookie cops on the scene responding to a call about a couple mowed down in the street. The car responsible for the hit and run never stopped and the driver never apprehended. He was also there to witness a much younger Bryann running to his older sister devastated and crying. The cop often wondered what ever became of the sad little boy robbed of his parents. Now he knew.

"Bryann, listen to me. The only time your head should be down is to tie your shoes. Otherwise you look weak. You're not weak are you?"

"No sir." Bryann replied.

"Then lift your chin, son. And remember, no matter what you did. How bad you screwed up, you always-always keep your head up, shoulders back and face it head on, like a man, understand?"

"Yes, sir." Bryann said immediately lifting his head. The last time a man spoke to him like that was his father and he immediately gravitated to the cop.

"I know about your parents. And I'm sorry for your loss. I also know you're not a bad kid. Just a kid, dealt a bad hand who's lost and in need of guidance. Which is why you've been given a second chance." He said sensing the child was in desperate need of a mentor.

"Yo cop, some of us succeeded despite overworked or absent parents. I somehow did! And so has my cousin!" Trig snapped.

"Bryann we are on a time clock. Every day we wake up we're closer to an expiration date. We don't have time to waste. So, what I suggest to you is to lose the sixth toe." the cop advised referring to Trig, worried that his bad company would corrupt Bryann's good behavior and handed him a business card. "If you ever wanna talk." Bryann eyed the card that read, Gainer Monroe Homicide Detective.

The squeak of his office door brought Bryann out of his daze. He blinked and saw Darrius walking out of the room.

"Hey! Where are you going?" Bryann asked.

Darrius turned on his heels. "You claim you want to help me. Finding me jobs and helping me to get my diploma is fine, but I come to you with real problems, and you don't do squat except lecture me like a afterschool special!"

Bryann leaned back in his chair and stared at Darrius, thinking long and hard about what had just been asked of him. It was obvious the boy was nowhere as tough as he fronted if he needed his social worker to save him. He lost count of how many times kids Darrius's age looked him in the eye and swore they were through with all the negative drama that came with thug life, only to turn around and do something incredibly stupid. Like get themselves killed. True, Darrius' environment had left its scars on him, but Bryann couldn't stop thinking about how half of Major City's black and brown men between eighteen and thirty-five were either in prison or the cemetery. And if he himself did not get a second chance from Gainer, how different his life could have turned out if he never took him up on is advice and called the number on his card. He stared at the paperweight he got for Father's Day with the caption that said, 'Do something kind today, whether big or small.'

"Okay. I'll help," Bryann said, hoping he was doing the right thing.

"Really? You will?" Darrius asked.

"Calm down," Bryann said. "I'm not promising anything except that I will try, for whatever that's worth. But first you've got to tell me everything that happened."

Reluctantly, Darrius told his social worker everything, about how Trig sent him to drop off a large supply of drugs and how he met up with Sugar along the way, then got knocked out from behind and woke up to discover he was robbed.

"How the fu-how could you be so stupid?" Bryann snapped catching himself. He was so disgusted with what he heard that he wanted to leap over his desk and give the boy an old-fashioned whupping. "Did you go to the cops?"

"The cops? That's a good one, Mr. Bonner. How that's gonna look? A drug runner going to the cops because he was robbed for drugs while getting his knob slobbed in an alley by a hooker and now he's scared of what the drug dealer who owns the drugs might do to him?"

"Okay, bad idea. So, where's Sugar now?" he asked.

Darrius hunched his shoulders. "I dunno. The whore is probably somewhere getting high with whoever knocked me out. I'll bet it was that crackhead Buster. There was enough shit in that bag to keep them zombies in space for weeks."

***

A car blasting Lil Kim's, 'Big Momma Thang' drove by a boarded up abandoned building that looked like it was made of wallpaper. Inside on the second floor, Sugar sat wide legged in a deep nod, clinging tightly to a glass pipe. But wouldn't let it slip through her fingers. "Now that's what I call a Sugar high." She snickered then pondered, "Hey what if the air we breathe is really a drug that makes us see a dazed version of the world. But when people take real drugs and trip they see the real world and that's why they're illegal? What you think?...Buster?"

Across the room Buster was stretched out on the floor rolling in his newly acquired wealth as high as a kite off the heroin he just shot up. Suddenly, what they had done hit him and he sprang up, wide-eyed, paranoid.

"What if he comes back looking for us?"

"Who Darrius?"

"No Avon bitch! Yes Darrius! Did you forget that he works for Trig? That motherfucker is crazy with a capitol K! And let's not forget about that sasquatch they call JackHammer with the big arms who works for him. Damn it, girl! What was I even thinking about letting you talk me into getting blazed in the building next to the goddamn alley we robbed him in? We got all this money—we could be sitting pretty in a motel somewhere instead of climbing through windows to get a quick fix."

Sugar rubbed her thighs and smiled at her man. "Negro, you couldn't wait either. So don't start blaming me. Besides there ain't nothing to worry about, baby. Darrius is a bottom feeder. A nobody. I wouldn't had chosen him if he was anybody important. As far as Trig is concerned, yeah, he's crazy. But that's Darrius' problem not ours."

"You know what you get when you cross a hooker with a genius? A fucking know-it-all!" Buster snapped.

"Aw, don't be like that," Sugar said scratching her arms and legs like she had a severe case of poison ivy, as her body began to call out to her for a second taste. She lit the end of her glass pipe that was black from constant use, then coughed and gagged when her lungs were blasted with a dose of crack. Beads of sweat rolled down her blank face. "That was a good hit," she muttered, then dropped her head.

Buster peered at his woman through his hollowed-out eye sockets and grinned devilishly. He knew that in this state Sugar would succumb to his freakish sexual appetite. Forgetting about the possibility of Darrius seeking revenge, he dropped his filthy pants then mounted her and began making sweaty love. In between grunts and moans, they were interrupted by the sound of wooden boards being ripped from the front door downstairs.

"Oh, shit! See, I told you he'd come back!" Buster whispered angrily.

"You're bugging. It's probably Mookie looking for a place to chill." Sugar replied unconcerned.

Something loud and strong entered the building.

"That does not sound like Mookie!" Buster said nervously.

Sugar remained quiet with wide eyes, fearing he was right. As the two listened in horror, floorboards creaked under heavy, earthquake-sounding footsteps that seemed to shake the entire building. The intruder ventured through the downstairs hall, noisily entering rooms searching for something. Unable to find anything or anyone the footsteps traveled up the staircase, each step closer, each step louder. The steps came to a halt outside of Sugar and Buster's room. Then slowly the doorknob twisted right and left. When the intruder discovered it was locked, an angry snarl that sounded part grizzly, part pit bull came from the opposite side of the door.

"Hey, man. No need to be like that. We only used a little of your stuff," Buster groveled to whomever, whatever it was on the other side of the door. The doorknob began twisting back and forth wildly. "And we'll pay you back! Honest to God!"

"And all your money's here, too. Every cent," Sugar added on the verge of losing it. "We was just playin', Darrius. But I'll take real good care of you, baby, this time I swear I will!"

Suddenly, there was a loud pounding on the door. Sugar screamed. "C'mon man, it ain't gotta be like this!" Buster pleaded, then remembered the gun he stole from Darrius and nervously pointed it at the door. "Hey! I got your gun motherfucker! So you better get the fuck outta here, or I swear I'll shoot!" Buster warned in a shaky voice. His weak threat had no effect, and the pounding continued until the door split down the middle. "Okay, motherfucker!" Buster shouted and emptied the entire clip into the door. Then there was a silence. Buster turned to Sugar and held a finger to his lips. He tiptoed over to the door and peeked through the bullet holes with no results. He put his ear up against it. "Hey," he whispered. "I don't hear anything, I think I got—" At that moment there was an explosion, and a something punched through smashing into the side of Buster's skull. One of his eyeballs shot out of its socket across the room and against a windowpane where it splattered like a bug. Its contents ran down like egg yolk. Orange, pink, red, and yellow exploded from inside his brain all over the room. An instant hemorrhage caused by the crushing of his larynx, erupted with vomit, blood, and bits of stringy layers of tissue.

Sugar screamed as she was splashed with blood and brain bits. Buster's lifeless body dropped to the floor like a marionette with its strings cut. Sugar looked down at him and gasped. It looked as if his head had been run over by a tank. More pounding and growling brought her out of the daze. One last punch and the door came off the hinges, landing on top of Buster.

By now, Sugar knew this wasn't Darrius. But if it was not him, who? A split second later she got her answer as the earthquake footsteps entered the room and a giant boot stomped on top of the door. The disturbing sound of Buster's bones and organs turning to jelly beneath the weight of the boots filled the room. Sugar cowered behind the couch, unable to believe her eyes. A huge shadow covered her like a blanket, and her bladder released warm urine. Tears ran down Sugar's face as she shook her head.

"No! Please, don't!" she screamed.

Ignoring her pleas, large, gloved hands circled her neck and lifted her into the air. The sound of bones popping and snapping were made as the intruder rang her neck like a wet cloth. Death came slowly for Sugar, like a ceiling fan coming to a stop, her legs kicking until they swung limply. She fell to the floor, her head now on backward and no longer dependent on crack to numb her emotions

After the mission was carried out, the heavy footsteps retreated from the room, back down the steps, and out the door, leaving behind fifty thousand dollars in miscellaneous drugs, one thousand and thirty-seven dollars in large bills, and two dead junkies.

Chapter 5

"I DON'T KNOW ABOUT THIS, Mister B. I mean, what if we get caught?" Darrius nervously asked Bryann as he searched the drawers of his desk.

"We have no other choice. You admitted yourself we can't go to the police. But if we can prove Trig has you and other minors selling drugs for him, they will listen. That's where the Dictaphone comes in... if I can find it."

"Yeah, but with this confession, don't that mean I will go to jail, too?" Darrius asked worried his confession would incriminate him.

"No, you're a minor. But it'll prove you were in fear for your life and left no choice but to sell drugs for him. I have some juice with a certain Detective on the force. He's helped me in the past. So, if I explain things to him, he can get you placed in job corps. And believe it or not it will be the best thing for you. You'll be off the street and able to get your GED, and maybe even college credits," Bryann said, as he spun around and checked the drawers of a five-foot-tall gray metal file cabinet." After slamming the last drawer shut, he declared: "It's not here. But I have one at my house."

Darrius rang for the elevator and glanced over at Bryann. Words couldn't express the gratitude he felt for the man who was sticking his neck out for him, and he made a promise to himself that when this was all over he'd get his GED and make Bryann and his mother proud.

The elevator door opened, and Roxy stepped out with a pencil behind her ear and cradling an algebra textbook and writing pad in her arms. In her hand was a brown paper bag.

"How sweet, you came to meet me. I once remember you saying how much you loved spice ham and cheese heroes, so I made us some for lunch." she smiled at Bryann hoping he'd appreciate the effort.

"Oh, crap!" Bryann said. With so much going on, he'd forgotten about his lunch plans. "I'm sorry, Roxy, but I'm not going to be able to tutor you today. Something came up." he explained.

Roxy didn't want to postpone her private lesson slash date and thought quickly. "But, I really need your help. I got this test on Friday and—"

"Didn't you hear the man J-Ho? He can't help you so make like a rash and break out!" Darrius shouted.

"J-Ho! Yo, who the hell are you talking to?" Roxy shouted.

"Darrius! Get on the elevator!" Bryann ordered through clenched teeth.

"But, Mr. B, I'm only sayin', we gotta bounce and she's—"

"Not now—right now!" Bryann yelled at Darrius, who rolled his eyes and did what he was told.

Bryann gently placed a hand on Roxy's shoulder. "He didn't mean what he said."
Roxy looked up at him with pursed lips and raised penciled- on eyebrows. "Well, okay, maybe he did. But he's an immature kid who still has a lot of growing up to do. Anyway, what do you say we do this tomorrow instead?"

"Tomorrow?" Roxy said, with forgiveness in her voice.

"I'll even bring lunch this time. Do you like eggplant parmesan? I made too much and my daughter isn't a fan of anything accept mac and cheese."

A *romantic* lunch cooked by her crush was even better she thought: "I love it! So, tomorrow, same time?"

"Same time." Bryann smile and boarded the elevator.

"Damn, Mr. B! She's on your dick so hard, Johnnie Cochran can't get her off!" Darrius wise cracked.

Bryann glanced over at Darrius with a look that stifled the young man. "Use your words and actions to uplift. Not tear down!"

"Sorry, I was just clowning." Darrius said dropping his smirk and avoiding Bryann's pensive stare.

'*If I didn't want Trig off the street so bad, I wouldn't even waste my time!*' But he knew he was lying to himself, knowing good and well that he'd help any sixteen-year-old kid in trouble, or anybody else older or younger for that matter. It was a part of his character he had no control over, like a reflex.

The long trek in silence came to a halt in front of Bryann's apartment building. Darrius was glad they finally stopped. He didn't know how much longer he could take walking with Bryann, who ignored him the entire way. He watched his social worker search through the keys on his crowded key ring, then unlock the door with the key marked "L."

The warmth of Bryann's lobby made the cold seem like a cruel hoax. Living in a filthy, rundown housing tenement all his life, Darrius had never seen a building as clean as this with its shiny floors and graffiti-free walls and piss free working elevator.

"Wait here. I'll be right back," Bryann instructed.

"Dang, I can't come up? I ain't gonna steal nothing from your crib."

"Did I say you would?" Bryann asked, mashing the elevator button.

"Then why you got me waiting down here like Brandy in Cinderella?"

"It would just be quicker if I went alone. Besides, the place is a mess." The elevator arrived and Bryann turned to Darrius,

"Give me a few minutes."

"Whatever, man," Darrius said dryly. He was disappointed he wasn't invited into Bryann's home. He pictured Bryann's place like Dr. Huxtable's on *The Cosby Show,* warm and cozy with nice furniture. And since he never knew his own father, he looked up to Bryann just like America's favorite TV dad.

Bryann unlocked his front door with the key marked "D" for door. It was Rita's idea to mark them and a very good one because he had so many keys on one chain. One day he'd get around to separating his house keys from his many work keys. Bryann headed down the hall into his bedroom. The room was dimly lit from the sunshine trying to force its way through the blinds. Still weary from this morning's activity, he shook off the urge to hibernate and went into his closet and pulled down a cardboard box from the top shelf.

He found old textbooks, cliffs notes, old exams (nothing lower than a B-minus), and more papers with grades just as impressive. Halfway into the box, he found the instrument that helped get him through college. Bryann unsnapped its leather case and pulled out the voice-activated Dictaphone.

When he was in school, Bryann, after working for a moving company all day, was in no condition to pay attention, much less stay awake in class. So every day before class he would arrive early and tape the Dictaphone to the bottom of the professor's chair and turn it on. Then he'd take a seat in the back of the room next to the window and put on a baseball cap and dark shades. He'd pull the brim of the cap down low enough to touch the top of the shades and lean comfortably against the wall. By the time the professor and students filled the room, he was comatose. As the professor spoke, the Dictaphone would record every word. When the professor paused, the recorder paused, when the professor spoke again, the recorder taped again. When the alarm on Bryann's wristwatch woke him, signaling the end of class, he'd hang around until everyone left, then remove the Dictaphone.

The toilet flushed, and Rita came out the bathroom.

"Rita?" Bryann asked surprised.

Rita turned and jumped. "Bryann, you scared me!"

"Sorry. What are you doing here anyway?"

"What am I doing here?" she repeated.

"Is there an echo in here? Why are you repeating everything I ask you?"

"Why am I repeating everything you ask me?" she asked. Bryann twitched his lips patiently, awaiting an answer. "Okay, I might as well tell you, but I just want you to know that you ruined my big surprise," Rita said.

"Surprise?"

"Yes, surprise. I had it all planned out. When you came home, I'd have a romantic candlelit dinner hot and ready," she took his hand and leaned forward then whispered in his ear, "and me too."

"Sounds great—there's just one problem," he said.

"Oh, no. Don't tell me you're working late."

"No, but we do have a rug rat, remember?"

"Not tonight we don't."

"Is that right?"

"Yup. Your sister's picking Bria up from pre-K and keeping her tonight."

"A child-free night, hmm?" Bryann smiled rubbing his goatee. "It's been a while since we had one of those."

"Tell me about it ... Now, what are *you* doing here?"

"Before I answer, why is their mold growing out of the windowsill?" he asked staring at the green growth.

"Hey, it's not mold. A week ago, Bria and I planted some seeds. In a few more weeks we will have either some cilantro, or some basil. I can't remember what's in each row, but I do know there's growth. Either way your daughter and I did that. Something is happening in the spirit of nurturing. But I'm teaching her that in life we may not always know what we are planting, we just keep sprinkling where we see the possibility of good. That little girl of ours just continues to inspire me. Ok mister, now your turn."

Bryann loved how his wife was always enlightening their daughter and raising her to be kind and conscious. He felt so lucky. So blessed. "This... I came home for this." He said holding up the Dictaphone.

"Your old recorder? What do you need that for?"

"Work stuff." He said.

"Oh. Well, make sure you have plenty of tape, too," Rita winked.

"Tape? Oh, I get it. To stick it under the teacher's chair." Bryann laughed, then stuffed the Dictaphone in his pocket, kissed his wife, and started to leave. On his way out he noticed some grocery bags on the counter. With a mischievous grin, he peeked into the bag.

"Bryann!" Rita called. "You're not snooping in the bag, are you?"

"Sorry." Bryann said, hoping the pack of mozzarella cheese he spotted was an indication that she was preparing her delicious baked ziti.

"Well stop. You already know about dinner tonight. At least let the meal be a surprise."

"Right. See ya later, babe."

Darrius jumped up with a lit cigarette between his lips when Bryann stepped out the elevator. "You sure took long enough," the young man complained.

"Sorry, I—" Bryann stopped in mid-sentence. Something was wrong. This wasn't the same young man he left to go upstairs. Now, he was all nervous and jittery.

"What? What is it?" Darrius asked, feeling guilty opposite Bryann's long stare.

"Are you on something?"

"Am I what? Aw, come on, Mr. Bonner!" Darrius sounded deeply insulted. "How could you even ask me that with all that's going on? Give a brother a little more credit than that."

"It's just that you're acting a little strange, that's all."

"Well, pardon me for being a little nervous, but it's not every day I set up drug dealers."

Bryann let it go but was not totally convinced the young man wasn't under some type of influence.

"So. You got this dickaphone thing?" Darrius asked, changing the subject.

"It's called a Dic-ta-phone, and, yes, I got it right here." He showed him. "So are you ready?"

"Man, that's how I was born."

"Good. Then let's go pay my cousin a visit."

Chapter 6

BRYANN AND DARRIUS STOOD IN SILENCE across the street from the red building with the red neon sign on the roof that flashed, THE VILLIAN'S HIDEOUT. Both were in deep thought about what they were preparing to do and what the consequences might bring. Over the wind's howl they could make out the sounds of partying from inside. All along the front, cars were parked and double-parked, and people caroused inside the hippest bar and lounge in Major City.

The front door opened, and the air filled with loud music as a young couple stumbled out. The young woman, giggling from one too many rum-and-cokes, had to be helped by her boyfriend to their black Navigator barricaded by a shiny silver Corvette. The young man cursed the Corvette's owner as he put his girlfriend in the passenger seat, then stormed around and got behind the wheel. His Navigator roared to life blasting Cypress Hill's 'Hits from the Bong', then smashed into the Corvette repeatedly. Once he was free, and the Corvette was demolished, he sped off into the night.

"So, Trig's in there, huh? Appropriate name." Bryann frowned, wondering if this was what was going on outside, than what lays ahead inside?

"Yup. It's his club. I hear it's real classy." Darrius nodded.

"Oh yeah. I'm sure it's filled with the finest Major City has to offer. So, you ready?"

"Hold up. I gotta take a leak first."

"They've got a bathroom inside, I'm sure."

"It'll just take a minute."

Something didn't feel right to Bryann. After staring into Darrius's eyes for a second, he said, "Okay, but make it quick." As he watched Darrius disappear around the corner, he was convinced the boy was hiding something. Five minutes later, Darrius reappeared.

"Aight, now I'm straight," Darrius said with a new attitude.

"What do you mean, now you're straight?" Bryann was positive he was high on something and studied him close before accusing him again. Then he found his proof. Peeking out from the edge of Darrius's right nostril was a white residue. "You little shit, you!" Bryann snarled. He made it a rule not to use profanity because he believed people who swore were frustrated because of their limited vocabulary and intelligence and didn't know how to express themselves. But this time his anger got the best of him.

"Here I am, sticking my neck out for you, and this is how you repay me, by snorting coke? How's that going to look—we're going in to talk to this man about sparing your life because you lost his drugs—and you're on them?"

Darrius was speechless. Once again, he fucked up. "Look, Mr. B. I'm sorry I blew it again, but I needed something to keep my nerves calm."

"Do you see me on anything?"

"No, but it ain't you who might get killed now, is it?"

"You don't know my history with my cousin."

Darrius nodded. "You're right, my bad."

Bryann shook his head, disappointed. "Just go on home. I'll do this myself."

"But I can't let you go out like that," Darrius said with a hyper flinch.

"We don't have a choice. Trig'll take one look at you and that's all she wrote." Darrius nodded and handed him a yellow card.

"What's this?" Bryann asked, accepting it.

"My cell. Hit me on the hip after it's all said and done."

"Hit you on the hip!" he repeated, beginning to feel used. "I should hit you upside your head. Now get out of here before I change my mind."

Darrius went to leave then stopped and turned to Bryann, "Can I ask you something Mista B? You're crazy smart. Why didn't you take like business classes in college and get one of those white collar, bougie, hedge fund jobs, getting stupid paid?"

"As opposed to just being stupid?"

"That ain't what I meant."

"I know you didn't. Look kid, for me being paid is waking up with food in your fridge, having people in your life who care about you and knowing you made a difference when you put your head back down at night."

"Ok. I can respect that. But I still don't get why you'd help me."

"There are a bunch of reasons I don't have time to go into right now. But the quick answer is, because you remind me of myself at your age."

"Me? Get out of here. No offense but you act white. I mean you wear a suit and tie. You been to college." the man child scoffed thinking they were as different as night and day.

Bryann sighed at his ignorance, "Darrius when black people display their intelligence and carry themselves with dignity, they are not imitating whiteness because intelligence is not an inherently white trait. Black excellence is real and has nothing to do with white proximity. And to answer your question, yes you. I was also a wise ass punk who thought he knew everything and didn't need anyone. And I was also manipulated by the same person manipulating you, who took advantage of my pain and suffering for his own personal gain."

Darrius had to admit, that was exactly who he was. "So then what happened?"

"My older sister's boyfriend happened. He was a cop who saw I needed a role model and stepped up to the plate. If it wasn't for him sticking his neck out for me after I got into trouble, I don't know where I'd be right now."

"So this is about settling a personal debt?"

"That and I believe in you."

"You what? I-I, don't know what to say to that." Darrius said in a soft voice with earnestness and utter confusion. It was the first time he'd ever been told that someone believed in him. On top of that it was coming from the first person he ever respected. "You really mean that?"

Bryann smiled at him. "Yeah kid. I do. Look, how's about we pick this conversation up later? After I go talk to the big scary bad guys inside."

"Oh yeah, sure-sure. One more thing, I never told anybody thanks before but I
really appreciate this." Darrius said and walked off.

Bryann nodded like he had this. Then sighed like he didn't. If word got back about this, he would definitely lose his job. If the people inside found out what he was up to he could lose his life. Then he thought about all the lives Trig destroyed and would destroy including Darrius'. He had to be stopped! Bryann opened his jacket and checked the Dictaphone one last time. He rewound it and played back a portion of the conversation he just had with Darrius. *Perfect,* he thought. *Darrius had no idea he was being taped, and hopefully neither will Trig.*

"It's show time," he said and headed toward uncertainty.

Chapter 7

THE DOOR TO THE VILLIAN'S HIDEOUT, was so red and shiny it looked wet from a fresh coat of paint. Bryann pushed it open and mechanically checked his clothes, relieved they weren't stained. Once inside he was greeted by DMX's song Party Up, rocking his ear drums. He looked around the smoky, loud, dimly lit bar and felt out of place He thought about how long it had been since he was in a nightclub.

The Hideout was divided into two sections. On the left side were cozy red leather booths overflowing with stylishly dressed people, laughing and enjoying themselves as they turned up drinks while grooving to the pretty ebony complexioned DJ spinning records behind her turntable station. On the right was a long glossy bar that trailed half the length of the place. Behind it was a black, thick-necked bartender with long processed hair. A thick, plush, blood-red carpet covered the floor, and the walls were painted in the same scarlet complexion.

Bryann made a beeline for the men's room and locked the door behind him. He splashed cold water on his face then looked at his reflection.

"Come on, you can do this! He's a man, just like you. Breathes air, just like you. Puts his pants on one leg at a time, just like you." Bryann affirmed himself as he tried to shake the rough images he remembered of Trig.

A sudden pounding on the bathroom door was followed by an even louder drunken voice: "Yo! Hurry the fuck up in there! This ain't no damn hotel!" One last splash of self-confidence and Bryann left.

Only the music was pumping louder and faster than Bryann's heart, as he made his way through the thick mixture of hard-working nine-to-fivers and party-all-night playas who hustled for a living. Once he reached the bar, he signaled for the bartender who was busy impressing a tipsy woman with his bouncing pecs.

"What'll you have?" the bartender yelled over the music.

"Hennessey, on the rocks," Bryann yelled back, thinking how much the bartender reminded him of the singers from the group Full Force, with his muscles and Jheri-curls.

Full Force disappeared but was back in a minute with a glass of cognac and ice. Bryann slid a ten-dollar bill toward the bartender. The bartender slid him his change back.

"Anything else?"

Bryann nodded yes. "Where can I find Trig?"

Full Force paused and flicked the toothpick in his mouth side to side, sizing Bryann up and deciding if he should answer. "Straight to the back," he replied. The way he figured, if the jittery man was one of Trig's many enemies, then his security would make short work of him.

Bryann turned up the drink, then placed an empty glass on the bar. He nodded a thanks and headed for the back leaving a tip on the bar under the watchful eye of a security camera.

After squeezing past a bevy of people he came to a clearing in the crowd and discovered there was a whole other section in the back of the notorious night club. The only one he found was a man in a black hoodie and sagging Tommy Hilfiger jeans playing a video game with his back facing the crowd.

Bryann headed toward the area, curious why everyone was packed in the front of the club and not back here where there was plenty of room.

"Can I help you?" an unfriendly, deep voice asked.

"Large dude." Bryann said after he spun on his heels and was standing chest to face with the biggest man he'd come into contact with in his life. Then the big man stood up and became bigger. "Larger dude." Dressed in a tight black T-shirt, he stood well over six feet nine inches easily and weighed three hundred pounds plus, with no trace of body fat. Physically, he was overpowering. But there was something else there that set him apart from other mountain-sized men who spent the majority of their day in a gym, and Bryann discovered it when his eyes traveled down his steel frame, forcing him to gasp when he noticed his arms. They were huge and swollen. Like they had a bad reaction to shellfish, giving him a comic book Incredible Hulk appearance. Luckily for the giant, he didn't share Hulk's beastly looks and instead was quite handsome with a smooth cinnamon complexion, dark, curly hair, and a goatee.

"Yo! Is you deaf?" the brick wall with eyes asked.

"If it's not any trouble, I'd like to see Trig, please," Bryann said, tearing his eyes from the freak of nature's arms.

"And you are?"

The walkie-talkie on the giant's hip crackled to life: "Let him through, JackHammer. He's cool."

Bryann looked over his shoulder and observed the man playing the video game holding a walkie-talkie up to his head. Then suddenly a strong hand went around his waist. Another grabbed his arm. "Hey! What are you doing?" he demanded.

"Fuck's it look like?" JackHammer snapped. "I'm friskin' you."

Bryann's heart pounded. If JackHammer found the Dictaphone, he was dead. One hand checked for a weapon, the other clamped around Bryann's hip like a vice grip, making him cringe.

"There's no need for this, I'm clean big man," Bryann

nervously said.

"Shut up!" JackHammer growled as he moved up Bryann's arms and closer to the Dictaphone in his inside pocket. "You look kinda nervous. What chu got in there?" he asked suspiciously, unbuttoning Bryann's coat.

"Nothing man. I told you, I'm clean."

"For your sake, you'd better be!"

In his head, Bryann began planning his own funeral. Closed casket.

"Hammer!" The walkie-talkie crackled, stopping the thick, hot sausage–sized fingers half an inch from the Dictaphone. "I said he's cool. Ain't no need to check him."

JackHammer slowly released his grip on Bryann with a vile look. "Enjoy you stay. I look forward to us meeting again."

"You know even though it was a compliment, it sounds more like a threat." Bryann said to JackHammer who stood there staring then twisted the cap off of a beer that wasn't a twist off. He exhaled, fixed his clothes then walked up behind the man who uttered the life-saving words into the walkie-talkie.

He was wearing a hooded sweatshirt and was armed with a red plastic revolver connected to a large virtual-reality shooting video game. On the wide video screen soldiers of fortune jumped out from behind digitized trees and boulders armed with bayonets, Uzis, and bazookas trying to kill their human nemesis. Each time a commando rolled into the line of fire he was blown into chunks of flying body parts.

"Long time no see. What's it been like, two, three years?" the hooded man said with his back facing Bryann, as if he had eyes in the back of his head. With a tap of the plastic trigger, he took out a helicopter and earned 500 bonus points.

Bryann swallowed hard, "So how'd you—"

"Mini-cams," The hooded man cut him off, pointing to the ceiling. Bryann looked up and saw a row of video screens mounted in a wide strip into the ceiling directly over the video game. A paratrooper swooped down and opened fire, taking him out and the words "GAME OVER" flashed, taunting him. "Shit!" he cursed, stepping to the side to reveal a four-inch TV monitor affixed to the console that captured Bryann.

Spinning around, Trig snatched back his hood to reveal a shaved head that rendered him simultaneously threatening and striking, showing off his chiseled features.

"Damn wack-ass game!" Trig fumed, tossing the plastic gun to the floor like a spoiled child and pulled out a real gun then aimed it at the game. Remembering he had a guest, he regained his composure, placed the weapon back where it came from, and turned with a sharp smile.

"So what's up, cousin, gimme some love!" he hollered with his arms raised, embracing Bryann with a tight squeeze and a blinding white smile that enhanced his dark skin. He was handsome, with boyish good looks and a set of soft eyes that gave a hard stare. He didn't have muscles like those in body-building magazines; instead, he owned a street build that made him large enough to get him noticed but small enough to slip away when necessary. "So, sit, sit," he offered, gesturing toward a booth. Bryann obliged, removing his coat and laying it across his lap carefully as he sat. "You hungry, thirsty?" Trig asked, snapping his fingers. A scantily dressed waitress scurried over.

"Nah. I had a drink at the bar," Bryann said.

"I know. So, you're still drinking Hennessey, huh? I stopped after it became as common as red Kool-Aid for every two-bit fake-ass gangster from the projects," Trig said, ordering a bottle of Moet. "So, what's been up? You still working as a hoe-cial worker?" Trig asked, scooting into the booth across from Bryann, blinging from the jewelry he adorned himself with. Besides the low-hanging diamond-laden chains around his neck and diamond rings on the fingers of both hands, he wore diamond studs in his ears, a heavy diamond bracelet on his right wrist, and a bold face watch in similar fashion on the left.

"Excuse me?" Bryann said pulling his eyes off his cousin's iced-out jewels.

"That's right: hoe-cial worker. Hell, after all you the one killing yourself for peanuts. Just like a ho that's getting pimped. And your wife, is she still working for the shitty—oops—I mean, the city?" Trig winked, cracking himself up.

Bryann was furious. Trig could have never accomplished half of what Bryann had. Yet he felt he could arrogantly sit there and insult all he believed in and worked for. The weight of the Dictaphone shifted, and he grinned as he thought how good it would feel taking him down.

"Yeah, I got a couple of pairs of socks with holes in the toes if that's what you're getting at. But other than that, I'm doing quite well, and I love my job." Bryann said through tight lips.

"Don't you mean you just over broke," Trig muttered.

"Excuse me?"

"The letters in job, that's what they stand for… Just- Over - Broke!" Trig shook his head and laughed out. "Man, that sucker's life made you soft. Got you all domesticated and shit. And judging by that doughy mid-section Dad bod you're rocking, I bet you don't even work out anymore. Me, I can easily bench press three hundred. Curl fifty and run five miles daily. But at least you're not prematurely balding. When my hairline started looking like George Jefferson's, I shaved it all off in favor of that Malik Yoba look. But at least my beard connects."

"Is that right?" Bryann said disgusted by his cousin's definitive personality.

"Damn. I can't believe you still say, 'Is that right!' Vegas would be touched. God bless the dead." Trig said, alluding to how his cousin still responded to practically anything with 'Is that right?'

Bryann picked up the phrase when from a slick street hustler he admired named Vegas. Vegas, who was a professional gambler, could turn ten dollars into ten thousand with the shuffle of a deck or roll of the dice. Although no one could actually prove he was cheating, people always said he had to be, mainly because they were themselves. His reply to their accusations was a long drawn-out, slick "Is that right? And when he was finally caught cheating, while staring down the barrel of a pistol, it was also the last thing he said before he was shot dead." Bryann began using the phrase as his own until it became, second nature for him to say. The waitress returned and placed an ice bucket of champagne before him, then left. Trig popped the cork and gripped the neck of the bottle and guzzled it like soda.

·"So, what brings you down here, cuz?" he asked, smacking his lips and wiping his wet, thin mustache. "Hmm ... let me guess. You had a rough day at the office and you wanna cop a bag of Mister Boombastic?" The annoyed look Bryann shot Trig made him grin. "No? Hmm, then the only other thing I can think of is you want me to spare that punk kid Darrius's life?" Trig winked as he took another swig.

Bryann's eyes narrowed to an inscrutable slit like a cat's. "Guess that explains the warm reception."

"That it does."

Just then a door opposite Trig's video game opened, and a beautiful young black woman with smooth skin in a poured-on candy red couture stepped out. She danced alone for a moment then she saw Trig waving at her and came over.

"Hey sweetie. So, who have we here?" she asked.

"Babe this is my cousin Bryann. We go back like eight-tracks, Cadillacs and Similac. Bee, this is my lady, Mary." Trig introduced proudly.

"Hello. Nice to meet you, Bryann," Mary smiled friendly, opening her arms.

"Nice to meet you, too," Bryann replied as she leaned in to give him an unexpected hug.

"Apologies, she's a hugger." Trig shook his head.

"So, you're the cousin my Mordecai always talks about when he reminisces about the bad ol' days." she said placing a red lip print on his head.

"Hey, what'd I say about calling me by my government name?" he said pissed.

"Sorry, Trig." She rolled her eyes.

"Anyway, this Buster may not look like it, but back in the day he was no joke. He had niggas petro. Straight up chin-checking fools. They used to say rumor has it, Bryann spells his name with two N's, for no nonsense! Hey, speaking of the bad ol' days how's your boy Warren doing? Heard he made Lieutenant at Wrong Path Penitentiary. Last time I saw him he was a bitch ass CO on D-block, escorting niggas to the yard and acting like he don't know nobody. Nigga must've forgot that where we're from, a bullet is a badge of honor and the gangs don't wear leather jackets. They wear scars. Like the one you got from Eddie Tift you're hiding under that beard." Trig laughed.

"What do you say we leave the past in the past," Bryann said, and Trig held up his hands in surrender, amused. Eyeing Mary, Bryann noticed a pair of tumor-sized gold earrings peeking from under her long curly weave and an engagement ring that featured a diamond the size of an acorn. "I see congratulations are in order,"

"Thank you. We're setting the date for next spring."

"Hey you know me. I'm quick to pull the trigger." Trig smirked.

"So, what about you? Are you married, Bryann?" Mary smiled.

"Yes, ma'am. Twelve years," Bryann grinned.

"Wow! He looks happy, doesn't he, honey? Think we'll be like that in twelve years?" Mary asked Trig and wrapped her arms around him.

Eyeing a Latina in a mid-drift top and belly-chain across the room dancing seductively to Bump N' Grind by R. Kelly, while shooting him a come-get-this look, Trig shrugged his fiancée from his shoulders. "Yeah-yeah, I guess. Look, check this out. Bryann and I got some catching up to do, so how's about giving us a minute."

"Sure, baby," she said, concealing her embarrassment, and then turned to Bryann. "It was very nice meeting you, Bryann. And next time you come by bring your wife. I'd love to meet her. Hey, perhaps we can all hang out sometime. Go bowling."

"Sure." Bryann smiled, knowing there was a better chance of his hitting the lotto on Mars than double-dating with Trig and his woman. "Nice girl," he said as Mary danced off in the direction of the crowd playing hostess.

Trig shrugged and gulped more champagne. "Eh, she's a-ight."

"She must be more than just a-ight' for your gonna make

an honest woman out of her." Bryann pointed out.

"How honest can she be if she's with me? But truth be told, I was boning so many chicken heads, hood rats, and project bunnies I started to feel like a goddamn zookeeper! Then I met Mary at a Busta Rhymes concert. Decent in the face. She used to strip so she comes with perks. Built like a porn star, got the bomb ass head, it's Vegas in the bedroom, no kids and keeps a clean house. I mean she can't cook worth a damn. I found that out when she seasoned the pork chops with ramen noodle packets. But who the fuck cares? It's not like I don't have a five-star chef on the payroll. So, I figured what the hell. You see, niggas be so quick to say bros before hoes. Clearly, they forgot that Tony killed Manny. Nino killed G-Money. Bishop killed Raheem. And Kane killed Able. But what niggas don't realize is Bonnie never switched up on Clyde. And I figured we all need a decent broad to make us look good. Besides, when you see tits like that you gotta have em. Gotta get em. Gotta keep em. You can identify, right, mister til' death do us part?"

"Actually, no. I married my wife for completely different reasons,"

"Other than bomb ass head, what else is there?" Trig snickered.

Bryann felt like his braincells were depleting every nanosecond they continued talking but reminded himself why he was here. "So, Mary doesn't strike me as the counterintuitive type. Does she know how your club was obtained?"

Trig snickered. "In the beginning I told her that I buy foreclosed property from the city. Fix it up and resell for a huge profit. But eventually after she got used to a certain lifestyle and I got tired of remembering lies, I hipped her to what's what. You know that mink coat you love? The ice on your ears and fingers? That phat Benz all your girls are jealous over? Well, it was all purchased courtesy of the base heads in Major City."

Bryann shook his head with disgust. "Wow."

"Cousin don't player-hate. Congratulate! Look around, do you think you could acquire what I have living that sucker's life you do? Peep my watch—the shit is so new there ain't even no tan lines underneath it! And my crib. That shit should be on MTV Cribs! Never do the envy, jealousy and insecure stuff. Be the hustler, well-wisher, the go-getter."

"Trust me, Trig I am hardly jealous. Once you hit a certain age, you become permanently unimpressed by a lot of shit. Yeah, you have a lot of nice things I can't afford working for a nonprofit. But that's all they are…things. I have an honest job that allows me to give back to my community, I married the love of my life, have a beautiful little girl, a roof over my head and the admiration and respect of my people."

Trig looked up from the blinged out, diamond bracelet on his wrist he was smiling at. "Huh? I stopped listening after you said, can't afford. But yeah, I suppose that other stuff you mentioned is something to be proud of too. As for me, I got Robin Leach–size caviar dreams, and the only way they'll come true is with cash money! I don't like to wallow in my ghetto upbringing but you better than anybody should know how rough it was growing up. Moms working as a maid for those snobby-rich white folks." he paused with a sneer as his early memories and the permanent scars poverty left, came back to haunt him. "I remember when she'd bring home their leftovers. Lobster, steak, filet mignon—it was all good, but we had to cut around the bite marks."

"Well, you don't have that problem anymore." Bryann said.

"Yeah, a lot has changed. But to this day I don't know how my moms did it. Shitty job. Being treated like less than. Always sick."

"It's called putting other's needs before your own. You should try it some time."

"Whatever. All I know is I was old enough to remember all of it and young enough to understand none of it. I remember when she had a really bad crisis and I had to call for help. The doctor at the free clinic is explaining to a kid how normal blood cells are round. But my mom's are shaped like a sickle or a question mark. They get attached and they tend to clog the blood vessel. This deprives the body of oxygen, and it causes intense pain. With sickle cell she's gonna have to go through this all her life. All I could think, was how poor people die and rich people live. And they have the same damn thing! Then in comes my father. The neighborhood joke."

"Uncle Sid wasn't a joke."

"Easy for you to say. Out of the Wise sisters your mom was the one who was actually wise. Walked around with her head held high, married your father, a radical cat who instead of crying about how unfair life was, did something about it and became a lawyer. Unlike my mother who cleaned toilets and married a loser."

"He did what he had to do to put food on the table."

"What he did was knock on neighbors' doors asking if they needed their crib painted or grass cut. Rummage through people's trash for things to sell like he was Fred Sanford. Then I gotta' face their kids in school. That shit was humiliating! Fucking kids teased the shit out of me! One in particular, always gave me the business. If it wasn't about my clothes, it was my Pops. He called him a pullman porter, whatever the fuck that is. You know years later I actually bumped into that asshole at a bar. Fucking Rodney Webber."

Bryann looked up. "Hey, I remember him. Captain of the football team. Last I heard he got a free ride to Hampton University. He was going places. Then he just vanished off the face of the earth. Whatever happened to him?"

"I happened to him." Trig smiled lavishly. "He was home for Spring Break and I bumped into him at that lounge everybody used to go to, Uncle Charlie's. We kicked it over a couple of drinks. He told me he was pre-med. Said that too many people warned him that NFL stood for Not For Long and that he needed a back up plan. He also said he was being spread thin from football practice and class and needed a break. So, I say no more and took him to a couple of parties. Introduced him to some friends. Got him laid. Gave him the VIP treatment. And at some point during the night when he was feeling on top of the world, I suggested he should try this new and cheap alternative to coke and weed called crack that had just hit the hood. At the time nobody really knew much about it. But I did. I was working for Fat Sam back then and had a crew working under me at the Roosevelt Houses. Needless to say crack was my middle name. He was reluctant at first but I swore to him by the time he was back at school it would be out of his system. Then I gave Rodney just enough, to beam up like Scotty for a week. But within a couple of days he was blowing up my beeper, already hooked. So, I sent him to my peoples. Instructed them, every time he comes by to give him whatever he wants. And tell him it's on the house. Courtesy of the Pullman Porter's son. Once he was hooked, I cut him off. By then he was a full-fledged junkie with a thousand dollar a day habit. After he lost his scholarship. His future. And his dignity. Family and friends cut him off. He sold everything he had. Then stole anything he could. Eventually he resorted to selling himself to those nasty boy-lovers cruising, down by the pier. Last I heard he caught the monster. But you want to know what the funniest part to the story is?"

"So, there's actually a funny part to all of this?" Bryann asked revolted.

"Right before he hit the pipe for the first time, the nigga turned to me and actually apologized to me for all the shit he put me through when we were kids. He said the guilt bothered him for years. And it was the main reason he came home instead of hitting Miami for spring break. He only went to Uncle Charlie's because after asking around, he heard I hung out there and was hoping to find me so he could apologize. I said dude, I had forgotten all about that. Water under the bridge. Now go ahead…Smoke up." Trig said diabolically and had a long, hard laugh reminiscing at how he destroyed a man's life. "What?" he asked his cousin sitting across from him looking appalled.

"Guess you were out of angel dust?" he said with a glare.

It took a minute, then Trig realized what he was referring to. "Oh man I totally forgot about that. Don't tell me you still tripping over that. No pun intended."

"So you can hold a past grudge but I can't?" Bryann shook his head. Trig shrugged. "And I don't think the offense matched the punishment."

"And I don't think he suffered enough." Trig shrugged.

"Let me know where I can contribute to your therapy bill." Bryann said shaking his head.

"I don't need therapy, I need money. I know why I'm not ok! But if you find me as insensitive as a toilet seat, then what would you have done instead Mister Judgmental?" Trig smirked.

"Nothing."

"Nothing? The guy who contributed to your shitty childhood is in your crosshairs and you don't pull the trigger?"

Bryann shook his head. "The best revenge is none. Heal, move on and don't become like those who hurt you. But in this case you could have taken a page out of Rodney's book, since he was remorseful, filled with guilt and apologized. Instead of snuffing out a potential Black doctor."

"How I see it, if he was that weak he had no business being a doctor no how. But how's about we move on from Rodney." Trig shrugged with no remorse. "This conversation reminds me of when my old man would come in, reeking of defeat. He'd pop open a beer, look at me and say, 'Boy, there are two kinds of people in this world, the givers and the takers. The takers may eat better, but the givers sleep better.' Which is why today, I have a full belly and haven't had a full night's sleep since the mid-eighties."

"I'm pretty sure you missed his point."

"Did I? Or did you? Then again, you always interpreted things differently, with your happy go lucky optimistic way of seeing a silver lining in damn near every situation. But I will say this. My father's work ethic was crazy. Rain, sleet, snow, hurricanes, lightning he was out there sun-up to sun down. Bouncing from one humiliating, low paying, back breaking, bullshit job to the next. Could be where I got my work ethic from. That and my love for Spaghetti Westerns." He said allowing the holster on his hip to show.

"So, when's the last time you saw him?" Bryann asked.

"Who, my father? Shit. When I buried my moms. But I send him an envelope each month faithfully, to keep the lights on and food in the fridge. Because he did that for us."

"Count your blessings." Bryann said reminding his cousin that his parents weren't with him in the physical, and he missed them every day. He also made a mental note to check on his uncle.

Trig rolled his eyes unsympathetically, "Trust me cuz, it's

overrated. That's why I swore, when I got older, never me. And I refused to gamble on college. Them egg heads bust their ass for years just to come out and bust their ass paying back student loans. And they're the lucky ones, cause it ain't a whole lot of jobs waiting for us black folks when we get out. Truth be told, all a college degree is good for is answering questions on *Jeopardy* as you scarf down greasy take-out in front of a twelve-inch black-and-white. However, if I was to go to college, it'd be Spellman."

"That's an all-women's school."

"Exactly!" Trig said with a devilish smile. "The other day some clown in a suit came in here bragging he was making six figures. So, I interrupted his conversation to burst his bubble and told him, that's only two hundred and seventy-four dollars a day. And Uncle Sam is taking half. Like I said fuck the legit path!"

"Sorry to hear you say that." Bryann frowned.

Trig eyed his cousin, "Oh? Well you didn't seem so sorry when my lifestyle came in handy this morning, right?"

"Excuse me?"

"No, excuse you! You had a situation early this morning with some vicious members of Gang Greene, correct?" Bryann's stunned expression answered Trig's question. "No need to answer. I already know. I also know that if it wasn't for me, that ugly bastard Big Ant would have snapped you in two like a bread stick."

Bryann felt embarrassed. He admitted Big Ant gave in rather easily, but he believed it was because he had stood his ground.

"You see," Trig continued, "I got eyes everywhere. I know everything. Like how you ladle slop, to the homeless at soup kitchens and play big brother to them snotty-nosed crumb snatchers on your block." Bryann glanced up suddenly at his cousin putting his business out there. "That's right, I know all about how you check their report cards and hand out money for candy and video games for every A they receive. Even when we was doing dirt, you always gave yourself freely with no thought of a reward. Like that time you gave that lady strung out pushing a stroller your money. Or when you pulled me off of that dude I was whipping on cause he wouldn't give up his wallet."

"He was an old man on a fixed income! You were literally taking food off his table."

"And that's exactly what I'm talking about. But you're wasting your time with them kids. Eventually, they'll learn about the power of the outlaw and that only with money, no matter how ill-gained, will they ever amount to anything. Which is why I don't understand why your waste your time."

"There are plenty of reasons. Such as to prevent little girls from choosing a pimp or a violent boyfriend to replace the father who wasn't around. Or to be a role model to the lost boys who look up to the drug dealers. Another reason is because of the greatest love of all." Bryann shrugged.

Trig lifted a confused eyebrow. "Say what now?"

"You have heard of Whitney's song, Greatest Love of All?"

"Once or twice when my girl played it at the crib. Wouldn't play it here though. Might cause a riot. So, what about it?"

"It's one of the best, most powerful songs ever written about self-preservation and dignity. Its universal message crosses all boundaries and instills one with hope that it's not too late to better ourselves. The lyrics are advice for kids to succeed in the future. Like the part that goes, everybody's searching for a hero. People need someone to look up to. A lot of these kids are looking for just that."

"And that's you, their hero?"

"I just want them to believe in themselves. Love themselves no matter what. So they don't end up being alone cause of the paths they take in life, or lose themselves in life's greatest struggles. Next time you listen to the song, listen to the crucial message."

"Umm-hmm." Trig sighed. Suddenly there was a loud commotion in the front of the club and Trig sprang to his feet. "Be right Black." He said and jogged toward the action then stopped beside JackHammer. "Fucks up?" he asked his one-man security staff.

"Some nigga giving Mary a problem about his bill. I was about to handle it!"

Trig glanced back at Bryann, who was watching him with curious eyes, and a devilish grin flashed across his face. "Nah. Fall back Hammer. I got this."

The hood anthem, 'Danger' by rap duo Blahzay-Blahzay ricocheted off the walls. But couldn't conceal the angry voices.

"Looka' here Ma, there's no way in hell my bill should come up to no forty-one fucking dollars and seventy-three goddamn cents! Not for no goddamn pitcher of beer and chili cheese fries! No way!" a tall dark-skinned Dominican man with dreadlocks cornrowed down his back was yelling.

Mary ran a hand through her hair and exhaled before responding. "Sir, please calm down. There is no need for you to use that language. Now, before you placed your order, you obviously saw the prices on the menu, correct?"

"No. I ain't bother to check shit cause I figured a pitcher of flat beer and soggy fries shouldn't come up to no more than fifteen bucks including a motherfucking tip!" he said, hoping to intimidate her with the two and a half feet he had over her.

As they went back and forth, no one noticed Trig silently move through the crowd, like a ninja.

"Look, sir. I apologize if you have a discrepancy with our prices. I suggest that in the future you pay closer attention to the menu before ordering. But the fact remains that you still owe me…hey! Where are you going? You haven't paid!"

The man turned his back on Mary and started for the door, then stopped and arrogantly spun around. "Obviously you don't know me," he said with an air of royalty.

"No, I don't. Should I?" Mary asked.

"Well allow me to introduce myself. The name's Crime. And as we all know…Crime don't pay." With the introductions behind him, Crime spun on his heels and continued toward the door, shoving people too afraid to move out of his way. He paused when he spotted a hard-faced Trig blocking his path smiling with a toothpick between his teeth, nodding to the music.

"Haters are like crickets, they make a lot of noise, you can hear them, but you can't see them. And when you confront them, they suddenly get quiet…Catch!" Trig calmy said then tossed something small and shiny at Crime.

Crime's long fingers snatched the object out of the air. He opened his palm and held up a .45-caliber slug.

"A bullet?" Crime said, confused.

"Yeah, a bullet. And if you don't pay my lady what you owe her, the next bullet you catch won't be in your hand…it'll be in your ass!" Trig said in a calm but threatening baritone and flashed the butt of his gun peeking from his belt for added effect. A silence swept over the room as spectators slowly backed away. Mary folded her arms across her huge bosom with raised eyebrows, waiting for tough-talking Mr. 'Crime Don't Pay' to reply.

Crime didn't graduate from high school. So he wasn't the smartest man in the world, but he did know that he was going to pay. One way or another! "Sheee-it," he said in a toothy, long, drawn-out wind. "Man, I was just clowning around, bro. No disrespect to your lady. Of course, I'll settle up."

The nervous expression on Crime's face called him a liar as he fumbled in his back pocket and pulled out a worn leather wallet. He withdrew a hundred-dollar bill and walked over to Trig.

"Motherfucker do I look like a goddamn waitress to you?" Trig growled with flared nostrils.

Crime stood before Trig trembling like a frightened child when Mary snatched the money out of his hand. It was moist with fear.

"See what happens when you mistake kindness for

weakness?" she asked, then stormed off to get his change.

With a twisted sneer Trig got up close and personal in Crime's face. "The change is her tip! Now bounce, you bitch ass nigga!" Crime tripped over his feet running, grateful he was alive. Trig turned to the staring crowd and shrugged, "I guess crime do pay!" he said causing an infectious laughter as partygoers returned to dancing and conversing as if a man's life wasn't almost snuffed out. Trig charismatically made his way through the crowd, proudly strutting like a black panther to the beat as adoring fans patted him on the back.

Back in the red booth, Bryann was angry with himself for being even a tiny bit impressed with how his cousin handled Crime. Ever since he walked through the door, he had been trying to block out the feeling of nostalgia and focus on what he came to do, but he couldn't shake it. Visiting Trig was like old times.

When he was twelve, life dealt Bryann a bad hand to say the least and took away both of his parents, leaving his older sister, Dee-Dee, and him to fend for themselves. It was then he began spending more time with his cousin Trig, who was two years older.

Trig was the black sheep of the family. He got his nickname on the streets for his love of guns. Buying them, collecting them, stealing them, and shooting folks with them, and he had spent half his life in prison. Raised in impoverished conditions with little supervision because his parents held down multiple jobs to keep a cracked roof over their heads, he was determined to lead a better life. So like so many other black men in the ghetto, he began dealing in illegal goods and narcotics. When he discovered his younger cousin was desperate for a role model and impressed with the lifestyle he led, he was more than happy to introduce him to his world. At first, he started Bryann off with small assignments, such as snatching purses and picking pockets, but the young man was a quick learner and advanced to armed robberies. And fueled by anger over losing his parents, combined with his muscular physique, he handled his own quite nicely in street fights.

Dee-Dee was at her wits' end. She could not control Bryann. It wasn't until Trig and Bryann found themselves handcuffed to a bench in the middle of a precinct that Bryann realized this wasn't a game. He no longer felt like the fearless rebel that he thought he was and instead he felt like the scared little boy that he really was. Trig on the other hand had been shackled to the same bench many times in the past. His name carved into the bench as well as the bored look on his face proved it.

Bryann stared at his sneakers in silence, regretting all the dirt he did that had him facing a lengthy jail term. A pair of patent leather shoes appeared before him. He looked up and met Gainer's disappointed eyes. He wished he'd listened to Gainer all those times he lectured to him about the dangers of running the streets. Now it was too late. Then a miracle happened.

Gainer told him he called on a lot of favors and got them off with the agreement that they would have to perform community service and agree to go back to school. If they were to sever the agreement at any time, the deal was off, and they would have to go to jail for a long time.

Bryann didn't know much about prison. The little he did know he'd heard from Trig, and it scared him. The stories of rape and murder flashed through his head, and he was more than willing to cooperate. Already, Trig had spent most of his voting age behind bars, and wasn't trying to go back either, so he agreed to the conditions.

As time went by, Bryann attacked his studies like a demon. He went from the dean's office to the dean's list. This was also around the time a certain young lady named Rita Rene Boone whom he had been trying to date finally gave into his persistence. With all these new interests, Bryann and Trig's relationship deteriorated, and they saw less and less of each other.

Trig found things to do to keep busy too, like getting deeper involved in the criminal element. Though the two were leading opposite lives, the one thing they had in common stood out—the desire to be the best at what they did. By the time Bryann married Rita and finished college, Trig had become a major player in the criminal world.

"Sorry about the interruption," Trig said, sliding in across the table.

"It's all right, I understand. Running a club can be dangerous." Bryann said.

"Dangerous? Who, that clown? Please! Homeboy was small potatoes. Now the Wolf Pack and Gang-Greene showing up here on the same night. That's dangerous! Them fools almost tore the place apart last month. If it wasn't for JackHammer and my other partner, Slam, I don't know what would've happened. We had to work it out so that one gang ain't here when the other is."

Half-listening to Trig ramble about trivial matters, he squeezed the Dictaphone, waiting for his cousin to incriminate himself. Trig reached in his inside pocket and pulled out a wooden box.

"Care for one? They're dipped in rum," he bragged, cutting off the tip of a Cohiba with a solid gold cigar cutter as he bopped his head to the baby making anthem, 'Get it On Tonight' by the smooth R&B crooner, Montell Jordan.

"I'm good," Bryann declined.

"Nothing but the best, baby!" Trig said, imitating his hero

Tony Montana, then sparked up, took a long pull on the stogie and blew thick smoke. "Shit! The Honeys is in the hi-zouse tonight! Yo, what the fuck were we talking about again?" he said eyeballing a beautiful dark-skinned black woman with runway looks and a vanilla smile while she danced to the beat.

"You were about to tell me that you were going to forget about the situation between you and Darrius."

"What are you a comedian in your off hours?" Trig asked bowled over laughing. "Nice try nigga, but your Jedi mind-tricks ain't working on me. I peeped what you were trying with that Greatest Love song meaning and facts bullshit. But fuck that! That fool allowed himself to get robbed for over ten g's of product. And do you know what he was doing when got, got? Getting a goddamn blowjob from a rooster."

"Rooster?"

"It's what I call hoes when any cock-a-do. And I hear it was Sugar. That nasty hoochie's syphilis has syphilis." he scoffed, cringing like he just chugged spoiled milk.

"Hey, you hired a dumb kid."

"Says the guy advocating for one."

"All I'm saying is what did you expect?" Bryann said calmly, opening the door for Trig to admit his crime."

"I expected him to carry himself like a man and not like a kid. I have plenty of other underage employees on my payroll, none of whom screw up as badly as him. And to think I hired him because logic dictates, the little brother of a successful drug dealer like Moola would be a good asset." Trig said so cavalier. *Finally!* Bryann thought. "But the thing about kids is, as long as they got a new pair of sneakers and some gold, they're satisfied."

"So, let me get this straight, not only did you employ the kid brother of a known drug dealer because you figured no assembly required but you are also using other kids to sell your drugs and you're exploiting them," Bryann said, choosing his words carefully so Trig would have to admit his crimes. Trig shrugged his shoulders and puffed. "Don't you get it? You're causing a genocide!" Bryann argued, again going for a verbal response that could be taped.

"Don't *you* get it? No matter what anyone says or does, the truth is that drugs have been around from the beginning, and they'll be here to the end! Why? Because people like to get fucked up! I'm a proud capitalist who knows that you could get rid of all the drugs. Weed, coke, crack, smack, dust, X, heroin, and so on, and it wouldn't mean shit! People would just come up with new ways to fry their brain cells!"

"Don't you feel any remorse for the countless people's lives destroyed by this genocide?"

"What, part of me saying I'm a proud capitalist did you miss? If it weren't for those losers, I wouldn't have all this," Trig said, waving an arm over his club.

"People are dying everyday thanks to you. Doesn't that bother you?" Bryann said with a look of disgust, trying to locate a drop of decency in his cousin.

Trig shrugged, "I feel like this. If you got strung out back in the eighties, I don't fault ya. You had no idea what you were getting involved in. Crack just came out, it was new, a cheap, quick high as opposed to coke. But, if you have seen with your own eyes generation after generation of addicts destroy their lives over a crack rock, and you pick up the pipe and say, 'Man, I gots to try me some of that!' then you ain't shit and you deserve what happens."

"Ok true nobody put a gun to their head and forced them to indulge. But you think the powers that be don't strategically flood our communities with dope, liquor stores and greasy fast-food joints on every corner when then know people are living in poverty, depressed and want to escape by self-medicating and eating themselves to an early grave?"

"Oh, so now it's my fault people have diabetes as well as a drug habit? I grew up under those same messed up conditions and I didn't fall victim to either."

"No, you just took advantage of those who did."

Trig sucked his teeth, "And I should feel sorry for *them*? Ha!"

"You should have Black communal accountability. Kids look up to you. They think you're a success, and the only way to lift themselves out of dire straits is to emulate you."

"And they're right. It's like, for some this game is a meal ticket, for others, like myself, it's a calling."

Keep talking, big mouth, Bryann thought. "Look, as a favor to me, lay off Darrius," he said, pretending not to hear the cold reply.

"As a favor to you?" he laughed like he just heard a joke. "What about the favor I did for you this morning? You rolled in here like a bad fart and didn't even say thanks. Nope, can't see it. Darrius knew what he was getting himself into, he's a victim of his own stupidity. If he had come to me and told me what happened, things could've been different, but how would that look, me letting him slide like that? I've got an image to uphold."

"Yeah, right. Like you would have forgiven him if he'd come to you and explained what happened."

"So what are you like an activist for the culture now?"

"I'm just a guy who cares."

Trig grinned and shook his head. "You know how funny it

is to hear you talk like this? Especially when you were such a badass back in the day. What happened to the guy who said, see me in a fight with a bear, help the bear; pour honey on me?"

"He grew up." Bryann shrugged recalling when he was an angry adolescent.

Trig grinned and put out his cigar. "Or he couldn't cut it. This is boring the shit out of me. Listen, tell your boy Darrius to pay me for the drugs he lost or deal with the consequences."

Bryann shook his head, not believing his ears. "Didn't you hear anything I said?"

Trig squinted into the bottom of the empty bottle of champagne. "Man, why are you sweatin' me? If you want to clean up all the drug dealing in Major City so bad step to Moola. He's the one making boat loads of Benjamins, not me. At least not yet."

"That's exactly why you should stop now. The police are aware of the goings-on of the Wolf Pack, and it won't be long before they are stopped. But nobody is watching you, and that's what's scary. It won't be long before you are on the level of the Wolf Pack and Gang-Greene."

"Thanks for the vote of confidence, cousin. But I'd like to think I am bigger than Gang-Greene."

"I see it was a mistake coming down here," Bryann said standing, careful not to let the Dictaphone slip out of his jacket.

"Remember when we'd get lifted over a couple of dime bags, drink more liquor than a college student and hit the streets daring anyone to be in our way?"

"I remember." Bryann sighed trying to forget.

"Do you also remember what the letters in the word poor stood for to me?"

"Passing Over Opportunities Repeatedly," Bryann rolled his eyes.

"Precisely. So instead of doing that, why don't you come and work for me? Apologies. Come and work with me. What do you say? After the work you put in back in the day, you wouldn't even have to get your hands dirty. It would be just like old times." Trig said extending his hand, waiting for a response with hope in his eyes. He desperately wanted to recapture his wild, carefree youth, and who better than the person he experienced it with, could make it happen? His family.

"Sorry, but I can't. See, I have this problem with a disc in my back, and I can't *stoop* that low." Bryann said leaving him hanging and rising to leave.

"Oh, cousin. One more thing," Trig said.

Bryann stopped but didn't look back.

"You claim you're all about helping folks. Having empathy, right?"

"What of it?"

"Just remember, empathy in this world, will get you killed."

Bryann walked off. He got what he came for. As his cousin walked away, Trig held up his hand with his fingers pointed like a gun and imagined he had Bryann in his sight.

"All in good time," Trig grinned.

Bryann made his way to the red steel door, clutching his blazer with the Dictaphone still taping. He felt the outside of his pocket with the recorder and found the stop button and shut it off.

"I knew you were hiding something!" JackHammer's voice shouted three decibels over the noise directly behind Bryann.

Bryann froze, instantly feeling sick with fear. A knot formed in his stomach, and he swallowed twice because his mouth had gone so dry there was nothing left to swallow with.

"What's in your jacket, chump?" JackHammer demanded to know.

Bryann was inches from the red steel door and thought of bolting, but fear of a bullet in the back prevented his feet from taking flight.

"So you just gonna sit there like you on the dock of the bay and act like you don't hear me! I said what's in the fuckin' jacket!" JackHammer repeated louder than before. People began to notice the action, and once again the festive mood in the club came to a screeching halt.

Bryann turned slowly and observed JackHammer snatch a man's jacket out of his arms by the bar. As he did so, a black .35 revolver dropped to the floor. JackHammer stared angrily at the gun, then grabbed the man by the scruff of his neck and dragged him over to a sign on the wall that said, *Do not bring guns in here. Come in peace. Failure to do so may result in you leaving in pieces!*

"Now, you look like a somewhat educated man, so I'm guessing it's safe to assume that you can read, can't you?" JackHammer asked in a furious tone causing the owner of the revolver to nod wide-eyed. "Okay then, read the sign!" he demanded.

"Do no—" the man began softly.

"Louder! I want everyone up in this piece to hear you. Now, from the top!"

Nervously clearing his throat, the man began again: "Do not bring guns in here. Come in peace. Failure to do so may result in you leaving in pieces."

"Very good. So then why in the hell are you up in here with the roscoe?" JackHammer asked, pointing to the gun on the floor. The nervous man parted his lips to answer, then clammed up when

JackHammer held up a finger. "Stop right there, and ask yourself this, will I tell the truth, or will I lie and get my teeth knocked out?"

The man took one look at JackHammer's arms, swallowed and said, "Well, what happened was—"

JackHammer shook his head and said, "I'm about to show you your brains on drugs, real quick!"

Crack!

The punch was like a rattlesnake's bite. Blindingly swift and deadly accurate. In fact, the blow was so fast the man didn't even realize he was hit until JackHammer snatched his ham hock–sized fist back and he tasted his own blood through his dislocated jaw. Bryann took that as a cue to slip out the door.

Mary came up behind Trig, who was enjoying the show, and put her arms around his waist. She flinched as JackHammer continued beating the screaming man and looked away.

"Where'd your cousin Bryann go?" she asked.

"He had to leave suddenly."

"Aw, too bad. I was going to ask him to call his wife and see if she wanted to stop by," she said, kissing him affectionately atop his shiny dome.

"Damn, Mary—isn't there something that you could be doing besides sitting up under me?" Trig said, shrugging her off him. Mary was used to the cold treatment and knew the display of affection earlier was for Bryann's benefit. Constantly worried about what other people think, Trig always wanted it to appear like every part of his life was perfect, even if it wasn't. She sighed and walked off to tend to her establishment.

Chapter 8

BRYANN ENTERED HIS APARTMENT SHIVERING, clutching his jacket tightly. After being shaken up by what he thought was JackHammer catching him in the act, he decided to leave the Dictaphone wrapped up. It never occurred to him how guilty he looked walking the chilly streets carrying a jacket in his arms.

Once in the confines of his living room he rewound the tape partially and excitedly shouted, "Yes!" upon hearing his cousin admit his crimes.

Something flickered in his peripheral vision. Bryann turned and noticed a trail of short candles lined up on the floor making a right into the kitchen then proceeding out and back down the dark hall. It also dawned on him that in his rush to check the tape, he failed to notice the only source of light in the whole apartment came from the candles.

He placed the Dictaphone on the coffee table beside Princess for her to guard, and he eagerly followed the candles into the kitchen. He stopped in front of the stove where a large dish was sitting on top. He placed a hand on the handle and squeezed his eyes shut. "Oh, please. Oh, please, let it be ziti," Bryann prayed to the food Gods. A smile broke over his lips when he raised the lid. He tasted the ziti, and his eyes rolled back. One more bite, then he followed more candles to the refrigerator and opened the door.

He found a bottle of merlot with a post-it note attached to it that read *Bring me along.* He grabbed the bottle and two glasses and continued following the candles down the hall. The candles stopped at the entrance of the hall bathroom. On the floor next to the candles was a second note that said, *Take off your clothes and get in here ... I'm waiting!* The sound of water splashing in the bathtub caused Bryann to tear out of his clothes.

With the wine and glasses in tow, Bryann bumped open the door, nude. As he entered, the fruity fragrance of burning black cherry incense entered his nostrils. More candles sitting on the sink and shelves illuminated the bathroom.

"Well, hello, handsome," a soft voice said.

Bryann turned and his eyes bulged. "I swear, God was showing off when he made you."

Sitting in the tub beneath a mountain of white bubbles, looking astonishingly beautiful, was his wife. After such a stressful day, her beauty was intoxicating. Shadows from the candlelight danced on her gorgeous face. She wore her hair sexily pinned up, leaving a couple of long strands to dangle. Never one to wear makeup, she only added a dab of lip gloss to enhance her radiant smile. The mass of bubbles broke up just enough to show a

glimpse of her breast and golden thigh. She was so lovely, she took
his breath away with her delicate cameo like features. Resting on
the edge of the bathtub was a saucer of jumbo strawberries covered
with whipped cream.

"Press play," Rita said sweetly.

"Huh? Press what?" Bryann said, hypnotized.

"The radio on the clothes hamper. Hit the play button."

Obediently, he placed the bottle and glasses down and hit
the play button on the CD player. Instantly 'So Blessed' sung
beautifully by Mariah Carey, filled the air. Bryann closed his eyes
and swayed, taking a trip back in time when they lost their
virginity simultaneously to the only people they would ever make
love to ever after. It wasn't long after that he got down on one knee
and told her he didn't know what kind of future he had, but he
knew he didn't have one without her. And when she said yes that
was exactly how he felt then and now... Blessed.

"Well, Mr. Bonner," Rita said, cutting her eyes seductively
at him, "Are you going to join me?" she asked and brought a
strawberry to her full lips and licked off the whipped cream.
"While it's still hot?"

Too overwhelmed to answer, Bryann swallowed hard,
nodded goofily and stepped inside the tub.

After a long, passionate embrace and a tender kiss, Bryann
poured some wine. "Here's to the love of my life, for the rest of
my life." He toasted over the romantic melody.

"And to our new baby, Ryann," Rita concluded, bringing
her glass to his with a cling.

"Ryann?" he asked.

"Well, yeah ... I mean, we named Bria after both of us,
right? So shouldn't this baby be as well? Besides, the name Ryann
could be a boy's or girl's name. It's, um, I can't think of the word."

"Unisex."

"Yeah, that's it. Ryann is a unisex name." When she saw
no reaction, she assumed he did not like the name. "Look, if you
don't like it, honey, we can choose another name."

"Hold on for a sec," Bryann said, pausing for a minute to
soak it in. "Ryann, huh?" he said. Rita nodded. A smile came over
his face, and they rubbed noses like Eskimos. "I love it. It's
perfect. And so are you," Bryann said, then moved in close to his
wife and began kissing and touching her all over her body as she
moaned from ecstasy.

"Don't ... stop," she moaned, biting her bottom lip.

Thinking something was wrong, Bryann stopped kissing
her. "What's wrong?" he asked.

Rita looked up with a wide-eyed, stunned expression and
put his hands back under the water where they were. "I said 'Don't

stop!'"

After forty-five minutes of drinking, kissing, cooing, and touching, the water was cold, the strawberries were half eaten, and the bottle was empty. Rita gently took her husband's hand, and, using one of her fingers, ran across the inside of his palm. It was her way of telling him she was ready to go to the bedroom to continue their celebration. Bryann picked up Rita and carried her down the hall, both dripping wet. The heat circulating throughout their home felt good against their skin as they air-dried. Gently, he placed her on their bed, which was as soft as a field of down. The drawn curtains on the canopy bed, and the view of the star-filled sky overhead set the tone just right as the CD changed and Whitney Houston serenaded them with, 'My Love Is Your Love.'

"Bryann," she said softly as he pat dried her off with a towel, kissing her affectionately on her back and neck. "Do you love me?"

"Yes, baby, I love you," he replied with a nibble on her ear. The feel of his stubble tickled her neck and made her quiver with delight. In return, the sticky sweet smell of Rita's perfume behind each ear was an aphrodisiac, making him want her more with each passing second.

"More than a car loves oil?"

"More," he said and kissed her breasts.

"More than a preacher loves God?"

"More."

"More than you love spice ham and cheese heroes?"

"So much more." He giggled.

"Now see, I know you're lying cause you once said you wanted to marry a spiced ham and cheese hero." Rita laughed.

Bryann looked at his wife with seriousness in his eyes, "You're the only person I've never told a lie to in my life?"

"For real? Ever? Not even a teeny tiny one?" she asked.

"Not even the teensiest of the tinniest. With you, I've always been honest."

"Wow. Me too. I always thought it was just me. And I love how after all these years later and I am still learning new things about you."

Bryann looked far into her eyes, kissed her passionately and whispered, "Baby we're a team."

"Team us?" she asked.

"Team us." He replied with a tender kiss.

"I love it when you do that."

"Do what?"

"Make my life better."

"Is that right?"

She was so much in love with this man that a tear of joy

came to her eyes. He was the only man in the world who could make her feel the way she did. It was a powerful mixture of love and compassion and ecstasy all balled up into one great tingly feeling, and she wanted her man to feel what she was feeling inside her body.

"Bryann, make love to me," Rita said as a tear fell, climbing on top of him and pulling the comforter over her shoulders.

Bryann smiled. Her body was soft in some places, firm in others. He could feel her warm breath on his chest and neck as she bent forward allowing her hands to move about freely beneath the comforter. Finding what she was after she lowered herself onto him and cried out from instant ecstasy. Bryann, too, let out a grunt, as his body welcomed hers then turned slightly and blew out the candle on the nightstand filling the room with pitch darkness.

Then for the remainder of the night; under the stars, with Whitney serenading them, husband and wife made passionate love and enjoyed their anniversary. Celebrating the beauty of Black Love.

Chapter 9

THE NEXT MORNING RITA AWOKE to find a dozen long-stemmed yellow roses and a small card that read *I love you* staring at her. Sitting up, she stretched with a smile as she inhaled the sweet-smelling flowers and briefly reflected on the previous night. After twelve years of marriage, she appreciated that her man was just as romantic and passionate as when they first started dating.

She reached over and removed a worn book from the drawer of the nightstand labeled *Memories.* Flicking past pages of old movie ticket stubs from her first dates with Bryann, love letters, and other mementos that no one else in the world would hold dear, she found a blank page and wrote *Twelfth Wedding Anniversary,* then pressed a yellow pedal between the pages. When they returned from the cruise the ticket stubs would join it. After slipping into her robe, she patted Princess and floated down the hall. From the bathroom she could hear Bryann singing Jackie Wilson's, 'To Be Loved,' off-key in the shower, giving Prince Akeem a run for his money. She giggled then continued to the kitchen for coffee.

Things couldn't be better, Bryann thought to himself as he showered. His anniversary last night was perfect, and he had in his possession the confession to finally get Trig off of the streets. As far as he was concerned, Trig was already behind bars, he was just too stupid to realize it.

Standing near the kitchen Rita noticed the Dictaphone on the coffee table and picked it up.

Bryann was finishing up his shower when his wife stepped in with him. "Good morning, King Bryann," she said with a kiss.

"Good morning, Queen Rita," Bryann replied.

"I love my roses. Thank you, sweetie."

"You're welcome," he replied, while eyeing his wife's body as the warm water ran from her hair all over her features. She looked like an Indian princess stepping from a waterfall. There wasn't a blemish, a pimple, or anything on her entire body. He was beginning to become aroused and began caressing her.

"Let's call in sick and spend the entire day in bed together," he whispered desperately, like he needed a fix, and she was a drug.

Rita bit her bottom lip as that feeling from last night was returning. Bryann knew the right places to touch her and make her instantly aroused. She grabbed his hand and pulled it away after a few more seconds of pleasure.

"As tempting as the offer sounds, baby, you know I can't. I took off yesterday and I know my desk is going to be piled sky-high with work. Just think, in a few more weeks we'll be in Jamaica making love morning, noon, and night."

"Oh, all right," Bryann said and climbed out the shower.

"Bryann."

"Yes?" he answered, hoping she changed her mind.

"I thought you said you needed your Dictaphone for work."

Bryann was stuck. He had totally forgotten about it on the coffee table. He couldn't very well explain to Rita that he'd been to see Trig. He knew how she loathed his cousin. Just last Sunday she fumed after reading an article in the paper about how a baby born drug-addicted and infected with AIDS had died. Rita immediately blamed Trig, although it could have been any of the drug dealers in Major City responsible for supplying the child's parents.

"I did. I mean I do." He said thinking technically he was telling the truth since he used it to help a client in need.

"So, you do or you don't?"

"I-I did but I still do. Why?"

"Sheesh no reason. I was just making sure you didn't forget it. Why are you acting like the Nixon tapes are on it?"

"That's crazy. There's nothing important on it."

"OK weirdo. So, there's nothing important on it." She repeated but it sounded more like a question than a statement.

"Yup that's what I said. Nothing is important on it. And you're the one who's being weird. In fact, I'm gonna call the weirdo police and have you booked on charges of being…weird." He said cringing when he heard himself say it.

Rita looked oddly at Bryann then snickered. "Babe, leave the jokes to Markeith."

"Got it." Bryann laughed awkwardly. He thought it was strange of her to ask what was on the tape and for a brief moment he worried that she had listened to Trig's confession, then quickly put his fears aside, knowing Rita would have reacted differently if she listened to what was on it.

Soon, husband and wife were dressed and left for work together. With the Dictaphone in his briefcase. Bryann hated himself for not being honest with his wife for the first time he'd known her.

***

"I wanna go to Bora Bora but I'm poora poora." A uniformed officer said to his partner getting an understanding chuckle.

"Who are you telling? Once I started spending my own money, I realized my mom was right. We do got food at home." His female partner replied.

Police were everywhere, like a scene straight from the six o'clock news. Standing around talking openly about sports, the job, the wife, the kids, and the mistress. Buying time until he arrived.

Major City's finest were confident in knowing they did their job, dusting for prints, covering Sugar's and Buster's bodies with sheets, outlining them in chalk, and putting up the all-too familiar *Do Not Cross* yellow tape in front of the building. A pudgy white balding coroner with a short ponytail was kneeled over Sugar's body, scribbling onto a small pad, ignoring the annoying questions shot at his back by reporters. Even if he did know how the couple came to such a gruesome demise, he wouldn't have told the vultures who circled the bodies hungry for an exclusive.

The sudden sound of heavy footsteps coming up the stairs brought the sound of conversation to a halt. All eyes switched to the door as the footsteps came closer. A man with a dark complexion, long hair, and badly in need of a shave and shower began trembling with fear.

"He's back! He's back!" the man shouted and ran behind two officers.

Every cop in the room put their hands on their guns and held their breath. In walked a six-foot surly bald black man with a thick goatee in a long trench coat. His presence demanded respect, and it was promptly rewarded. A sigh of relief passed from the lips of the cops, and they removed their hands from their holsters.

The pudgy coroner rose to his feet with a grunt. "Damn, I'm feeling my age. Gainer, be kind to your knees cause you're going to miss 'em when they're gone. Mines are writing a check my back can't cash."

"I'll try to remember that. So, who do we have?" Gainer asked. His rugged exterior told of a man who had seen a lot of horrifying things in his twenty-two years on the force and become numb to it.

"That would be Miss Carlotta Ross, aka Sugar."

Gainer lifted the sheet, unfazed by her head almost twisted off. "I assume that the other body over there must belong to Buster Riley?"

"How'd you know?" Gus asked. A veteran in the field of street death, he had been squatting over bodies as long as Gainer had been solving how they were murdered. He considered his work a grim but exciting privilege, being paid to encounter the most intimate details of human struggle and death.

"These two are—eh, were—inseparable," Gainer informed him. "In addition to being a hooker and pimp they were also con artists. She'd lure guys into alleys with the promise of sex for a few dollars. He'd be waiting to knock the chump out with a two-by-four. The horny bastards were so excited about getting a blow job for practically nothing that they were easy prey. My guess is they finally messed over the wrong person's money." He shrugged, sure of himself.

Gus shook his head. He never could figure out why some folks went to such great lengths to make a couple of bucks when it would be so much easier to fill out an application at the post office. "I always say, people are gonna do what they want no matter what, so we might as well box it, sell it, and tax it. Anyway, according to the zombie over there that freaked when you walked in—"

Gainer cut his eyes in the frail man's direction who was enjoying his ten minutes of fame talking to reporters. "His name's Warren Sanchez. And at the rate he's going, you'll be zipping his body bag closed real soon.

"Geez, Gainer. Is there anyone in Major you don't know?"

"Decent citizens," Gainer winked.

Gus snickered, "Well, Warren was in a nearby room sleeping off a hangover when he heard a noise. He said he came in here and found the lovebirds like this."

"Did he get a look at who did it?" Gainer asked.

"Yes and no. Whoever did it was already halfway down the stairs. He did mention something about the guy being huge with hands as big as manhole covers. At first I shrugged it off as just crazy junkie talk, but then I got a good look at the bodies. Come here, lemme show you something." Gus led Gainer over to a wall where photographers were flashing away. He shooed them away so Gainer could get a better look, then pulled back the sheet covering Buster. An empty needle lay beside his body. "Guess he died in vein, huh?" Gus said, grinning with his usual flair for poorly timed humor.

Gainer frowned, then eyed Buster's smashed head. "Damn, nasty way to go out. A sledgehammer to the mug piece," he said, rubbing the salt-and-pepper beard connected to a short, tight fade.

Gus made a loud buzzing noise like the wrong answer on a quiz show. "Sorry, try again."

The detective squinted at Buster's head more closely and couldn't believe his eyes when he saw the row of deep dents inches apart alongside Buster's smashed jaw. "Wait a minute! You got to be shitting me! Are those ... knuckle prints?"

"Right you are, sir," said Gus. "We found him under the door."

Gainer glanced over. A cop was dusting the door for prints, and he noticed the large hole. "Manhole covers, huh?"

"But who, or should I say what, could cause this kind of damage? Cause this damn sure ain't human," Gus asked.

"Only one person comes to mind," Gainer grunted. The cell phone on his hip rang, snatching him out of his thoughts. In one fluid motion, he removed the phone and flipped it open like a gun from a holster. "Talk to me .... Hey, Bryann." His mood changed, and Gus was amazed to see a bit of joy in the hard man's face. "You got what? You sure? But how in the hell did you—boy, are you crazy? I don't believe you did that! Do you know the risk you took? You sure he admitted to everything? And you got it all? You played it back? Okay, okay—meet me in front of the station house at—" Gainer pulled his sleeve back. "Eleven-thirty. And, Bryann, although I'm not that thrilled with the way you obtained his confession, I am real proud of you, son. You hear me?"

"Thanks," Bryann said behind his desk, staring at the Dictaphone. "Yes, I promise I won't let it out my sight, Gainer ... okay ... uh-huh, eleven-thirty. I'll be there."

Chapter 10

TRIG WAS LISTENING THE AUDIO NOVEL, Rich Dad Poor Dad, educating himself on how to use money as a tool for wealth development. He and Mary were sitting at a red light, Her frustrated body language and spaced-apart distance between them told she was unhappy, and his said he was oblivious.

He suddenly noticed flashing lights in his rear-view mirror, and heard loud sirens. "What the fuck!" Trig snapped as a squad car screeched up beside them.

A hyper cop jumped out with his gun drawn, "Hands, where I can see them!"

"What's the charge? Driving while black?" Mary asked.

"Out of the car, Trig! We finally caught you red handed!" the cop smirked.

"Congratulations you caught us, talking." The bald black man laughed so hard he put his fillings on display.

"Watch that mouth, before I remove your lips. Won't be enough of your black ass left to stick in a cigar box. Let's go, now!"

"Yasuh Mista Officer Sir. Whatever you say boss. I said it before, and I'll say it again. The justice system is a Goddamn joke! And police have entirely too much power with little to no accountability." Trig rolled his eyes as he and Mary reluctantly held their hands out the window and complied.

Trig knew the charge was trumped up so they could get him into the station house where he would find out the real charges. He also knew that whatever they said they saw him doing he'd have an alibi for. That's what paid witnesses were for. As he was cuffed and placed into the back seat of the vehicle, Trig instructed Mary, not to worry. He told her to continue on home, alert the fellas and he'd be home later. She nodded with fake concern, but wished he were going away forever.

***

Gainer waited patiently across the street from his precinct beneath the digital Citibank clock that announced it was Wednesday, September 17, eleven forty-six, twenty-two degrees. His Rolex, a gift from Dee-Dee, called the bank clock a liar with eleven-fifty. He was a statue, oblivious to the bitter cold as he took a pull on his fifth Marlboro of the day, a habit he had been trying to quit for years. A police van pulled up, and two cops in riot gear got out and came around the back. The van wobbled and shook as cursing and pounding came from within. Gainer squinted his eyes for a better view as one of the cops nervously unlocked the doors.

Instantly the doors flew open and JackHammer leaped out the van with his massive arms bound behind his back with chains. He plowed into the closest cop and sent him flying through the windshield of a parked car. Other officers charged the hulking figure and were swatted like flies. With his cigarette dangling between his lips Gainer came running up and, reaching in his coat, brandished a 9-millimeter.

"Whoa-whoa! No need for all of that!" Trig yelled from the back seat of the police car that pulled him over as it came on the scene. "JackHammer! Chill out, man!"

"Trig?" JackHammer asked in a slurred voice, still groggy from the taser and beating he received after refusing to come along peacefully.

Trig protested as he was removed from the car. "Yeah, it's me! Now be easy, big man. We ain't do a damn thing wrong! I promise you, we'll be home before the Wayans Brothers comes on. These pigs is just busting our balls. History has proven that they themselves have committed some of the worst crimes ever, but have convinced the world that we are the threat!" Trig rationalized then turned to Gainer, who was still drawn on JackHammer. "You can put your manhood away now, dick-tective. I've got the situation under control. And whatever the charge is my receipts are properly categorized." he smiled.

Slowly, Gainer lowered his gun. His expression showed how much it pained him not to pump a few rounds into the giant. Trig and Gainer traded vile looks as he and JackHammer were led inside the precinct by a small army of officers.

"Some people are only alive because it's illegal to shoot them," Gainer muttered, keeping his eyes on Trig until he was gone.

An ambulance pulled up as Bryann came walking up the sidewalk and over to Gainer. The two could pass for father and son, as Bryann greeted the older man with a warm hug.

"What happened?" Bryann asked as cops helped removed their fellow officer who JackHammer hit, from the windshield.

"Never mind that. You got the tape?" Gainer asked. He was even more anxious than ever to bust Trig after their brief exchange of words a few minutes ago.

"Right here," Bryann said, producing the Dictaphone.

"Excellent. Now let me hear that bastard dig his own grave." Bryann rewound the tape to the beginning and was about to press play when Gainer noticed a white limousine pull up across the street. "Damn! There's no time. The mayor's here."

"The mayor? What's she doing here?" Bryann asked, surprised.

Secret service men hopped out and secured the area, then whisked a middle-aged black woman in a smart business suit inside the precinct. Bryann had no idea his little tape could produce someone as important as the mayor.

"If she can put away a major dope dealer in the city, she's guaranteed re-election," Gainer explained.

"Is that right. And all I did was risk my neck capturing his confession."

"Hey, what can I tell you? Get into politics."

"Maybe I should. It doesn't seem that hard a job. It's not like I'm flipping burgers or anything with real responsibility."

Gainer chuckled as a stone-faced Black man with captain stripes on his sleeves marched up and he quickly straightened his posture.

"Captain Miller, this is Bryann Bonner. He's the one I told you about who taped Trig's confessing about pushing drugs over on the South Side," Gainer said.

The Captain squeezed Bryann's hand firmly. "So, you're the son Gainer never had. Good to meet you. Well, I'm sure Gainer has already told you that we are not supposed to encourage this type of thing. And normally we follow certain protocols when apprehending and charging suspects. But these aren't average suspects. And this isn't an average situation. So, in this case things have been handled differently. And off the record, good work. That slippery son of a bitch and his crew have violated almost all the laws that we as a civilized society have put into place. But **you**, he didn't see coming." He turned to Gainer, who stood by smiling proudly. "So where's this tape? You heard it right? His voice, nice and clear?"

Gainer and Bryann traded nervous glances. How could he tell his Captain that he had never even heard it when he sounded like he was about to give him a parade and key to the city? The detective blew hard and spoke. "Um, yes, in fact I was just listening to it for the second time as the mayor pulled up. And just like Bryann said, Trig admitted to everything. Selling drugs, using kids as workers, everything. By Trig's own admission, there's enough evidence on that tape to send that bastard and a lot of others away for a long time."

"Okay Gainer, I trust you. And I don't need to tell you what would happen if we called the Mayor down here for nothing. But you said you heard it."

"With my own ears," Gainer said.

"Well, that's good enough for me. In fact, I want to hear it for the first time when he does," the Captain smiled, then the three continued down the hall.

When Bryann entered the room, he could not believe how

many important people were in attendance. Seated at a long table was Mayor Ellise Smiley, political activist Reverend Augustus Smalls, District Attorney Ruben Gregory Carreras, and a sad-faced black woman Bryann recognized from the news and talk shows, as Alma Jackson. The mother of an eleven-year-old boy named Archie who exited a bodega with friends at the exact moment an altercation ensued, and gunfire erupted. Archie was hit by a stray bullet and killed instantly. After her son's death, Alma turned pain to purpose and anger into advocacy by founding MASK, Mother's Against Senseless Killing. Armed with a mega-phone, a long-sleeved t-shirt with her smiling son's image under the caption, 'Sleep In Heavenly Peace', a determined grieving mother formed an alliance with other mothers who also lost their children to street violence. The band of women in pain started a crusade against gang violence, organizing rallies and headlining protests to get illegal guns off the streets in hopes that no other mother would have to endure what they had.

"Jeez, Gainer," Bryann whispered. "You invited everyone except God and Santa Claus."

"God was busy, Santa's outside parking his sleigh," Gainer whispered back.

"Can I have everyone's attention, please?" Captain Miller asked. "Now, as you all know, the quality of life in Major City has taken a dramatic turn for the worst in the last ten years."

"We can thank Mayor Smiley for that!" Reverend Smalls attacked, pounding a fist on the table as his double chins shook like Jell-O. "Cutting programs that kept kids off the street, taxes at an all-time high, homelessness, unemployment escalating, but you aren't suffering, are you? Pulling up in a stretch limo off of the taxpayers' money! Disgusting! Then again, what do you expect when you've got a Republican for a mayor?"

"I know *you* aren't accusing anyone of shady operations, Augustus!" Mayor Smiley yelled, rising out her chair. Her security rushed to her side like bookends. "Because if you want to bring it to the table, I'm sure all those trusting members of that racket you call a church would like to know what really happens to their donations, Mr. Lexus-driving, fur coat–sporting, diamond-pinky-ring-wearing, teenage skirt chaser!"

"Enough!" Captain Miller shouted over the two feuding like siblings. "We are not here to debate over the job the mayor's doing," he continued, as the mayor and Reverend rolled their eyes. Bryann shook his head in disbelief and better understood why the city was falling apart. Holding the room's attention, Captain Miller continued. "The reason this meeting was called at such short notice is that it has come to my attention from my number one detective, Gainer Wilson, that we have in our possession the weapon to finally take out Mordecai Wise better known as the slime ball drug dealer who goes by the name, Trig."

"I'm appalled his name is Mordecai." Reverend Smalls scoffed at the thug having the audacity to have a Biblical name.

"You've got something on Trig?" Alma Jackson asked in a timid, hopeful voice.

"Yes ma'am, I do." Bryann said compassionately.

"Praise Jesus." She rejoiced.

"And you are?" the Reverend inquired.

"The man who did the job no one else could," Gainer said proudly, throwing an arm around Bryann's shoulder.

"So, what's this weapon?" the mayor asked.

Gainer nodded at Bryann and he pulled out the Dictaphone and placed it on the table.

"Ladies and gentlemen," Gainer said. "What you're looking at is the device that secretly taped Trig's confession to all the little sordid nasty things we knew he was doing but could never prove."

"Let's hear it then," Reverend Smalls demanded.

"Not until the guest of honor has arrived. I want your faces to be as surprised as his when you hear what it has to say." Gainer interrupted.

"So, Captain Miller, have you heard this tape?" Alma Jackson asked anxiously breaking the unnerving silence.

"No, ma'am I have not. But Chief detective Gainer has. I've watched him rise from cadet to top cop, and now the most valued and honored Detective of this department. Working tirelessly protecting people, carrying out intelligence-driven policing strategies, helping to develop several lasting reforms, all while giving back to the city's communities. And I hope he will succeed me when I eventually retire. So needless to say, if he says he has the confession to put away a crime lord, I trust him wholeheartedly."

"So then you've heard it Detective?" D.A. Carreras asked.

Gainer blew smoke into the air, then paused as if he was hesitant to respond. For the first time it dawned on him how big of a risk he was taking on something he had never heard. He hoped Bryann knew what he was doing. "Yes … yes, I did, as a matter of fact. I was just telling the captain I heard it for the second time before we came in. And believe me, Trig confessed to it all. The drugs, the kids working for him, everything."

The paranoia was returning to Bryann as he listened to Gainer lie, and he went to sit in the back, away from it all.

"No, son, I want you to sit there," Gainer said, pointing to the empty chair at the end of the table. "That way when that bastard goes down, he can look at the man responsible square in the eye!"

Bryann did as he was instructed, while the feeling that something was terribly wrong grew stronger and stronger.

"You're to be commended, young man. What you did was quite tenacious. Your selflessness and putting others first, has made the streets safer for the city." Mayor Smiley said to Bryann as he took the seat beside her.

"Yes, I agree. I've got to give credit where credit is due, Mr. Bonner. You are a brave young man and I, too, am impressed." Reverend Smalls said.

Bryann smiled and nodded a meek, "Thank you," uncomfortable with all the attention. All he wanted was for Trig to get what was coming to him and to go home to his wife.

"Brother, you don't know the half of it," Gainer interrupted. "The social worker standing here risked his life to help out a young kid he learned was in serious trouble with Trig. Oh, and by the way, did I mention that he has blood ties to Trig? They're cousins. Bryann practices humility and selfless acts on a regular basis and everything he does is for other people. He's incapable of doing the wrong thing." This impressed everyone even more, and nothing but praises were tossed at the brave young man who valiantly put law and common decency before misplaced loyalty.

"I'm not perfect." Bryann meekly said.

"Officer Bills, would you be so kind as to go get the man of the hour." Gainer confidently said to an officer who obediently nodded and exited the room." He then noticed the distraught look on Bryann's face. "Hey, are you gonna be able to do this?" he whispered in Bryann's ear.

"Oh, sure, I'm cool." he said, not looking the part.

"Tell me now, because I sent that uniform to get Trig."

"No, I came this far, I've got to see it to the end! Besides, I want to see the look on his face when he hears his own voice on tape."

Gainer placed a strong hand on Bryann's shoulder. "I'm proud of you, son."

"Thanks," Bryann half smiled at his surrogate Dad. "I'm kinda proud of me, too."

The door opened, and the conversation came to a halt as the officer escorted in an arrogant-faced Trig with his wrists cuffed before him.

"Wow, so many important people in one place. What is this a surprise party for me? What's the occasion?" Trig asked the room, deflecting their obvious hate toward him with a bright smile.

"Your downfall!" Alma said with conviction in her trembling voice. A week after burying her son, the single mother learned that the shoot-out that robbed her of her only child was allegedly between members of Trig's crew and a rival gang. But no arrests had been made because no witnesses were willing to come forward for fear of retaliation. And from that moment on, she lived for the moment when she could look into the face of the man she held personally responsible for her hurt and pain and serve him a plate of retribution.

"Hey! It's the angry lady from TV! Huge fan. You and McGruff the crime dog need to link up. Take a bite out of crime." Trig smiled savagely.

"Bastard!" Alma hissed and broke into tears.

"Young man you're everything but a reflection of Jesus and better hope that the Lord is merciful come judgement day!" Reverend Smalls said as he consoled Alma.

"Show some got-damn respect, punk!" Gainer said, then pushed Trig toward the far end of the table, forcibly sitting him down.

"Easy Old Steed. Just part of my charm." Trig smiled up at Gainer, then looked down the table, making eye contact with Bryann with a pensive stare. "So why am I the one in cuffs but you look as nervous as a long-tailed cat in a room full of rocking chairs?" he asked his cousin who silently looked away. He shrugged then noticed the mayor. "And I'm surprised that you're even taking part in this circus, Mayor. This is no way to treat your constituents."

"Last I checked ex-felons can't vote. So, you are not a constituent." The Mayor replied.

"You got me there Elise. But you can't just be snatching brothers off the street for no reason. I got rights you know!"

Gainer snickered, the closest thing to a laugh he could muster. "Oh, you have rights! You have the right to shut the fuck up or so help me, I'll plant my foot so deep in your ass you'll have to open your mouth so I can tie my laces!"

"So, do you like stand in the mirror in your boxers and practice saying corny shit like that every morning?" Trig sized the furious man from head to toe laughing and was snatched out of his seat by his collar. "Hey-hey! This is Egyptian silk! Highly sensitive to the oils in poor people's fingers."

"Simmer down, Gainer. We got the bastard dead to rights." the captain said to Gainer who looked like he was two seconds from throwing away his career.

Trig looked unconcerned by the threat. "Look, I've been cooperative up till now, but I'm growing tired of this shit! So either tell me why I'm here or let me go," he said.

"Trig," the Captain started. "They say confession's good for the soul, so care to make this easier on yourself and tell everyone in the room what it is that you do for a living?"

Trig unscrewed his face and grinned widely. "Oh, sure. I'm a male escort, and your wife is my number one customer. She's putting me through law school."

Gainer pounded the table with a big fist, upsetting a pitcher of water and causing everyone to flinch. "You think this shit is funny?"

"Actually yes, I do. Since you kidnapped me off the street and threw me in a cell without probable cause, violating my civil rights. Threatened my safety but have yet to tell me what this is all about. So, care to?"

"You tell us, since you're the filthy piece of shit drug dealer who uses kids to push his poison."

Trig's smirk was erased like a blackboard at the end of a school day. "I don't know what you're talking about."

"Oh, really? You sure about that?" Gainer asked up in his face.

Trig flinched back and said, "As sure as my high-priced attorney is going to enjoy this easy pay day."

"What if I told you that I have proof? And what if I told you that there was no denying the circumstances? And what if—"

"What if, what if, what if! What if a buzzard had a piano in his ass, then we'd have music in the air! Look, if you got proof, big man, bring it! Otherwise uncuff me because my time is non-refundable. Non-exchangeable. And non-transferable." Trig said, daring them to present this evidence he hoped did not exist.

Everyone at the table began trading smug looks like they knew something he didn't, except for Bryann who couldn't shake that bad feeling. "Proof? Funny you should ask that," he said, ignoring the gut feeling. "Because that's just what I was taking care of the other day at your tacky club."

"Look at you, showing out in front of company. I knew I should have let JackHammer whip your ass!"

"Aha! So you admit your guilt?" Gainer accused.

"Don't 'aha' me! The only thing that I'm guilty of is trusting my disloyal cousin."

"I'm disloyal? That's rich. You know there comes a point where loyalty becomes ignorance!" Bryann blasted back.

"To hell with you Bryann! And quit twisting my words around Gainer, cause I ain't admit to shit!" Trig shouted, jumping up defensively. Gainer slammed him back down in his chair. "Ya'll see that right? Fucking police brutality! Look, I'm being framed! I mean … yes, Benedict Arnold came by my legitimate social club to see me, but no, I ain't admit to no drug dealing."

"Is that right?" Bryann said.

"Yeah, that's right! You know what? Fuck this!" Trig said

and got comfortable and poured himself a glass of water.

"So you just gonna sit there, not care in the world?" Gainer asked.

"I don't yell fire til I see flames." Trig shrugged and sipped. Bryann placed the Dictaphone in front of his cousin. "Fuck's that?" Trig asked.

"Your three-alarm fire." The Detective grinned then proudly nodded at Bryann.

Bryann nodded back and rewound the tape in the Dictaphone. Trig's smug look was slipping. His eyes nervously darted around the room. "Whatever is on there won't hold up in court! It's inadmissible evidence!" Trig said trying to conceal his worry.

"Not once they hear this!" Bryann jammed his thumb on the play button. *"Hey, baby. Last night was great. I'd marry you all over again. I hope Ryann is a boy so he can grow up to be just like his daddy. Look, I know you wanted for us to take off and stay in bed all day, and I am sorry I couldn't. But just think: In a few weeks we will be on the sandy beaches of Jamaica. In the meantime, listen to this, and remember I love you."* Bryann was frozen, and Gainer had to switch it off for him.

The room was so quiet Bryann could hear his heart racing as the color drained from his face. In all the years he'd heard his wife's beautiful voice Bryann never thought he'd see the day when it was a horrific sound. But when he heard her message taped over the information he'd risked everything for, he felt just that. He looked to Gainer who mouthed, *'What the fuck?'*

A sinister laugh came from the opposite end of the table, taking Bryann out of his daze. "That was soooo sweet! Cousin you're a lucky man. Congrats, you should share this with your matching pajama Christmas pics." Trig laughed. "But one question: What's it got to do with me?"

"That's what I'd like to know!" the mayor snapped.

Bryann was slack-jawed, gawking from shock. Gainer, stared on through bewildered eyes. The captain glared at them both.

"But it's on here! I heard it with my own ears!" Bryann said as he rewound the tape to the beginning. Nervously fumbling, Bryann pressed play and the Dictaphone betrayed him again, this time repeating the conversation he and Darrius had about Darrius's using cocaine before visiting Trig, which he thought he had erased.

"Oh cousin-cousin-cousin. Tsk, tsk, tsk" Trig taunted.

Gainer pursed his lips, then lit a Marlboro to conceal evidence of fast heartbeats. Trig laughed louder, tilting back, almost falling out his chair. For the next ten minutes, a shouting match ensued as everyone demanded to know why they were summoned here and lied to by the so-called number one detective. Gainer reluctantly admitted he didn't hear the confession and apologized for bringing everyone here under false pretenses. Immediately, Captain Miller distanced himself, saying he knew nothing of this and was as shocked as everyone else.

After allowing a brief cooling period, Gainer went on to explain that knowing Bryann as long as he has, he's come to respect and trust him, which is why he lied. He also said that he honestly believes Bryann taped Trig's confession, but it was obviously erased or why would he go through all this. Not to mention the fact that everyone in the room knew Trig was guilty as sin without having to even hear the tape.

"And again I ask, where's your proof? Cause even though I ain't no lawyer, I been in and out the court system enough times to know that an accusation does not prove guilt. But I do know all this here equals a nice lawsuit, people losing cushy jobs and pensions." Trig explained with the newly found confidence of someone who saw they were clearly out of danger.

"Look, maybe my tape doesn't have his confession like I said, but he's lying!" Bryann pleaded to the room. "Ask him! He said for Darrius to come and work for him!"

Trig stayed calm, never blinking. "And that's true. I did." Bryann looked confused as Trig continued. "You said Darrius desperately needed a job." Trig turned to the people seated around him with an innocent look. "I was once a misdirected youth so I remember what it was like when you don't have many options, and when my cousin told me about a young man in desperate need of a job, I gladly offered him one in my *legitimate* candy store. Had I known this is how I would be repaid, I may not have been so eager to help. I feel so betrayed."

Bryann couldn't believe what was happening. The change of events was miraculous. This morning when he left his apartment everything was going his way. And now, he wished he'd never even gotten out of bed. "Wait no! That's not true!"

"Ok I'm confused. A minute ago you said I suggested the boy come and work for me. I admit I did and now that's also a lie?" Trig shrugged.

"Come on—this is bullshit! He knows we're not talking about selling candy at a damn candy store!" Gainer screamed.

"Not another word, Gainer!" Captain Miller said through clinched teeth as a throbbing vein appeared in the middle of his forehead. Trig sat back in his chair enjoying the fireworks.

"What about JackHammer, sir?" Gainer asked discreetly.

"What about him?"

"He's caged up downstairs."

"Why? Who ordered his arrest?"

"I did, sir. A local prostitute, Carlotta Ross, aka Sugar, was murdered yesterday along with her boyfriend, Buster Riley."

"And?"

"Well, I have reason to believe Trig ordered his bodyguard, JackHammer, to murder them."

"And how did you come to this conclusion?"

"Well, an informant told me that Sugar and Buster stole some of Trig's money and drugs. Then they turned up dead. Beaten by someone with powerful hands. And his righthand man fits the description." Gainer said, purposely leaving out that Bryann was his informant.

"So I get arrested while driving black and my boy gets arrested for having big hands while being black. Seriously the only way to change the system is to agitate it." Trig yelled.

"Shut up, you!" Gainer said, two minutes from handing in his badge just so he could pound Trig's face in.

"Do you have any proof? Witnesses?" Captain Miller asked.

"Well, no. But, come on, captain you've seen the damage that gorilla can do with those freaky arms of his! The doctors at St. General's dubbed their accident ward the Hammer Pavilion because of the injuries he's given out!"

"Well I'm sure they all deserved it!" Trig added.

"Boy, if I have to come over there so help me—" The phone in the corner interrupted Gainer.

Captain Miller snatched the receiver as everyone in the room spoke in hushed voices. Bryann scanned the room, uncomfortably avoiding Trig's constant stare. The slamming of a phone jolted him out of his daze.

"Well, detective, it appears you're gut feeling must've been something you ate," Captain Miller fumed. "That was forensics. No fingerprints, no DNA and that large amount of cash and narcotics you mentioned was left behind."

Gainer twisted at Trig, who smiled and hunched his shoulders, holding out his hands to be unshackled. "But what about the officer he almost killed bringing him in?" he reminded his superior Officer.

"You mean the officer who violated Hammer's civil rights by beating, tasing and dragging him in here the way he did?" Trig asked.

Captain Miller sighed anticipating the headlines in the paper and worse, being met with the heaviest legal artillery from all of this. "Let them both go."

"But sir."

"I said let them go!"

Trig stood and shook his hands to get the feeling back in

them. "Here's where you say sorry." He smiled at Gainer.

"Put away the dental work and get the hell out of my face!" Gainer said with contempt.

"No hard feelings, Dick-tective."

"I should have left you in that cell to rot, all those year ago!" Gainer hissed.

"Perhaps. But then I would have never reached my full potential." The smooth criminal smiled then stopped before Bryann and eyed him from head-to-toe grinning. "I remember back in eighty-six, when you consoled that girl who cried after the challenger blew up."

"Ingrid Littlejohn. And I remember when you made that insensitive joke about NASA standing for 'needs another seven astronauts.'" Bryann glared.

"I was trying to make y'all laugh."

"Nobody saw the humor in a spaceship filled with heroes exploding."

"Even as kids when we were ripping and running, you always had a heart for protecting people and dropping wisdom. I could tell you wanted to spend your life trying to save everyone. But you can't. And it's a long disappointing ride. Sorry I thwarted your holy moral mission. But do me a solid. The next time you're handing out words of wisdom to our future leaders in the neighborhood, you tell them this for me, the real enemy can be right in your face and the whole time you're overlooking it because you love them."

"The love we had is long gone." Bryann glared.

"Point missed. But don't say I didn't warn you. Oh well. See you 'round…cousin." Trig said then turned to address the pissed off room. "Dang ya'll look salty. But I get it. You all probably see me as many things. Sketchy, wild, arrogant and insensitive. But all I am is a Black man living in America trying to rise above the statistics. However, contrary to what you all must think about me, I'm really not such a bad guy. In fact, some people find me a joy to be around."

"Like who, your junkie customers?" Gainer asked.

"Biggest fuck up of your career and you still manage to crack jokes. Actually, I have a softer and more sensitive side. And to prove it I won't sue, you crooked sons of bitches! Yo cousin, one little tidbit for you to pass on to them little street urchins you love so much, you can be lied on, talked about, and plotted against and still come out a winner." He said and exited laughing.

"Sanctimonious bastard!" Gainer swore.

"We are living in a time where Satan doesn't even hide anymore. And the world still can't see him." The Mayor said. The rest of the room emptied as she gave the captain a look.

Shit traveled downstream as the Captain passed down the disgusted look to Gainer. "Bryann, could you please wait for Detective Washington outside?"

Bryann turned to Gainer with a concerned look then to the Captain. "It's my fault! Blame me!"

"Oh, trust me I do! But luckily for you, you don't work me. Now if you don't mind," The Captain snarled.

"Go on kid. You don't need to see this." Gainer said to Bryann with a long winded sighed.

Bryann sadly nodded then exited and the door slammed behind him. The entire precinct became quiet as the captain was overheard yelling and screaming at Gainer at the top of his lungs for using poor judgment and embarrassing him the way he did. As he listened, Bryann felt low and all he could think about was if Gainer would ever trust him again. After the eternity long, tongue lashing was finally over, Gainer came out and walked over to Bryann who was sitting on a bench, staring at his shoes.

"This looks familiar," Gainer said. Bryann looked up and around, then realized he was sitting on the very same bench he was cuffed to with Trig years ago when Gainer gave him a second chance. He sighed when he found Trig's name carved into the wood. "Well, guess who's no longer chief Detective?"

"What happened? They didn't fire you, did they?" Bryann asked nervously.

"Nah I was demoted. Lost practically all my vacation time too. Your sister's gonna love that, since she was talking about us going away next summer to Italy. Honestly after the royal ass-chewing I just received, I almost wish he did can me. And I think he would have, too. However, with everything going on in the streets right now, the Captain knows he can't afford to lose me. Even if, as he called me, his number one fuck up. He knows I'm still the best detective this precinct has."

"What happens next?" Bryann asked sympathetically.

"I'll be the running joke throughout the precinct until somebody else screws up. Which should be in the next ten minutes. They wanted to contact your job and throw you under the bus. But I used my one and only favor with Captain Miller to stop them. No sense in both of us being miserable at work." Gainer conjured up a half smile.

"I messed up royally," Bryann said, dropping his head into his chest.

"Yeah, we both did."

"And to top it off, Darrius is as good as dead, and it's my fault."

Gainer loosened his tie and flicked open the silver monogrammed lighter Bryann gave him for his birthday when he was a kid, then lit another Marlboro and took a seat beside him. "Nobody's gonna die. We'll put a patrol car outside his door."

"Will there be one there a month from now? Or how about a year? What about after he gets married, huh? Cause soon as they stop showing up, Trig'll be waiting. He ain't stupid, and he holds grudges!" Bryann knew his tone was out of line. A silence followed his outburst as Gainer blew a smoke ring, then flicked the cone of ashes onto the floor. "I'm sorry," Bryann said.

Gainer waved it off. "Your heart was in the right place."

"But not my brain! I should've checked it one last time. Dammit, Rita! She has no idea what she did. No idea!" Bryann vented.

"Easy, son. She obviously didn't know what was on the tape or she wouldn't have done it. Just like you obviously didn't know it was erased. So cut her some slack. She's not the one who dropped the ball. We did. Come on, I'll see you out." Gainer said, tapping Bryann on the leg.

As the two neared the front, young men, angry and shackled together, were being escorted in. The sight of young lives being wasted upset Bryann, and he came to the realization that even if he did get Trig off the streets, there were many others that would gladly fill his shoes. He began wondering if he was wasting his time.

"So, when are the police gonna show up at Darrius'?" Bryann asked flipping up his collar now that they were outside.

"They should be there now. A squad car will be in front of your door tonight, too."

Bryann looked at Gainer like he was speaking a foreign language. "My place? What for?"

"Just as a precaution. You said yourself Trig holds grudges. And I don't like how he said see you 'round. Sounded like a veiled threat."

"Aw he's not going to do anything."

"You really want to take that risk with your family? Rita? Bria?"

"God, it just keeps getting worse and fucking worse! I just want to fast forward to the part of my life where everything's better." Bryann said, massaging his temples as a police car pulled up.

"You mean the part where your wife is pregnant with your second child? That better part? Look don't go home and make a fuss about this. There's too much to be happy about. Regardless of what happened back in there." Gainer advised.

"Yeah sure." Bryann half nodded. With all that happened, he almost forgot about her being pregnant.

"Hey, Trig may have won the first battle, but the war's still on," the detective said. Bryann forced a smile at Gainer's inspirational words

"It's just that I was certain we had him, dead to rights!"

"Remember this my boy because it'll serve you later. The only certainty on this planet is that no one is ever what they seem. Now go home to your family."

"How come you're being so easy going about all this?" Bryann asked angry with himself for everything.

Gainer took a pull on his cigarette then blew a cloud and placed a comforting hand on Bryann's shoulder. "Cause it hasn't changed the way I feel about you. You made a mistake. It happens."

"But this was a huge mistake."

Gainer smiled. "Yeah, it was. But don't regret past mistakes and decisions, good or bad. Because they led you to where you are today."

"Not sure I see the silver lining." Bryann frowned.

"Well, think of it like this. Because of a mistake you once made, I met you and fell in love with your sister. And now we're family. If I could do it all over again, I wouldn't change a thing. So, instead of regretting what happened today, I prefer to think that it happened for a reason. A reason we'll learn, later. Got it? And speaking of your sister, let's not mention this to her. I've already had one ass cheek chewed off."

"You and me both." Bryann nodded in agreement, then got in the back seat of the squad car waiting to take him home and pulled off.

Across the street, Pig stuck his finger in a bar-b-que sauce packet, then into his mouth and sucked it clean watching with vested interest.

Chapter 11

THE RIDE HOME WAS A LONG ONE. All Bryann could think of was how upset he was with his wife. Deep down he knew she wasn't to blame, but he was too furious to think rationally. He had the police let him out on a corner so he could phone Darrius. When Darrius heard the news, he thanked Bryann for nothing and slammed the phone down. Bryann was so upset he let everyone down that he walked the rest of the way home with the police trailing him.

When Bryann opened his front door Bria came charging at him, arms flailing.

"Daddy! Daddy! I had fun with Aunt Dee-Dee and Unca Gaina last night. We made popcorn and baked cookies! And look, I made this for you at school today. It's for you and Mommy's annie-verseree," she blurted without coming up for air, then held up the drawing she'd made of her family including the family's pet cat.

"Where's your mother?" Bryann asked, without so much as a glance at her masterpiece. Bria's mouth hung open at her father's indifference.

"Hey, stud muffin," Rita said cheerfully, walking out of the kitchen. "I didn't feel like cooking tonight so I brought home sandwiches from Perez' bodega. They were all out of spiced ham. So I got you a chopped cheese instead. Not good for you but good for the soul. I called you at work today. Markeith said you were working in the field. I swear, he's a trip. Every other word out his mouth was about some girl, and then he turns around and asks me to hook him up with one of my girlfriends from my book club. Like that would happen! What I'd like to know is how he gets so many women with his skinny behind? Me personally, I like my man with some meat on his bones. Oh, and speaking of my book club, we're currently reading Misery and there are a lot of differences from the book and movie. Did you know that in the book Annie uses an axe to cut Paul's foot clean off before moving to his thumb as opposed to taking a sledgehammer to his ankles like in the movie?" she said, throwing her arms around Bryann and kissing him.

"Is that right?" Bryann replied coldly.

Rita released him, sensing something was wrong from his stiff body language. "Hey, what's up?"

"In the back—now. We need to talk," he said, then stormed down the hall.

"Oooh I get it…we're roll playin?" she joked, attempting to lighten Bryann's sullen mood. He looked back, rolled his eyes, then continued down the hall.

Bryann's mannerism and tone unnerved Rita. She looked at Bria's sad little face still holding on to the drawing she waited all day to present to her father. "Bria baby, go into the living room and play with your cat."

"Okay Mommy."

"Rita!" Bryann's voice roared, making Rita and her daughter both flinch.

When Rita entered the bedroom, Bryann was staring out the window at the night, focused on the fire escapes lined with flowerpots, sheets, and towels, flapping on clotheslines. He glanced up and saw Rita standing behind him in the reflection of the window.

"What's the matter? Is everything all right?" she asked, concerned.

Bryann spun on his heels and faced her with dark eyes. Gainer told him to let it go. But he couldn't. "No, everything is not all right. Thanks to you, everything's totally fucked up!"

Rita was flabbergasted. In all their years of marriage he never once raised his voice at her. Now here he was not only yelling but cursing too. Another side of him she was not used to.

"What did I do?" she asked in a shaky voice.

"Look familiar?" he asked, holding up the Dictaphone.

"Your old tape recorder," she said. Then it hit her. "I left you a message."

"Yeah, no shit!"

His sarcasm was painful to her ears, and it was written all over her face. "What, you're mad because your secretary heard the message? I put a note on the Dictaphone saying 'play me' so only you'd hear it."

"I didn't see a damn note!"

"Why are you being so mean? I thought you would like it," her voice cracked.

"Like it? Because of your cute little message a boy's life is in danger, not to mention how you made me look like a total idiot in front of Gainer and the mayor and everybody!"

Rita was totally lost. "Gainer? The mayor? What-what are you talking about?"

"Hello? The message you made! You taped over Trig's confession," Bryann snarled, showing no mercy as he took his anger out on his wife.

"Wait-what…I-I don't understand. You saw your cousin? When? Why?"

In the coldest voice he could summon, Bryann told her everything. Why he was home in the middle of the day, why there were cops in front of the building, and the real reason he needed the Dictaphone.

"But you told me the tape was blank," she said, fighting back tears.

"Well, obviously there was something on it!" Bryann bellowed with misplaced anger. When he saw Rita's eyes swell, he knew he'd gone too far, but he could not stop. He was angry with himself for not having the same attitude with his cousin earlier. Angry with himself for not double-checking the tape, and angry that his parents weren't here. "Bottom line is you had no business messing with my things!"

"Bryann I'm sorry," she pleaded. "I-I didn't know." Rita choked as tears started to fall. She was hardly passive, and anyone else would've been abruptly put in his or her place speaking to her in this manner, but this was Bryann. The love of her life. Her soulmate.

"Baby, please lower your voice." she begged as her mascara ran down her face.

"Oh please! We're seven walls away from another ear."

"Well could you please calm down."

"Calm down? This day has been one huge disaster, and you're asking me to calm down?" With his mind clouded by rage, Bryann savagely threw the Dictaphone against the wall, shattering it into pieces of flying plastic and metal. Rita flinched and started crying uncontrollably.

"Mommy?" Bria called from the doorway wide-eyed. "Why are you crying?"

Before Rita could makeup an excuse, Bryann turned on the child. "Bria! Didn't your mother tell you to stay in the living room?" Bria nodded. "Then what are you doing in here?" he demanded causing his daughter's beautiful face to drop, filled with unimaginable sadness.

"What the hell is wrong with you Bryann, don't you yell at her!" Rita said.

Bria frantically looked from right to left at her parents screaming. Her whole life she only saw them express love and affection toward each other. This was alien to her. She frowned and dealt with the situation the only way she knew how, crying.

The sound of her wailing made Bryann realize just how far he'd gone.

"Have you lost your damn mind?" Rita asked angrily, no longer crying. She picked up her child and consoled her. "How dare you come up in here yelling and carrying on like a mad man! And over some worthless hoodlum! Now, I don't know what possessed you to see that misogynistic, poor excuse for a man named Trig, but I can tell you, it wasn't worth it! And as far as taping over his confession goes, you told me the tape was blank so how in the hell was I supposed to know what was on it?"

Everything she said was true. He didn't have the right to blame her for today's disaster. "Rita. Baby, I'm sorry," Bryann said, feeling horrible about his behavior.

"Yeah, you're *sorry* all right!" she said, rocking Bria who'd stopped crying and was now sucking her thumb with red cheeks stained with tears.

"Baby, please forgive me. It's just that I've wanted to take Trig down for the longest for what he's done. You know that. And I thought I finally had, but then when I heard your message, I was so mad."

"Bryann please! That's no excuse. We are your family and we love you. I work in the courts every day, and I see criminals who have committed heinous crimes get off scot-free, and it bothers me too but I don't come home and scream at you…or our daughter." She placed Bria down and went to her closet.

"Bria. Daddy's so sorry he yelled at you, okay?" Bryann said. He felt so bad he wanted to cry. Bria sniffled with red eyes and nodded yes. "Do you forgive me?" he asked, holding out his arms.

"Yes," Bria said in a sweet voice and hugged her father.

Bryann lifted his daughter and closed his eyes then kissed her, momentarily forgetting his problems until his wife walked past him with a suitcase.

"Whoa-whoa…wait, w-what's going on?"

"I think it's best if I stay at my parents for a little while. While we both cool off."

"Rita, no, please, you don't need to go,"

"Yeah well think it's best if I do."

"Okay, but for how long?"

"That's up to you."

"Up to me? I don't even want you to go!"

"Look, Bryan, until you can get past this thing with your cousin, we're going to see more days like this, and I think it best if we weren't here. For Bria's sake. You scared her. And she doesn't need to see her father acting like that."

"Wait, baby you don't think I would ever?..." he couldn't even say the words.

"No. Of course not! But the way you lost your temper, it scared me too."

"Well, isn't this the pickle on the crap sandwich that is my day!" Bryann blurted out but got no response from his wife. "How's this going to look to your folks? The day after our anniversary, you and Bria coming over in the middle of the night?"

"I'll make up something," Rita dryly replied.

"And they'll see right through it."

She tossed her bag on the bed folded her arms and looked

directly into Bryann's eyes. "Fine. Then look me in the eyes and tell me you'll let the police deal with Trig and you're through with your crusade against him."

Bryann faced her and his eyes dropped. He may have been able to camouflage the truth when it came to the Dictaphone but telling a major lie straight to her face was something he was not capable of doing.

"Just as I thought! I'd never do anything that would disrupt or jeopardize my joy, hope or peace, which is my family and that's what you did!" she said, disgusted.

"I'm sorry. I just saw a kid who needed my help. And it reminded of when I did and what Gainer did for me."

"Bryann, I love you. I love how you're kind to others with nothing in it for yourself. I love your intense inability to see reality because you're too busy believing your ideals. I love every part of you. And for the first time since I've known you, I saw a part of you I didn't love."

"I'm so sor-"

Rita placed a finger over his mouth to stop him mid-apology, "I am not going to allow you to take your anger and frustration out on our daughter and me. This is something you have to work through alone." She said then planted a kiss on his frowned lips. "Come on Bria, we're going to see Grandma and Grandpa."

"Yay! C'mon, Daddy!" Bria cheered.

Bryann put on a fake smile. "Um, Ladybug, Daddy's gonna stay here."

Bria frowned. "No Daddy, you come too."

Bryann glanced up at his wife. Her face said she wasn't changing her mind, but her eyes were indecipherable. "No, sorry baby, Daddy's gotta get up early in the morning."

"Okay," Bria said, pouting.

Bryann turned to Rita while she was locking her suitcase. "Rita?" he called, in a voice that she knew was going to be followed by him trying to persuade her to stay.

"No, Bryann," she said, grabbing her coat. "I've made up my mind."

Bryann silently watched his wife call a cab, then helped them downstairs with their bags. The cab was already out front waiting on them. The police protection was parked across the street, drinking coffee out of a thermos, and eating bologna-and-cheese sandwiches. Rita noticed them and glared at Bryann.

The cab driver got out and put the bags into the trunk. Bryann couldn't take his eyes off of Rita. She was beautiful in the night wind as her hair frolicked about her face. Certain strands knew just where to lay to give her that stunning angelic look that made her male coworkers hate Bryann without ever meeting him. With a loud slam of the trunk, the two were snatched from their moment in time and the cabby was ready to leave.

Bryann kneeled before Bria. "Okay, Ladybug. Now, you be good and listen to Grandma and Grandpa."

Bria kissed her father. "Okay. Don't forget to feed Princess," she mumbled over a wide yawn and stretch.

"I promise I won't."

"Call me," she said, holding a tiny fist with her thumb and pinky sticking out, up to the side of her face the way she'd seen her parents do.

"First thing tomorrow. I love you, ladybug."

"I love you too, Daddy," Bria said, then climbed into the back seat.

Bryann rose to his feet in front of Rita. She stared into his sad eyes, and for a brief moment the world stood still, and it was just them. He wished he could go back in time and do things differently.

Bryann mouthed 'I love you,' as a single tear trekked down Rita's cheek. She then got into the cab beside Bria, who was starting to doze. Fighting the urge to beg his wife to come back upstairs, Bryann told the cabby to wait a second and went over to his police protection. He asked the cops if they would mind escorting his wife and daughter to her parents safely, then come back. Although it was against direct orders, they agreed. He apologized for his behavior earlier, and they pretended they didn't know what he was talking about. After one last glance at his family, he signaled for them to go.

As he watched the cab pull off and round the corner followed by the police car, Bryann thought how a perfect day ended so miserably, and how for the second time today Trig won.

Chapter 12

THE NEXT DAY BRYANN CALLED HIS DAUGHTER as soon as he got to work. He told her he missed her and assured her that her cat was fine. After they spoke, he asked to speak to her mother. Rita didn't have much to say except that she was running late and had to go. Bryann hung up feeling defeated and stared at a picture on his desk of them. He then called Darrius to see how he was and if he was ready to talk. With loud music blasting in the background, a young woman explained he was there but left after someone beeped him. Bryann hung up and hoped she would remember to tell him he called. Afterward, he worked diligently on some cases. At one-thirty, he helped Roxy get over her phobia of algebra while dining on leftover ziti he brought from home.

The end of the day finally came, and he prepared to go home. The reality of going to an empty apartment depressed him. The longest time he and Rita had ever been apart since they were married was the three days the doctors kept her at the hospital after giving birth to Bria because she lost a lot of blood and they needed to watch her in case she needed a blood transfusion. Even then he stayed until the nurse ordered him to go home and get some rest because she knew he'd be back at his wife's side first thing the next morning. On the way out, he passed Miss Crawford's office and heard a familiar voice. He stuck his head in the door and smiled for the first time all day.

"Hey, you know the rules—no laughing permitted on the premises," he smiled.

"Hey, you!" Veronica Valentine said, happy to see Bryann. The bruises on her face had all but healed and she looked like a new woman.

"You look good. How are things?"

"Couldn't be better. Thanks to Miss Crawford, my son and I are in a super nice shelter over on Blake Street called, Rise of Broken Women." Veronica said.

"Hey, I know that place. It's run by my friend Aida Rodriguez. Nice lady. She and I interned at Covenant House together." Bryann said.

"She's a sweetheart."

"She is. And speaking of your son, how is he?"

"He's doing great. My sister has him right now."

"And your husband?"

"Well, he's pretty upset that I left him."

"Is that right?"

Veronica nodded vigorously. "Yup. The police were there while I packed my stuff in case he started bugging out or something. And so was Miss Crawford. You should've seen her—

Danny was trying to talk me into staying, and she was right there in his face telling me not to listen to his shit. And Mrs. Torres got me this terrific lawyer who's advising me about restraining orders and legal matters concerning my baby."

"Didn't I tell you Miss Crawford would take care of you?" Bryann asked.

"You was right. She's my she-ro. She showed me that I ain't gotta take no mess from a man. That's why I stopped by to thank her—and you too—for helping me take back my life."

"We aim to please, ma'am," Bryann bowed, feeling good about making a difference in someone's life.

The faint ringing of Bryann's phone came down the hall. He checked his watch, it was five-forty. Everyone knew he got off at five-thirty.

Bryann wished Veronica and her son all the luck in the world, then excused himself. Bursting into his office and overanxious to speak to Rita, he neglected to turn on the light and fumbled about in the dark. Finding the phone, he snatched it up.

"Hello? Rita?" He sounded winded. There was no response on the other side. Just silence and heavy breathing. "Hello? Hello? Who's there?" he asked again.

The breathing on the other side turned into a low maniacal laughter. "Watch your back."

"Who the hell is this?" The voice sounded camouflaged, like the person on the other end was speaking through a handkerchief. There was more silence and heavy breathing. "Don't make me come through this phone! Who is this?" Bryann demanded.

There was more laughing, then the phone slammed down.

Bryann stood silent in the dark with the receiver in his hand. Gainer was right, he was in danger.

***

A week had passed. Nothing changed. Rita was still not ready to come home, and Darrius had not turned up. Every couple of days the phone calls restarted, and that worried Bryann because he had no face to match with the whisper. But instead of upsetting anyone, he decided not to say anything and hoped it would stop.

***

"Now, let me get this straight. All I gotta do is work the night shift here until I make Trig's money back, and then we're even? And afterward, I can continue working and start getting paid again?" Darrius asked. At first when he received the page, he hesitated to return the call, but he knew he could not keep running

122

forever.

Kool G Rap's Road to Riches was playing in the background as a lean, dark-skinned man with his hair braided in cornrows nodded in response to Darrius's question.

"Yo, Stutter'n Squint. You tell Trig I gladly accept his generous offer," Darrius said, unable to believe that his problems were finally behind him.

"Yo, you mu-mu-muther fu-fu-fucker, quit c-calling me sss-stu-sstuttering sssquint before I ku-ku kick your assss!" Stutter'n Squint said, shooting small missiles of saliva everywhere with a fidgety eye.

"Nigga you sound like you got tongue redundancy." A man nursing a tall boy of beer said and the room came to life from the laughter of Trig's workers at Stutter'n Squint's expense.

"You know none of this mess would have ever happened if it weren't for your social worker playing Matlock," Slam said, placing the one hundred fifty-pound dumbbells he was curling down to light a cigarette.

Darrius became quiet, and the room eyed him.

"Wait a minute. Darrius, you didn't know he was going to tape Trig, did you?" Slam said.

"Nah." Darrius shook his head visibly upset.

"Damn, that's just bad ghetti-quette." The muscular man said shaking his head.

"On everything I was just as shocked as all of you were when I found out. I only wanted him to talk to Trig for me. Since they're family, I figured Trig might listen to him. I had no idea he planned to use my problems as a way to settle his own personal beef," he said.

"I don't know what you were thinking, going to him any goddamn way. This is the underworld! If you got beef you supposed to handle it yourself, not run to your social worker for help like some little kid in a ABC afterschool special." Slam said.

Suddenly the front door burst open, and the room jumped as JackHammer entered. Due to his colossal frame, combined with his magnificent arms, he looked like a whole different species as he turned sideways in order to fit through the doorway. Nervous glances were exchanged. Even though everyone in the room was on the same team as Jackhammer they couldn't shake the tense feeling they got whenever he came around. Trig strolled in behind him without a care in the world. And bringing up the rear was Pig, devouring a slice of pizza.

"Damn! It's as cold as Eskimo pussy out there," Trig said, shivering beneath a full-length mink coat.

"Eskimo puh-puh-pussy. That's fuh-funny," Stutter'n Squint snickered out loud, but the silence and cold glare from Trig informed him he wasn't looking for laughs. "Yo somebody, put on the news." He ordered.

A kid quickly fiddled with the radio knob until he got the twenty-four-hour news program.

'A twenty-three-year-old man was found fatally shot in the lobby of an apartment building of the notorious Roosevelt Houses. Police were called to the location at around eleven thirty pm. The victim was taken to Bayview Community Hospital where he was pronounced dead. His name has not been released, pending family notification.'

Trig shook his head and snickered. "They're talking about Drake. I heard that fool got popped fighting Pookie over that hoe Jasmin. Now he's dead, Pookie's on the run and she's with a new nigga." He paused and eyed the huge heart tattoo on Stutter'n Squint's right bicep that said, 'Valerie'. "That's your woman's name?" he asked. Stutter'n Squint nodded a meek response. "I don't know what kind of sex makes a nigga wanna tat a bitch's name on him, but I ain't had it yet!" the bald black man scoffed then directed his attention to Darrius, who was nervously avoiding eye contact. "So, look who's come out of retirement."

Darrius swallowed hard before speaking. "Hey Trig. I heard about your offer, and I accept. And I just wanna say that I am sorry for all the trouble I caused you. I had no idea Mister Bonner was gonna tape you. I was just scared."

"After the way my cousin double-crossed you, you still respect him enough to call him 'Mister' but not the man who you've come to begging for forgiveness?" Trig eyed Darrius with a sneer.

"Sorry, Mister Trig." Darrius said.

"Nah, sounds dumb." Trig said, shaking his head. "You know all this could have been avoided if your goofy ass would have come to me in the beginning. Now I got cops clocking my every move."

"Trig, five-o just rolled by," JackHammer informed him, staring out the window.

"See? That's exactly what I'm talking about!" Trig complained, pointing at the window. "I don't need this aggravation. My life is stressful enough as is!"

"Trig, please man, I'll do whatever you want. Work as long as you want."

"Sorry, I can't risk it, you're too hot. Before we may have been able to work something out. But now…" Trig shook his head.

"Quiet as it's kept, you need to raise the fuck up out of here," JackHammer said. "Because I'm sure them cops saw you come up in here."

Darrius headed for the door, then paused and looked back,

biting on his bottom lip. "So, Trig, what about the money I owe?"

"What about it?"

"I'm saying. If I can't work it off, how am I going to repay you?"

"I'm only interested in hearing your problem once. Our next conversation has to be about solutions."

"So, I still gotta pay?"

Trig looked flabbergasted. "Still gotta pay?" He turned to his crew. "Can you believe this guy? He loses my stash, sic's my bitch-ass cousin on me, gets me arrested, now I'm under surveillance, which fucks with my money and he's asking does he still have to pay! Yo thanks for adding levity to a tense moment." He chuckled then turned to his large-armed goon. "Yo Hammer, is Swifty still hanging around?"

"Waiting for you boss man." JackHammer replied.

"Cool. You know what, you look like you could use a workout. Darrius, you wanna see my boy JackHammer hit the heavy bag? Sure you do. Come on." Trig said not giving Darrius the option to decline and lead the way.

The group went through a door into a dark room in the back. Trig switched on the light and Darrius gasped. A body bag was dangling from the ceiling, but the sand was removed and a fat black man with his mouth gagged was stuffed inside with his head poking out of the top.

When he saw Trig, he tried to plead his case but the wide piece of tape covering his mouth prevented him. Everyone laughed except for Darrius. Although it was hard to make out exactly what he was saying, it sounded like he was pleading for his life.

"Shh, I already told you buddy, it's all good. I never get mad at someone for being who they've always been." Trig rationalized then glanced at a nervous Darrius. "Darrius meet Swifty. Swifty, was once my trusted numbers ninja. And his job was to oversee the day's take. Sad. You can have all the degrees in the world but if you don't have a hustler's mentality, ambition and most importantly common sense you'll be lost."

"Yuh-yuh-you fuh-fuh-fuck-"

"Yes, we know Squint! He's fucked!" Trig sighed impatiently cutting Stutter'n Squint off midsentence. Swifty mumbled something incoherent that sounded like more stifled begging. "When Swifty was a kid, he was put in advanced math courses after solving a Rubix Cube in less than 3 minutes. In fact, the two of you have something in common."

"Wuh-we do?" Darrius stuttered.

"You also sound like you have a lot in common with Stutter'n Squint too." Trig laughed. "But the thing you have in common with Swifty, is that he too owed me money."

"Owed?" Darrius repeated confused, wondering was Swifty able to pay him back, and if so why was he bound, gagged, and hanging inside this bag?

"Uh-huh. He thought nobody would notice if while counting my money, he helped himself to a little taste. I swear, some people just drain the fucking nice right out of you." Trig walked up to Swifty and shook his head then addressed the room, "Don't lie to an over thinker. It never ends well. Such people have trained their brains to look for holes in a story. If shit don't make sense, they will think about it over and over until it makes sense. I'm that person. I pay attention to shit you wouldn't even think I'm paying attention to. Like when as little as a penny is missing cause he was moving decimals back and forth on the books so he could afford to send his kids to an uppity prep school. When I confronted him about the math not matching, he begged me to give him a chance to repay him. But like I told him, if you condone sucker shit, you a sucker too! Still, me being the nice guy I am I said okay, here's what we'll do… JackHammer needs a new sparring partner. So, just work out with him and we'll call it even. He agreed. Didn't you Swift?" he asked and Swifty mumbled something. "My bad." Trig said and removed the tape over his mouth. "You were saying?"

"I agreed to what you made sound like me being humiliated. Not killed! Please Trig! Don't do this!"

"Swifty, you're a numbers man. You should know the best math you can learn is how to calculate the future cost of your current decisions!" Trig said.

"I swear on a stack of Bibles six feet high I didn't take a dime of your money!"

"No you just took what you thought you deserved!" Trig sneered and placed the tape back over his mouth as Swifty mumbled something incoherent which sounded like, *'Fuck you!'* "Two things I can't stand. A liar. And aa liar that gets mad when you don't believe the lies they're telling you!"

Trig nodded to JackHammer. The large brutish man whose punches were equivalent to a Nissan Pathfinder at top speed, cracked his knuckles, walked over to Swifty, ignored his whining and shoved the bag. As it swung away, he jumped into a boxer's stance and planted his stone fist in the center of it hard! He then began throwing a typhoon of body crushing, bone breaking hooks and combinations that shook the room. Everyone but Darrius watched with glee as Swifty was being tortured. His eyes met Darrius' and pleaded for mercy. Darrius looked away but could hear the man crying as he was being beaten to death. Over the cheers of Trig and his crew, Darrius heard one loud, final punch and Swifty exploded like a blood-filled meat suit. The room became eerily quiet. Darrius opened his eyes and immediately regretted it.

Swifty's head was slumped forward, and he was no longer begging for his life, because it had come to a painful end. A hole at the bottom of the body bag was leaking with a foul combination of blood and feces.

"So, how was the work out?" Trig asked JackHammer.

"Ok. But I'm gonna need a new work out partner." The big man replied, wiping his gargantuan sized fists clean with a red rag.

"The sooner you figure out which chairs don't belong at your table, the more peaceful your meals become." Trig sighed then turned to a weak looking Darrius. "Enjoyed the show? You know the exercise I hate most, running out of money. You will lose weight in two days. Which is why I don't care if I'm at the top of the Urban food chain, I still need what you owe me. Now run along."

Darrius slowly walked out then paused and glanced at Swifty, picturing him being JackHammer's new work out partner.

"Duh-Duh-Dead muh-man wuh-walking." Stutter'n Squint said. Snickers filled the room as Darrius dropped his head in shame and left.

Stopping by the liquor store for a bottle to calm his nerves, Darrius drank and vented about was how Bryann wrecked his life. The more he drank, the more he thought about it, the more it infuriated him. Why did he have to screw this up? He knew how important this was—that it could mean his death.

By the time he got home the bottle was empty and it was decided. Some way, somehow, he'd get even with Bryann Bonner.

Chapter 13

BETWEEN THE CONFINES of West 187th and West 189th Streets, some of the vilest and most despicable acts in Major City took place. A nightmare land of pimps, prostitutes, dope fiends, and dealers; this three-block war zone lined with burned-out buildings and garbage-filled lots where people with no bathrooms or homes relieved themselves, was an intense jungle of crime and corruption. And it was also where the Wolf Pack operated its highly successful drug cartel.

Each block had four workers posted like border guards on every corner—spotters to take the order from the customer, couriers who fetched the product, and muscle-bound enforcers who collected the money.

Last but certainly not least, standing on the roofs of the dilapidated buildings were the lookouts who howled like wolves to warn the street dealers below against danger from police sneaking up to make a bust.

One of the lookouts, a twelve-year-old who'd seen more death and misery than some Vietnam vets, was the first to notice the army of Gang-Greene dressed in dark green army camouflage, rounding the corner. Without a second thought, he howled at the top of his lungs, alerting his comrades.

The door of a small shack where the Wolf Pack warmed themselves against the bitter cold, burst open. The rap song, Time's Up by street poet O.C. filled the air, as angry, crazed youths filled the streets. The gangs faced off in the middle of the street trading threats, not promises! A bronze-complexioned man, handsome beyond words, adorned in a butter leather jacket, Gucci and jewels that earned him the name Moola, stepped before Big Time, the leader of Gang-Greene. With a stunning woman on each arm, five o'clock shadow on his chiseled face, toothpick between his teeth and an arrogant smirk, he eyed his rival from head to toe, unfazed.

"Guess it's obvious, I come from a long line of cool niggas." Moola smiled as his team laughed.

"Or bitch ass niggas. Depending on how you see it." Big Time retorted as his team laughed louder.

"You know what's beautiful about the nineties? Is that sistas don't have to do much to be considered beautiful." Moola said ignoring the diss and kissed the neck and hands of his female companions. "So, Big Time! To what do we owe this unexpected visit?" he asked with a pompous smirk.

"Don't play with me, Moola. You know why the fuck we're here!" Big Time snapped in a deep voice befitting someone his size.

A slight thuggish-looking man with a ponytail stepped out of the crowd and began to laugh uncontrollably, displaying sharp gold fangs, earning him his nickname Fangs.

"Actually, we don't. Unless that last whipping Moola put on you wasn't enough, and you want another?"

Members of the Wolf Pack began snickering, inciting Gang-Greene, who were already looking for an excuse to attack. Big Time held up a hand to calm his crew and instructed his men to, "Chill."

"Read my lips," Fangs continued. "You're trespassing on private property. See, this all may have been yours once, but that was the past and this is the present. You lost it to us fair and square, remember? Or are you suffering from that shit white people get when black people bring up reparations, selective amnesia?"

Big Time wished he had amnesia, unfortunately for him, he remembered everything vividly. Once upon a time, Gang-Greene was making money hand over fist from selling their product on the very same streets. It was the perfect location—two blocks east was the check-cashing place. Three blocks west was a seedy motel where the bottom of the barrel thrived. And somewhere in between was a drug rehab that none had ever made it to.

The first of every month they kicked themselves in the rear running to cash their welfare checks and spend it on a quick escape. For Big Time and his crew life was one big party, financed with other people's misery. That is, until Moola saw an opportunity and challenged Big Time to a one-on-one fight for ownership of the streets. And according to the codes of the street, if someone challenges you for what's yours, you either defend it or lose it. Within minutes, Big Time had succumbed to Moola's lightning-quick hands and lost it all. Now the man who once preceded his own reputation for being the kingpin in Major City, was reduced to scurrying around dark alleys pushing nickel and dime bags. Sometimes he thought about how much easier it would be to wear a paper hat and flip burgers.

Big Ant stepped beside Big Time to show his loyalty. "I hate to be the bearer of bad news, but things are going to turn out different this time."

"Big Ant, is that you?" Moola smiled devilishly. "What's your big ugly ass doing here? The way I hear it, Trig's got you wrapped around his crooked trigger finger." Bama and E-Murda traded looks. Now they realized why he let Trig's cousin punk him that morning.

"Yo suck a dick nigga! Trig did me a favor once and I returned it by not pounding his people's head in!" He turned to Big Time. "C'mon bro, just give me some tissue, and I swear I'll wipe this shit out of your life for you!"

Big Time put a gentle arm around his shoulder and appreciated his loyalty. "Patience, Big Ant, you'll have your time with that loser once I've gotten our block back. But right now, this is between me and Moola."

"Who you callin' a loser?" Moola shouted as his women restrained him. "Only losers I see are you G.I. Joe wannabe bitches. You want me so bad? Fine! I could use the workout anyway!" Moola kissed each of the ladies on the cheek, palmed one of their asses like a basketball then began removing his jewelry, angrily handing it over to Fangs. With his knuckles bare, Moola began bouncing on his feet, psyching himself up for the fight.

Big Time tore out of his camouflage jacket like a rage monster, and Moola noticed he was far more developed than the last time they fought. He wondered if his knuckle game had improved as well.

Big Time prepared to charge when Moola paused. "Hold up. If I lose, you regain control of the block, right?"

"Isn't that how you got it in the first place?" Big Time said in a fighting stance.

"Yeah, but I'm saying, what if I win again? What do I get this time?"

"Don't worry, you won't. Now, let's do this!"

"Slow your role. I can't see it. You can't come to the gambling table empty-handed."

"Well then, what do you want? It's obvious by all the cars, bitches and jewels you aren't hard up for money, Moo-lah."

"Well, there has got to be something you have that I want. Let me think. Hmmm. Hey Fangs, c'mere."

"What's up?" Fangs obediently stepped up.

"What was that you called our friend here last night when we was getting our drink on at The Villain's Hideout?"

"That would be, *Small Time,*" Fangs laughed, reflecting.

"Yeah, Small Time, that's type funny. I tell you what." He said turning back to Big Time. "If you win, you get everything—the block, my customers, the whole enchilada, but—" he held up a finger. "If I win, your name will forever be changed to *Small Time.* Deal?"

Everyone was quiet, waiting for Big Time's answer.

The stakes were high. All Big Time had left was his name, and if he lost that, he might as well be invisible. But he couldn't back down, or his crew would lose the little respect they had left for him. Besides, he'd been training hard for this, and he knew this time he could beat him. Big Time stared at Moola's hand, then at the anxious faces of his crew who begged for a fearless leader. It was no secret he was jealous of Moola's killer good looks as well as the fact he somehow managed to pull in double what he did when he was in control of the block. He stared him down and was met with a strong, confident smirk from Moola.

"Okay, deal," Big Time said, half-hesitant as he shook his hand for all to see.

"Bet." Moola said, raising his fists. "Now I'm ready!"

A man hobbled out and sized up both men, "Listen up! This is a war zone. No holds barred. No truces. You rock til you drop! Chew the meat and spit out the bones! Only the fittest survive! Understood?"

The two nodded then circled each other with fists raised defensively. Then without warning, Moola moved in and faked a punch to the head and buried his fist inside Big Time's stomach. Big Time let out a grunt. It was all he could do to keep from folding on the floor. Moola followed up with a left hook to the jaw. Big Time could feel the pain ricochet through his skull as the cheers of the Wolf Pack rang in his ear.

"When this is over, I'm going to buy you a big-ass neon sign that says *Small Time* in blinking letters. Matching license plate too." Moola said and threw a couple shots that his opponent slipped.

Over Moola's shoulder Big Time could see Big Ant standing there with a look of disappointment. He couldn't let his friend down. He refused.

"Save your money bitch—you'll need it!" Big Time said and delivered two quick blows, sharp as daggers, to Moola's exposed chin that dazed the cocky boxer. He then pivoted on his shoe and caught him in the chest with a right cross, making him step back. Gang-Greene went wild.

Moola's chin held up, but his smug look was erased. For the first time he had doubts of the outcome and by the concerned looks on his men's faces, so did they. Their livelihood was in jeopardy. Shaking it off, the two men swung wildly, then collapsed into clinches and finally resumed battle as the cycle began again.

"So, no more smart remarks, Moola?" Big Time huffed with newfound confidence. "I worked hard for this. It's over, Moola!"

"Don't count me out just yet," Moola hissed back. The suave drug dealer had been street-fighting for years. Same as his opponent. Except looser and dirtier. When Big Time left himself exposed for a moment, a back spinning kick landed squarely on his chin. Moola then moved in and unleashed a right to his body and a deadly uppercut to his chin, reminding everyone of his power. Then, with deadly control, the smaller man faked a blow to Big Time's midsection and came around with a swift right across his nose. There was a pop followed by a gush of dark blood as his world went sideways and Big Time collapsed to the ground like a bag of rocks. Moola raised his hands and bounced like Ali as the crowd moved in. The boy from the roof appeared in the sea of faces, took one look at the defeated man on the ground and pointed at him laughing.

"Get up! You want some more?" Moola asked standing over Big Time.

Big Time sat up, lightheaded. His crew's eyes urged him to get back up. But the stabbing pain from his busted nose forced him to shake his head. It was over. Through blurry vision he searched the crowd for Big Ant but couldn't find him. He felt like a loser. A green jeep with camouflage designs rounded the corner and stopped before Big Time. With motionless expressions, Bama and E-Murda got out and helped their leader to his feet. Krystal dropped her head, ashamed.

"And this is why I always say, never do something permanently foolish just because you are temporarily upset. That being said, oh Small Time?" Moola called in a teasing voice. The men carrying him stopped so he could turn around. His nose and shirt were caked with blood and dirt. Moola got up in Small Time's face. "This is the last time we play this game, you hear? Come marching up in here like George Washington again, and I'ma send you back like Abe Lincoln got it?"

Mucus poured out Small Time's nose and he sniffed it back into his nostrils. Baby tears arose in his eyes, and he pitifully stared at the ground and meekly said, "Got it."

"Good. Now go to the hospital. You look like shit." Moola laughed as he watched Big Ant help Small Time into the jeep and pull off. The law of the jungle had prevailed, and Moolah remained supreme in his followers' eyes.

The remaining Gang-Greene members turned and left with their heads hung low as the Wolf Pack screamed "Bitch-ass losers!" at the back of their necks. There was nothing they could do but accept defeat. Nearby, a figure in the shadows that had been watching the whole time chomped down on a cigar. Before he could light it, a burning match was raised to it by way of a massive forearm. The figure took a pull on the cigar then blew smoke. "All in good time."

Chapter 14

BRYANN STOOD in front of his building, numb from the freezing night temperatures. The thought of going upstairs to an empty apartment with no one to greet him but the cat depressed him. He needed to be around people who loved him. He needed to go home. After walking thirty minutes across town, he arrived on the splintered front porch of the two-story house he grew up in. He fumbled for the key he hadn't used in over a month, then unlocked the front door.

"Dee-Dee? Gainer?" he called out, but no one replied. He opened the closet next to the front door and hung his leather parka on the rod beside three of Gainer's bulletproof vests. "Hello? Anybody here?" he called again. "Beautiful," he said, feeling let down that no one was there to greet him in his hour of need.

Dee-Dee's house was so stylishly decorated Martha Stewart would have been impressed. Plush wall-to-wall carpeting matched perfectly with the chocolate brown leather sofa and love seat. The end tables were covered with family photographs. The walls were adorned with beautiful African paintings and masks. In the corner was a 30-gallon aquarium with a bed of blazing blue gravel and bright tropical fish. On a polished-glass coffee table sat souvenirs from the many tropical islands Dee-Dee and Gainer had visited. Making the picture complete was a giant flat-screen TV.

Bryann stepped down into the sunken living room, loosened his tie and collapsed on the sofa. He grabbed the remote control off the coffee table, then sat back and propped his feet up. He switched on the TV and channel-surfed, stopping at a commercial in which a father was taking his daughter trick-or-treating. It reminded him of the approaching holiday, and he hoped Rita and his daughter would be home by Halloween. He knew his wife didn't want to talk. But he had to try, something. So picked up the phone and dialed. When a familiar woman's voice answered on the first ring, he was pleasantly surprised and shocked she answered his call. He took it as a positive sign and immediately began pouring his heart out.

* * *

Rita never thought in a million years when she left her parents' home for good that she'd be back and certainly not under these circumstances. She hated it. Hated lying to her parents about why she showed up in the middle of the night with their grandchild and a suitcase. Eyes puffy and red from crying. And she hated that look her mother gave her that said, *'see I was right!'*

But what she hated the most out of everything, was not waking up next to Bryann. The longest they'd gone without sleeping in the same bed ever since they were married, was when he and Markeith went to Washington DC to attend the Million Man March and he stayed overnight at a Howard Johnson's. Even then, they stayed on the phone talking all night and left the receivers on their pillows because neither could sleep without hearing the sound of the other's breathing. Now here it was, close to a month of her sleeping restlessly next to her daughter in her childhood bed with a brass headboard. She needed an escape and noticed the time, then turned on the radio to listen to her favorite program.

'Goood evening Major City! Ya'll know what time it is! It's time for Edutainment Radio! With your hosts, Keema Valentine.'

'And your boy Mikey Jay!'

'Mikey, can I start the show by saying, I cannot believe how fast the year is zooming by? My husband and I are almost finished with our Christmas shopping.'

'Dang already, you do realize its only October, right?'

'Look, say what you want but come Christmas I won't be scrambling to find something cause I'll be done. All I will have to do is decorate."

"Aight, I'll give you that. It makes sense when you put it like that. Well, I haven't even started mine yet. But then again, it's not like I have a lot of gifts to buy anyway. Just you and my momma.'

'You would if you went out and met someone.'

'I'll have you know that I went out last weekend to a house party. But when I got there, I was like Looorrrd please tell me these aren't the only women you got! Gotta be some more in the back! And why is it Black people never want to teach you how to play spades? They just say, you don't know how to play spades, really loud after you've already said you don't know how to play spades. And then start telling people you don't know how to play spades."

"So, you don't know how to play spades?"

"I'm not speaking to you."

'You know you love me Mikey. Ouch!'

'You ok over there co-host?'

"Yeah, I'm good. My back's a little stiff. You don't realize how old you are until you sit on the floor to wrap Christmas gifts, then try to get up.'

'Wait a minute you wrapping them already too?'

'Didn't I just tell you I don't like to scramble?'

'Alright, well if you gonna be down on the floor wrapping you gotta exercise. Or in my case sex-ercise.'

"Clifford and I are fine in that department. But back on the gifts real quick. I am this close to not giving my youngest daughter hers.'

'Oh Lawd. What'd Tamara do?'

'It's not what she did. It's what she said! She gon' ask me, what year I was born. So I told her 1966. This heffa says, dang Ma were you a slave?'

'What the hell!'

'That's what I said. Then her butt gonna walk away laughing. Alright then, we will see who is laughing come Christmas morning when she ain't got no gifts under the tree.'

Rita cracked up at the radio hosts antics, while sipping on her herbal tea.

'Too funny. So, listeners, we're gonna take a quick station break to pay some bills and play a song or two. In the meantime, if you have something on your mind. A question you'd like to ask one of us. Like, what was slavery like?'

'I hate you!'

'Or a comment feel, free to call us at 555-0155. We're here to talk to you, encourage you and listen to you.'

'WTLC 105.7 FM, Edutainment Radio. The show that entertains and educates.'

Prince's Little Red Corvette played, and Rita reminisced about the time when she and Bryann went to see the movie Purple Rain. He walked in unsure about her celebrity crush's debut and walked out a fan. But when they went to go see his next movie, Under the Cherry Moon even she had to admit that it was whack. And his third attempt, Graffiti Bridge. Whacker! A couple more songs that took her back to her childhood played and she was caught in between happiness and sorrow.

'You're listening to WTLC 105.7 on your FM dial, Edutainment Radio. The show that educates and entertains. I'm Keema Valentine and we're back. So, Mikey I just took a call from a listener with a serious problem he's hoping we can help him out with. His name's Mister Bee and he's currently separated from his soul mate Misses Bee.'

'Oh no. That's terrible. What happened he got caught cheating?'

'I don't know, let's find out. Caller, are you still there? Hello? Mister Bee?'

'Yes? I'm here.'

Rita spit out her tea like a Three Stooges skit, when she recognized Bryann's voice.

'So, Mister Bee, Keema tells me that you're in the dog house. Separated from your wife.'

'Yeah-I am.'

'Wow you sound like you're in a lotta pain buddy.'

'I am. I really miss my wife.'

'So, what happened did you step out of the marriage and get caught?'

'Huh? No way! I'd never cheat on my wife!'

'Okay-okay. My bad. Don't come through the radio. I just assumed because that's usually the reason most women leave.'

'I apologize for the outburst Mikey. But no, I didn't cheat. I made a huge mistake that I'd rather not go into. I was trying to do what I thought was the right thing. And it backfired severely. People got into trouble, and I made things much worse. When I got home, I took it out on my wife. And our daughter. I said things. Things I didn't mean. Stupid things, that I shouldn't have. And I raised my voice at them. So, she thought it was best if she and our daughter left.'

'Mister Bee how long have you guys been together?'

'Twelve years. We were high school sweethearts.'

'Aw, true love. Just like my husband Clifford and me.'

'Is that right?'

'Yeah. So, I know what you're feeling. Mister Bee I think she needed some time away so you could get yourself together and work on yourself. Not to mention your child doesn't need to see her parents arguing.'

'I agree Keema. Mister Bee, you sound like the type of brother who puts his family before everything. Am I right?'

'Yes Mikey. I love my wife and little girl more than life itself. There's nothing I wouldn't do for them.'

'Aw, I'm gonna cry. Mister Bee I'm willing to bet she misses you as much as you miss her. I'm assuming she's not taking your calls?'

'No ma'am, I've tried but she just isn't ready to talk.'

'You can't rush her. She's hurt.'

'Yeah…trust and believe, she's not the only one.'

'Say man, did you try flowers? Gifts?'

'No Mikey. That'd be pointless. Ri-I mean Misses Bee's not the type who you can give her some roses or jewelry and it'll erase everything that happened. She'd be insulted. You gotta come correct with her.'

'And rightfully so. Misses Bee sounds like a woman after my own heart. So Mister Bee, is that why you decided to try calling us?'

'Yes. This is her favorite radio show, and she listens to you guys all the time. In fact, the two of you have gotten her through some trying times. So I thought…well maybe, I dunno, if I called you, she'd listen and hear me out. That's even if she's listening.'

'Well Mister Bee, I truly hope she is listening to us right now. And if you are Misses Bee, woman to woman, for what it's worth; I've taken countless calls throughout my lengthy career from guys who messed up claiming they're sorry. And I gotta be honest, this is the very first time I don't need convincing, I actually believe him.'

'You know, I was thinking the exact same thing Keema. And I'm a guy who messes up on the reg.'

'I can tell by the sincerity and pain in your husband's voice that he's truly sorry and wants his family back. Now I'm no relationship expert, nor do I claim to be, but like that lady on the train said to Lisa McDowell when Prince Akeem apologized for hurting her, go on honey…take a chance. So that being said, Mister Bee, the stage is yours. Tell your wife and soulmate what you're feeling.'

Rita leaned into the radio, along with the countless other listeners across Major City waiting to hear what Bryann would say.

'Ok thanks guys…Hey Baby, I hope that you're listening, um. I just wanted you to know that with all my heart, I am sorry for the way I behaved that night. I was wrong and it was entirely my fault. It's been really hard living without you and ladybug. I miss you both so much. Baby, please come back home.'

'Wow brother, I pride myself on being a man's man and you got me over here feeling some kinda way. On the real, Keema and I are rooting for you. Is there a song we can play for you two?'

'Sure, Since I Lost My Baby, by Luther Vandross.'

'You got it brother. Peace'

"Good Luck Mister Bee. And give her, her space. When she's ready she'll be back. And remember, you can't go back and change the beginning, but you can start where you are right now and change the end.'

'I will. Thank you guys.'

The phone rang. Bryann picked it up. "Hello?"

"You play dirty." Rita said.

The sound of her voice made the hairs on the back of Bryann's neck stand up and his throat constricted. He closed his eyes and mouthed, *'thank you'*. "Hey. How are you?" he asked.

"Fine, and you?" Rita said.

"I've been better, and I've been worse. So, what are you doing?"

"Just sitting here, listening to you on the radio."

"Yeah. I just got off the phone with them a little while ago. They said it would air in about ten to fifteen minutes. I didn't know what to do. I was desperate."

"Life would be so much simpler if we could live it backwards." She said. Bryann could hear, Luther singing, softly in the background.

He closed his eyes and listened to the music along with her, wishing that she was right there beside him. "Hey-I."

"Hey-I." They both began simultaneously then giggled together. "You go first." Rita started.

"No, please. After you." Bryann insisted.

"…I was going to say that Bria misses her daddy," she said after a long silence.

"Her daddy misses her… and her mommy," Bryann whispered. As he waited for her reply the seconds seemed like hours.

"Look Bryann, I—"

"Come on, Rita. You can't honestly tell me you don't miss me as much as I miss you."

"Don't be silly Bryann, of course I miss you. But after the way you behaved, then calling my parents' house yelling and carrying on the way you did—"

Bryann sighed. It was embarrassing to be reminded of what he did and he decided not to mention it to Keema and Mikey. A couple of nights ago, after a long, rough day, he stopped at the liquor store on the way home. By one-thirty in the morning the room was spinning, and he picked up the phone. Rita's father answered half asleep and was rudely awakened by his drunken son-in-law demanding to speak to his wife. Rita got on the phone and a shouting match ensued, awaking everyone. Including Bria, who cried when she saw her mommy crying.

"Look, I'm sorry," Bryann said humbly. "It's just that the bed's too big without you."

"I just need time."

He recalled Keema's advice and pulled back. "Okay…okay fine, no pressure. So… is everything okay with the baby?"

"Yes, the doctor said the pregnancy is coming along just fine."

"Good, so where's Bria?"

"She's playing with the kids next door. They have a new kitten."

"Oh no, now you're leaving the cat too?"

"Ha ha, very funny. Hold on, I'll go get her."

"No, don't bother. She's probably having fun. Just tell her …Just tell her, that daddy loves her, and I'll call her tomorrow." he said choked up.

"Okay, well…goodnight, Bryann."

"Rita, hold up. I … love you."

"I love you too, Bryann." Rita hung up, then dried her tears. She looked up and her parents were standing in the doorway. "So, you heard?"

Her mother nodded and opened her arms. Rita walked over to her and had a long cry in her embrace, as her father rubbed her back and kissed his daughter on the top of her head then wrapped his arms around his family.

"It'll all work itself out Baby Girl." He promised.

***

With nothing interesting on cable, Bryann went into the kitchen and grabbed a cold Heineken. The thought of going back across town was not too appealing, especially when his old room was upstairs. He walked up the stairs and down the narrow hall passing his parents' old room, which remained closed since their death. He tapped on the door. Called out, 'Sis? Gainer?' then peeked in Dee-Dee's room, the door of which was opened partially—but no sign of his sister or her boyfriend.

Bryann entered the last room at the end of the hall. The sight of his childhood room made him sigh. It remained intact as he had left it when he moved out at eighteen to marry Rita. One wall was covered with vintage pullout posters from *Fresh and Right On* magazine of Salt-N-Pepa, Big Daddy Kane, LL Cool J, and other rappers who were big in the '80s. The other, had multiple Jet Magazine beauty of the week pages neatly taped from the ceiling to the floor.

On his dresser were photographs of him and childhood friends he had not seen in years. Beside his bunk bed was a dusty weight bench, and in the far corner was a desk and chair. On the table was a heart-framed picture of a teenaged Rita posing with one hand on her hip.

"God, there ain't nothing on the face of mother earth more beautiful than a black woman in a summer dress," Bryann complimented, staring at the picture on the edge of the bottom bunk. He thought about all the times that he and Rita gave each other hickey chains on the very same mattress while Dee-Dee thought they were studying. The combination of the beer and the long day had taken its toll, and Bryann pulled off his pants and got as comfortable as best he could on the small mattress, then drifted off to sleep.

The next morning, Bryann awoke to his old Mr. T. talking alarm clock warning him *"I pity the fool who don't rise and shine. Now get outta bed or yo butt is mines!"*

He half-opened his eyes and mumbled, "Coffee."

As he shuffled down the hall in his boxers, Dee-Dee's bedroom door opened, and she strutted out naked, glowing from early lovemaking. When she saw her brother she screamed to the top of her lungs. Gainer charged out the bedroom, stark naked as well. The sight of his older sister and her boyfriend buck naked made Bryann shut his eyes and holler as well. Dee-Dee ducked back in the room and reappeared in a housecoat.

"Bryann! What are you doing here?" Dee-Dee demanded,

tying the belt tightly around her waist.

"Going blind!"

"You scared the hell out of me!"

"Sorry Dee-Dee, but I didn't feel like sleeping in an empty apartment," he replied.

Dee-Dee sighed, and looked at her baby brother through sad eyes, instantly feeling his pain, and hugged him. "So I take it you two are still separated?"

Bryann nodded. "It's going on a month, Sis. I go to see Bria after work, but Rita will suddenly have something important to do and make herself scarce."

Gainer threw an arm around Bryann. "Give her time, son."

Bryann nodded but didn't feel any better then looked down at his sister's boyfriend who was still nude. "Um, Gainer? You wanna put something on?"

At the breakfast table, Bryann played with his eggs and moped. Dee-Dee sat across from him silently watching him, thinking of the right thing to say without mothering him. The two looked nothing alike. Favoring their father, she was dark-skinned and had an identical cleft in her chin as he did. She wore her hair in neat shoulder-length box braids that complemented her strong elegant African features. At forty-four, she was in excellent shape because of a strict regimen of healthy food and exercising three nights a week.

As Dee-Dee watched her brother she remembered it like it was yesterday, the day she went from being a carefree twenty-six-year-old with no responsibilities to the sole legal guardian of her brother. She had just gotten in from work, to find the living room packed with relatives and police. And then she got the heartbreaking news, that a drunk driver murdered her parents. The only comforting news was that they died on impact and didn't suffer.

Family and friends of their parents offered to take Bryann in but when he ran crying into her arms, there was no way she was about to allow that. Right then and there she knew that she had to, grow up and raise him herself. A decision that even with it's ups and downs, she's never regretted.

"Why don't you move back home until you two make up?" Dee-Dee offered. "There's plenty of room, and we'd love to have you—right, Gainer?"

Still replaying the morning's embarrassing scenario in his mind, Gainer reluctantly nodded, "Uh-yeah, sure." He knew he had no choice but to accept it if that was what his girlfriend wanted. Even though he felt she babied the young man too much, that was one place he never challenged her because he knew he would lose. With the absence of a father, he tried to instill things in him that she felt Bryann needed to be a man. He was proud when the young man became responsible and moved out on his own instead of letting his sister wait on him hand and foot. He believed Bryann should go home and work things out with his wife like the responsible man he helped raise him to be.

"Nah. That's okay, sis," Bryann said, finishing his coffee. "Last night I was feeling a bit lonely. I'm cool now."

A smile formed at the corner of Gainer's lips as the man he helped raised came forward.

"You sure?" Dee-Dee asked, eyeing the loud green tie that clashed horribly with his lavender shirt.

"Yeah, I'm sure. Besides, after this morning, I know you two like your privacy." Bryann winked at Gainer, kissed Dee-Dee on the cheek, and left for work.

Chapter 15

"KID, DY-NO-MITE! What was the name of Arnold's goldfish?"

"Shit! Was it George? Lincoln? Regan? Wait, I remember. Abraham! Name the band Re-Run was busted trying to tape at a concert."

"The Doobie Brothers. Come on man you're insulting me. I bet you didn't even realize Roger didn't have lenses in his glasses. He wore empty frames before RUN DMC. Now ask me a tough one."

"Okay, mister smart ass. What apartment did the Jeffersons live in?" Markeith asked Bryann with a raised eyebrow.

"Aw, man, please. Twelve D." Bryann replied like it was common knowledge. "Name all of the daughters on the first episode of the Cosby Show," he asked Markeith.

"And you accused me of asking easy ones? Okay, there was Sandra, Denise, Vanessa, and Little Rudy."

"Wrong! There was no mention of Sandra on the first episode. They didn't even introduce her until episode ten of the first season. In fact, in the very first episode, Claire asks Cliff why do we have four children and he says cause you didn't want five." Bryann laughed as Markeith sucked his teeth in defeat. "So let me hear it."

"Before I do, what page is the beauty of the week in Jet magazine on?" Markeith asked knowing there was no way his goody-two shoes friend would never know about the page featuring scantily dressed gorgeous black women, that turned boys into men.

Bryann smiled and said, "Dude growing up, my entire wall, top to bottom was covered with gorgeous Black queens from page forty-three."

"Fine. You're the king of Ghetto Trivia." Markeith admitted reluctantly, rolling his eyes at the game they came up with.

"Thank you, thank you. I'd like to accept this award on behalf of all the talented and beautiful Black actresses and actors who, to this day, still don't receive the recognition they deserve." Bryann laughed holding up a stapler as his office phone rang and he answered. "Bryann Bonner speaking,"

"If I were you, I'd watch my back," the muffled voice from before said.

"So, you're back. What happened to you? I missed you," Bryann replied sarcastically.

You fucked with the wrong one. I'm gonna get you, punk-ass bitch!"

"Is that right? I'm sooooo scared!" Bryann said, causing

Markeith to look up.

"You think you're funny? But I got something for that ass. Best believe!" the caller warned.

"Well, I have a tough time believing anything that's whispered over the phone. Tell you what, put a little base behind your voice, and maybe I'll become concerned." Bryann said. The caller hung up, and Bryann slammed the phone down, swearing under his breath.

"What was that all about?" Markeith asked, concerned.

Before Bryann could respond the phone rang again. He furiously snatched up the receiver. "Listen up, jerk-off! Why don't you be a man and tell me who you are, so I can put my foot square in the center of your—"

"Bryann! Do you know who you're speaking to?"

Bryann's face turned pale. "Rita?" he said softly.

"Yes, Rita! What's that all about? Bria called you, then handed me the phone, frantic, saying Daddy was yelling at her."

"Shit!" Bryann closed his eyes and wondered could things get any worse. "I'm sorry—I thought it was someone else."

"Obviously. But who?"

"Someone—I don't know who—playing jokes over the phone. It's probably this piece of garbage that was beating his wife—I had her and their baby placed in a shelter. It's nothing I can't deal with."

"You sure?"

"I've dealt with his type before. Goes with the territory. Let me speak to Bria." Bryann explained to his daughter that he thought he was talking to somebody else and that he wasn't mad at her. She quickly got over it and wanted to know when he was going to take her shopping for her Halloween costume for next week. This year she wanted to dress up as her favorite superhero the beautiful African American teenager and defender of her planet Krotoa, Nubiana Princess Power.

He promised he'd pick her up the next day after work, then asked to speak to her mother. He expected Rita to say she wasn't ready to come home yet, but he still had to try. To his surprise, Rita admitted she hated sleeping without him too and was ready to come home, if he was ready to treat his family right. Forgetting Markeith was in the room with him, Bryann became so excited he began to tear up. Rita said she wanted to go costume shopping with them and maybe pick up a little sexy something for him, too. Bryann hung up feeling a surge of happiness through his body.

"They're coming home Markeith! My family is coming home!" he said, throwing a fist in the air and dancing around like he just scored a touchdown.

Markeith stayed quiet with a sad face.

"What's up with you?" Bryann asked.

"My place is being fumigated, and I was about to ask if I could bring a honey over to your crib tonight," Markeith said, then winked with a smile as Bryann playfully shoved him. "What? She had a friend for you,"

Bryann laughed out loud.

* * *

"Okay, let me get four dimes of rock, a nickel bag of sess, and a little Mexican brown," the foul-smelling junky said, as though he were placing an order at a fast-food restaurant.

Slam nodded and produced all the narcotics the basehead desired. After the transaction was made, he sat back down on the milk crate and vegetated in front of a small TV and continued watching Living Single.

"Damn, Kyle. You's a fly muthafucker." he said licking his lips.

Darrius strolled in. He had just paid a junkie to threaten Bryann on the phone for the third time, and each time he did Bryann seemed less and less intimidated. He needed a new approach to getting even with the man who, in his warped mind, ruined his life.

"Slam, my man! How's it going?" Darrius greeted the bored weightlifter with his hand extended.

"Boy, are you crazy? What are you doing here? Didn't Trig say for you not to come around until he said so?" He rose with his hands on his hips.

Darrius noticed the feminine mannerism of Trig's number two bodyguard but refused to go there. "I know, but it's been a week, and I can't take another day of sitting in the house with that damn chicken head girl!"

"That's your problem, chump! Now take your young ass home before Trig finds out you was here."

Right on cue the door opened and Pig came through, followed by Trig. Darrius swallowed hard at the sight of the fierce-looking black man. "Hey, Trig," he said frightened, covering it with a pitiful smile.

Trig moved toward him wearing an evil grin. "Darrius, just the person I was looking for."

"You were?" Darrius and Slam said simultaneously.

Trig nodded. "I figured out what you can do to get back in my good graces."

"What? Anything! You name it, Trig, and consider it done. I'll do anything to prove my loyalty!" He brown-nosed like an attorney trying to make partner.

"Anything?" Trig said, walking over to a velvet picture of dogs shooting dice on the far wall. He pulled back the picture and revealed a safe with a face like a digital clock built into the wall.

"Anything!" Darrius repeated, sounding sincere.

"Remember, you said it," Trig said, then began pressing the numbers on the combination of his digital safe directly in front of Darrius's wide saucer eyes. Slam, who knew the combination along with Pig, wondered why his boss was entrusting a punk kid with information it took him and Pig years to be trusted with, but decided not to question it. Trig withdrew a large wad of money from the safe and wrapped it in a red rubber band, then tossed it across the room to Pig. "Take that to Mary," he instructed Pig. "Tell her it's for the club, not her." Pig nodded and left. "Now Darrius," he said, shifting back to the young man. "About that job. I want you to know I'm only asking this of you because I think you have what it takes to pull this off."

Darrius felt good that Trig had so much confidence in him. "Trig, I told you, man, anything you want just ask. No problem."

"Okay, I want you to steal my cousin's house keys and make copies for me without him noticing. Can you do that for me?" Trig asked.

Darrius became numb. True, he was angry with Bryann, but he still liked and respected him, and he knew stealing his keys meant putting him and his family in extreme danger. "But what do you want his keys for?" he asked in a low voice, already knowing the answer.

"Don't concern yourself with that! Just get me the damn keys, boy! Can you do that?" Trig asked in a deep voice. The look on his face dared Darrius to defy him.

Darrius glanced over at Slam, who looked unconcerned and chugged his beer.

"Well, what's up, kid?" Trig asked, inching forward as if he were preparing to strike. "And might I add, *you owe me.*" Darrius closed his eyes and nodded. A sinister smile etched on Trig's dark face. "Good man."

Slam turned to Trig. "So you got a connection for him to get the keys made?"

Trig smirked. "Yeah fool, it's called a *locksmith.*"

Darrius wasn't a religious person, but for the first time in his young life, he asked God to forgive him.

Chapter 16

THE NEXT MORNING FOUND BRYANN IN GOOD SPIRITS. Roxy noticed the change in his behavior as he cheerfully whistled while standing by her desk sorting his mail. Seeing an opportunity present itself, she reached in her purse and withdrew a small bottle of perfume and spritzed her neck. She then unbuttoned the top two buttons on her brown knit top and arched her back to make her medium bust appear larger in the push-up bra.

"So, aren't we in a good mood?" she asked, hoping he'd notice her efforts.

"Yeah. I know, I haven't been myself lately. My wife and I have been going through some problems," he explained.

"That's too bad," Roxy said, sounding like she was sorry to hear the news but secretly cheering inside.

"But yesterday we made up, and tonight she and my daughter are coming home."

"I see," Roxy said, unable to hide her disappointment. "That's awesome."

"I know, I can't wait to see 'em." Bryann was so happy he failed to notice Roxy's phony reaction. "But enough about me. Did my tips help you with your math class?"

"Huh? Oh, yeah. I got a ninety-five on my last test."

"That's wonderful! I'm proud of you. I told you if you work hard, you can achieve anything and everything."

"Not everything," she said sarcastically under her breath.

"I'm sorry?"

"I said 'thanks.'" Roxy smiled. She was still thinking about his wife returning to him. Thinking if she were his wife, she would have never left him, and that if she were given the chance, she'd make Rita past tense. She couldn't stand it anymore, seeing him every day and wanting to tell him how much she cared for him. The other boys she dated were just that—boys. But Bryann was different. He was handsome, intelligent, and educated. A perfect package aside from the loud clothes he wore, but so what. She decided she was going to tell him how she felt, right now. Just lay it on the table and deal with whatever happened. At least she wouldn't have to keep it bottled up inside anymore. "Mista Bonner?" she said in a hoarse voice.

"Roxy please, call me Bryann, all my friends do," he said with a wink.

Good sign, she thought. "Okay Bryann, there's something you should know, I—"

"Yo! Mister Bonner! I need to talk to you." Darrius' voice made the two look back. Roxy sighed at his bad timing.

"So, look who decided to walk back into my life," Bryann

said.

"I need to talk to you in private," Darrius said.

Bryann turned back to his receptionist to show her she wasn't overlooked. "Roxy, you wanted to tell me something?"

With Darrius standing before her, staring down her throat, she felt awkward. "I just wanted to... thank you again for your help. That's all."

"Oh, well yeah sure, anytime."

Darrius knew that wasn't what she wanted to say and snickered. Roxy felt embarrassed and dropped her head.

Up in Bryann's office, Darrius explained that he was sorry about acting like an ungrateful ass when all Bryann was trying to do was help him. He also said that he heard Trig was looking for him, and he went to stay with a new girlfriend which is why he couldn't be found. He went on to say he wanted to get out of the thug life for good and go back to school, so if that messenger job was still available, he'd gladly take it.

Bryann was ecstatic. Just the other day he got into a debate with a frustrated co-worker who said kids are just different these days, blaming the 'anything goes' mentality as the root of dysfunction. But he disagreed and explained that he'd met all kinds of kids throughout his career as a social worker. Many were incredibly smart and accepting of others. What's changed is a society with lowered expectations, lack of discipline and an acceptance of disrespect. Bryann went on to say that by giving kids boundaries, expectations, rules, limits, rewards and consequences, they will rise to the challenge and exceed your expectations every time. He wished Miss Glass-half-full was around to witness Darrius, to prove his theory.

"Now, this is what I want to hear," Bryann said smiling. "It makes everything worth it." Bryann jotted down a phone number and handed it to Darrius. "I will arrange for your placement test for the GED program. In the meantime, here, call this number tomorrow morning and ask for Kimayla Stokes. She's a good friend of mine and owns a messenger service. She's given jobs to countless young men like yourself who want to make a change. And deserve a second chance."

Darrius accepted the number and rose, anxious to leave. Bryann came from behind his desk and hugged the young man, patting him on the back. "Words cannot describe how proud I am of you, Darrius," Bryann said. Darrius thanked him but could not look him in the eye and left.

Inside the elevator, Darrius took out the keys he had lifted from Bryann's pocket when they hugged, and went through them until he found the ones marked front door and lobby. Luckily for him, his social worker was the affectionate type because he did not have a clue how he was going to get his keys. He pulled some pieces of modeling clay out his other pocket and mashed each key into the clay to get a print of it. When he got downstairs he told Roxy that he found some keys by the elevator and handed them to her and left. Roxy wondered why someone like him would even care if someone lost his or her keys.

After getting the keys made from the clay molds, Darrius tried to shake how Bryann said he was proud of him. He had to stay focused on what he had to do to stay alive, so he decided to sniff some coke to ease his mind. When he finally got to the candy store, a group of people were standing around as Trig viciously smacked a young pregnant woman in the face.

"Bitch, I wouldn't show you my dick in a photograph!" he hollered as a teary-eyed woman ran off, clutching her jaw while bystanders pointed and laughed. "Can you believe that shit?" Trig asked openly. "Damn funky bitch gonna tell me her welfare check is late and she ain't got no money for blow, but she'll *blow* me till my toes curl! Please! I screw junkies out their money, not instead of their money, know what I'm sayin'?" In the midst of the laughter, he noticed Darrius in the crowd. The young man nodded and held up a set of keys on a key ring. "All right—let's break this shit up!"

Wedged in the back seat between Slam and Pig, Darrius sat in silence, wondering where he was being taken, but decided against asking Trig who still seemed angry about the junkie offering herself to him. The silence was making him crazy, and he turned to Slam to strike up some conversation.

"So, Slam—how'd you get so big? You look like Arnold Schwarz-uh-nigga," he kidded, hoping to lighten the mood in the car and score points for his humor. No one laughed.

Slam glared over, annoyed with the boy's question and mumbled, "Good food."

"What kinda food?" Darrius asked, like he was interested in training with him.

"Prison food!" Slam snapped back.

"Oh, okay, never mind," Darrius whispered, sinking in his seat.

JackHammer pulled up on a raw dirty block, desolate and unfamiliar to Darrius. Everyone got out and lined the sidewalk.

"The keys," Trig said.

"Oh yeah, here you go. Keys to the castle." Darrius said as he tossed them to Trig.

Trig caught them and studied them in the fading sunlight, then cracked a smile. "This will do nicely. Good work. So Darrius, let me ask you something…how does it feel betraying the only person in the world who still gave a damn about your ass?"

"What are you talking about?"

"I'm talking about how you're a traitor by definition. Are you not?"

"What do you mean?"

"I mean your brother don't give a damn about you because Moola is too busy enjoying himself and making moola. And your moms gave up on the both of you, which left my bleeding-heart, soft ass cousin Bryann. The only one left who still had faith in you, who wanted to see you do something with yourself, and you betrayed him, cause right here in my hand I am holding the keys to where he and his family live. So, I was curious to know, how does it feel?"

The weight of what Trig said felt immense, but Darrius fronted with a simple shrug of his shoulders. "Well, to be honest with you, he drew first blood when he tried to tape you, so I don't feel nothing."

"You don't feel nothing huh?" Trig smirked at his crew.

"No. My loyalty is with you," the boy answered, trying to sound like a man. Inside, he felt like garbage.

"But didn't he record me so he could help you? In fact, didn't you come to him asking him to protect you from me, and he put it all on the line to help you?"

Darrius thought quickly, "Well yeah, but I figured if I showed you how your cousin was living then you'd know I had your back."

"So what you're saying is that you will betray people who will risk everything to help you, but I can trust you?"

"That's exactly what I am saying."

"So, I can trust a traitor?"

"Um, yes but no because I'd never betray you."

"Going to my cousin, was betrayal!" Trig snarled then exhaled. "Darrius, you ever heard that expression, God takes care of babies and fools?" Trig asked.

Darrius shook his head, "No. What does it mean?"

"I'll tell you later." Trig chuckled as his crew stood silently behind him staring at Darrius like well-trained attack dogs awaiting the command to kill. "First, I want to tell you a story. I couldn't have been any more than five and my old man took me to the park one Sunday afternoon. I ran up on the slides and yelled down to him, 'I'ma slide down backwards, Daddy. Catch me, okay?' he said, 'Come on son, I'll catch you, *trust me*. So my trusting ass let go and, BAM! I hit the ground and busted my head wide the fuck open. Now I'm sitting there in the dirt crying and bleeding like a little bitch and through the snot and tears, I ask him, 'Daddy, why ain't you catch me?' And you know what that old bastard told me?" Trig asked then hocked up a loogie and spat it on the ground next to Darrius' shoe. "'Rule number one, don't trust anybody as far as you can spit!" After his cautionary tale, the cold-blooded killer opened his jacket and revealed the butts of his guns.

Darrius was as nervous as a cow in a meat factory and backed up in fear. "Come on Trig! Man I did what you asked, why you gotta do me like this? I proved I'm useful." he pleaded.

"Come on Trig, why you gotta do me like this?" Pig mimicked Darrius with the same high-pitched, scared and trembling voice.

"You're about as useful as a backstage pass at an MC Hammer concert. Look, nothing personal. For what it's worth, you were an important pawn in my game of chess." Trig said.

"Game, what game? I don't understand," Darrius said, two seconds from running.

"No matter! But I'll tell you what. Since you did come through for me, I'm gonna give you a running chance. All you got to do is make it to the end of the block before I count to ten. And to make it even easier, I'm gonna turn my back." Trig said and did an about face.

Darrius studied the distance he was expected to sprint down and knew there was no way he'd make it to the end of the long, barren block before ten. He turned to Trig's men who were making a joke of the situation by running in place, pointing and laughing.

"All right Darrius, you ready?" Trig asked.

"Please Trig, don't do this man!"

"One!" Trig said in an even tone.

"Trig… man come on, please!" Darrius begged.

"Two!"

Darrius turned to Pig with a look of utter horror on his face. "Help me, man!"

"You still standing there? Your ass better turn into cartoon smoke!" The overweight man strongly advised.

"Three!"

Realizing he was wasting precious time, he turned and raced down the block at top speed. The space of the sidewalk he had to cross appeared to stretch a mile and he panicked he would never reach the opposite side. By the time Trig reached eight, Darrius was almost at the end of the block and in the home stretch. Slam, Pig, and JackHammer had to give credit to the young man who was only a few feet away from saving his life.

"Nine!" Trig shouted.

Darrius was inches away from victory and could see the corner. Unable to breathe because his lungs were bouncing against his chest like bongos but still finding the strength to push his aching legs, he was beginning to believe he would make it and live. His foot was just about to touch the corner when Trig yelled,

"Ten!"

He then leaned forward as if he were about to touch his toes and pointed two snub-nosed .38 automatics between his legs letting off a round from each gun simultaneously. Darrius was running hard when he heard the shots, then felt his legs give out and hit the ground. When he tried to stand up he could no longer feel his legs. He turned over and his eyes bulged from shock. Blood gushed out from where his legs used to be like an open fire hydrant. Then he looked over to his left and stared at his legs lying on the ground for a full two minutes before screaming at the top of his lungs.

JackHammer's Navigator backed up beside Darrius and Trig stepped out. Darrius turned over and crawled away, smearing the sidewalk with a messy trail of pink flesh and red blood.

Careful not to muck up his alligator shoes, Trig pushed him over on his back with his foot and pointed a gun in his face. His eyes wide like a deer in the headlights

"This is fucked up!" Darius cried, tears running down the sides of his face from pain and fear.

"No. This is life. And I'm very well versed in it! But you're gonna be aight."

"I am?"

"Remember when I said? God takes care of babies and fools. Well luckily for you, your ass is both!" Trig smiled and raised his gun.

"Come on Trig please! Don-"

BLAM!

Trig ignored his begging and squeezed the trigger shooting Darrius point-blank, removing half his face. Another bullet put a dark hole over his heart. Slam and Pig got out of the cruiser, carrying garbage bags and duct tape.

"Make sure you wrap him up nice and tight," JackHammer ordered. "I just got my whip reupholstered, so I don't want a drop of blood spilled in my ride."

Trig lit a cigar and stood by watching. His plan was beginning to take effect.

Chapter 17

A GREEN JEEP, IDENTICAL TO THE ONE THAT TOOK Small Time to the hospital after his loss to Moola, came flying top speed toward the pool hall the Wolf Pack used as a hang out. A cockeyed man in a leather Wolf Pack jacket recognized the Gang-Greene vehicle and brandished ammo. The jeep stopped in front of the pool hall and a large package was tossed out, then sped off. With guns drawn, he cautiously walked over to the package wrapped in garbage bags, pulled back a corner of the plastic and his eyes bulged at the discovery. For a brief moment he froze while staring at the object, with his hand clamped over his mouth to prevent throwing up. In an instant, fear crept over him as he recognized what he had just uncovered.

"Where's Moola? I need to see Moola! Yo Moola!" The cock-eyed Wolf member rushed into the pool hall shouting. The infectious beat of 'Insane in the Membrane' by Cypress Hill, had turned the pool hall into an all-out party, as the frantic man's eyes banged and rolled in their sockets like pinballs. In his pursuit he failed to notice Fangs and bumped hard into him, almost knocking him down.

"Peek-a-Boo, what the fuck! Watch where the fuck you're going before I hit you hard enough to make you see straight!"

"Where's Moola?" Peek-a-Boo demanded, ignoring the threat.

"Nigga he's in the bathroom with some bitch, why?"

Peek-a-Boo didn't answer and rushed toward the back. Fighting past people, he made his way to the bathroom and pounded on the door. "Moola, you in there? Open up! Moola?"

Inside the bathroom, Moola grinned at his reflection in the mirror, smoking a cigar while having sex with a beautiful woman from the rear. An ashtray was resting on the arch of her back to catch his ashes. Peek-a-Boo's yelling was throwing off his stroke. He became upset and snatched open the door without covering up.

"What nigga? And this had better be important!" he said angrily.

"It's about your brother, Darrius," Peek-a-Boo said between gulps of air.

Moola let out an annoyed sigh upon hearing his little brother's name. "I know you didn't interrupt me for this shit. Is that pain-in-the-ass back here again begging to be a Wolf? No… I done told him already it's not gonna happen. Look…you tell him I said for him to go home before I kick his little ass." He laughed as the girl he was screwing, unashamed about her nudity, walked up behind him and stuck her tongue in his ear while stroking his dick.

"I—I can't tell him that," Peek-a-Boo said, trying not to

notice.

"And why the fuck not?"

"…Because…He's dead."

Moola pushed the young lady away and turned to Peek-a-Boo with a blank look hemming him by his collar. "What the fuck did you say? Nigga is this your idea of a fucking joke?"

"No Moola! I'd never joke around with you like that." The cockeyed man said frightened.

Outside the pool hall, Moola stared at the remainder of his little brother's face and fought back tears to protect his image. Fangs silently stood beside his best friend. The crowd from inside had trickled out onto the cold streets as word spread quickly of the young man's death. Moola stormed over to Peek-a-Boo and snatched him by his collar.

"Who did this?" he demanded through clenched teeth.

With one eye appearing to look to the left while the other eye focused straight ahead, Peek-a-Boo nervously said, "I was out here holding down the front when this jeep comes flying up. I recognized it from the one that picked up Small Time after you had whupped his ass cause it had that same army print all over it. I was about to bust shots, but it stopped, threw a package out, then sped off. I checked to see what it was and found him."

"Did you see who was driving?" Fangs asked shaking with fury.

Peek-a-Boo shook his head. "Uh-uh—the windows was tinted."

Fangs could see the pain in his friend's face and placed his hand on his shoulder. "Don't matter who was driving. It's obvious who did it, and they'll pay!"

Moola was too emotional to speak and glanced back down at his brother. All he could think about was how he was ready to brush him off for some woman when he heard he was outside. Unable to hold back the tears, he dried his eyes with a backward swipe of his hand as the flashing lights of the approaching police cars lit up the scene.

* * *

The ground in King Park was covered with a vibrant carpet of brown, orange, yellow, and red leaves that the fall picked from the tall trees. Squirrels scurried about, gathering acorns to store for winter as their gray and black pelts protected them from the chilly breeze. Half-absorbed in Bebe Moore Campbell's latest romance novel, Rita kept a watchful eye out for her daughter from a nearby bench.

"Bria, honey don't run off too far," Rita warned the happy

child as she chased behind a flock of sparrows without a care in the world.

"'Kay, Mommy!" Bria yelled over her shoulder. Every time she came too close, the tiny sparrows looking for a meal on the ground would fly off a couple of yards then land. Bria snuck up on them, and when they flew away, she found herself standing before a tall man in a black trench coat. She looked up, and her mouth dropped open.

Suddenly, Bria screamed, and Rita leaped up calling her name. Her eyes became heavy with tears as she watched the man she married hold their child close to his heart. Bria was so overjoyed to see her Daddy she couldn't help but scream. Rita came over, and without a word, wrapped her arms around her family and kissed them.

* * *

Bria clutched the shopping bag containing her Nubiana Princess Power costume as she attacked her banana split in the booth of the cozy restaurant. 'Your Home is in My Heart' by Chantae Moore and Boyz to Men, was playing over the sound system.

"I can't wait to wear my costume," she told her parents between spoonfuls of ice cream.

"Neither can Mommy," Rita whispered, winking at Bryann as she referred to the sexy red satin-and-lace lingerie she'd bought while he and Bria were shopping for her Halloween costume. Dressed in the leather trench she had gotten him, Bryann wiggled his eyebrows at her in response. It had been a long time since they made love, and he was eager to end the stretch.

"So, don't you think it's time she knew about the b-a-b-y?" Rita said.

"I guess now is as good a time as any," Bryann replied wiping chocolate syrup from his daughter's face.

"Bria. How would you feel about having a little brother or sister?" Rita asked.

"I dunno," Bria replied with a smile and shrug as she crammed a spoonful of ice cream and sprinkles into her mouth.

"Well, the reason Mommy asked is that she's going to have a baby," Bryann added.

"For real?" Bria asked, looking oddly at her mother.

Rita nodded her head. "That's right sweetheart, inside of Mommy's tummy is your new little brother or sister."

"Why is the baby in your tummy, Mommy? You swallowed it?" Bria asked.

Rita cut her eyes at Bryann for help. "Don't look at me," he said, grinning. "Personally, I would've gone with the stork theory."

Rita grimaced and slightly stuck her tongue at him, then turned back to Bria trying to figure out how she was going to explain pregnancy and childbirth to a five-year-old.

"Well, Ladybug, it's like this," Bryann said in a gentle voice. "God put the baby in Mommy's tummy to sleep until it's ready to be born. And next year the baby will wake up and come out Mommy's tummy. And do you know who the baby's going to want to see first, when it wakes up?

"Uh-uh. Who?" Bria asked, wide-eyed and fascinated, leaning forward.

"Why big sister Bria, of course. And that's when you'll meet your new sister or brother."

"I hope it's a sister," Bria said excitedly. "The lady next door to Gramma and Grampa has a little baby girl. Her name is Jasmine Marie."

"Wow, what a pretty name," Bryann said. "So does this mean you're happy about the baby coming to live with us?"

Bria nodded her head and hugged her mother, then lovingly kissed her stomach. "I can't wait to see my new sister or brother."

"That should hold her, till she's older," Bryann whispered with a wink thinking how kids are a gift parents get to unwrap every single day and he couldn't wait to unwrap his new child.

Right at that moment Rita knew she made the right decision to come back home. She smiled over at her husband and mouthed, *'I love you.'*

'Love you back', he replied and felt like the luckiest man alive.

She leaned in and planted a kiss on his lips causing their daughter to grin with delight. "Yay." Bria said happy.

Bryann's cell phone rang and he frowned at it for interrupting the moment.

"Hey you, tell your side-piece not to beep you during family time," Rita teased.

Bryann winked then looked at the number on his phone. "I gotta take this. Be right back." Bryann explained and walked outside. After a brief conversation he returned to the table a different person.

"So which one was that?" Rita asked, keeping the joke alive.

"It was my job," he said quietly. "About Darrius."

"Is he?" she asked without asking.

"Yeah," Bryann nodded morbidly.

"Oh, honey—I'm so sorry," Rita said, hoping there wouldn't be another episode.

"What happened?" Bria asked.

"Eat your ice cream, Ladybug," Bryann instructed.

"Who did it?" Rita asked.

"They don't know yet, but I got a hunch he's bald, black, and has an itchy *Trigger* finger."

Rita looked up from her burger when she recognized that, '*I can't sit here and do nothing*', tone in her husband's voice.

"Now Bryann don't go doing something permanently foolish because you're temporarily upset. I'm sorry about what happened, but we both know he was hardly an altar boy. It's a shame that yet another young man of color has lost his life to the streets, but I work in the courts and see it all the time. Just yesterday I watched a boy no older than Darrius get handed down a sentence so long, that by the time he finally gets out, Bria will have graduated from college. Like the judge said to him, if you don't want to go to prison don't commit a crime."

"Oh please. Like this country doesn't systematically ensnare people of color into the mass industrial complex through poverty and neglect, but I digress. Look, I gotta go see Darrius' mother. Pay my respects." Bryann said in a disgusted tone.

Rita kissed and hugged Bryann goodbye and assured him she was okay with his leaving. He told her he wouldn't go if she had a problem, and she told him not to be silly. He made her promise three times she would be at their apartment when he got home. She said she'd be waiting up for him in the lace lingerie and smelling of perfume. He promised he wouldn't take long and left.

Chapter 18

BRYANN STOOD IN THE CEMETERY just a few short days after learning of Darius' death, thinking about how morbid his surroundings were, especially with Halloween only three days away. As he and a small group of the dead boy's family and friends stood silently in the chilly air, a Priest uttered a few words about Darrius being at peace. Bryann glanced up and noticed Moola hiding his guilt behind dark shades and a full-length black mink coat.

A teenage boy with long braids, wearing a black t-shirt that said RIP Darrius, hit play on the boombox he was cradling. The song Life Goes On by Tupac, Darrius' favorite rapper played.

A girl who looked no older than sixteen wearing gaudy jewelry and a head full of blond Shirley Temple curls, cried out, "My man is gone!" Bryann recognized her voice as the girl he spoke with over the phone.

Dressed in a black dress and veil, Darrius's mother stood off to the side, alone looking like a stranger at her own son's funeral. It was evident the thin, wrinkled lemon-skinned woman wanted no part of her oldest son Moola and his lucrative drug business by the simple-looking clothes she wore.

Bryann walked up to her with a solemn face. "Miss Banks, I just wanted to personally express my sympathy, not only for your loss but also for the frustration you and your other family members have encountered."

"Family? Them low-life crack dealers over there ain't no kin of mine!" she snapped, showing no shame as she pointed at the group of adolescents standing off to the side. "For years we've struggled to get our young black men to the front of the bus, only to find them in the back of the hearse. But I wanna thank you Bryann, for trying to put my boy on the right path."

"He was a great kid."

She smiled at his kindness then threw a single rose onto her son's casket as it was being lowered into the ground and gave into her tears. As Bryann stepped up and consoled her, he couldn't help thinking of a poem Darrius once wrote titled, It's a Jungle Out There. Although he couldn't remember the entire poem, one verse stood out in his mind:

The beloved life that took your mama nine months to make
But with the flex of a finger took nine seconds to take.

"Mama?" Moola called to his mother, walking toward her.

Miss Doris Banks, single mother of two, survivor of breast cancer and a telephone operator for over fifteen years, stood face-to-face with her first-born son. She once envisioned him making her proud by walking across the stage to receive his high school then college diplomas. Now she could barely stand the sight of him but tolerated seeing him long enough to say exactly what was on her mind.

"You had one job Maurice! Be a big brother! That was it! Why couldn't you do that?" the heartbroken mother sobbed.

"I don't have a good answer for you Ma. I wish I did. I hope you can forgive me." Her boy whispered with his head down.

"After I busted up your car in hopes you'd wake up and stop selling that poison, I kicked you out. Then I put this dress I'm wearing on my dresser. Because I knew I'd someday wear it to my son's funeral. I just never imagined it'd be my youngest."

"Momma I'm sorry."

"The only one you can ask forgiveness from is Jesus. Because I wish it was you in that damn pine box. Instead of my baby. All he ever wanted was to be like you. But in a way now he is. Cause you're dead to me!"

Moola never said a word as the only woman he ever loved in the world walked out of his life for good. Calmly, he removed his Versace shades and glanced over at Bryann. Then he placed the frames back on his face and slid into the passenger seat of his Yukon beside Fangs, who was smoking a blunt and listening to, 'Dear Mama' by Tupac. He stayed focused on Doris, as the haunting lyrics mirrored his own turbulent relationship with his mother. And he too like Pac, 'wanted to take her pain away'.

"Give her some time. And you're lucky. My mom's has cirrhosis of the liver, sleeps on rubber sheets, gets turned over by strangers and has a picture of me on her nightstand." Fangs said trying to make him feel better in his own twisted way and offered him some weed. "Where to?"

"Just drive nigga." Moola whispered morbidly and accepted the blunt. Sitting in his expensive truck worth the cost of a small house, he recalled when he saved up his money from working the corners to buy his first car. A white Mustang Cobra with gold rims, complete with matching rims, Alpine speakers and a car phone. He hid it from his mother. But quickly learned, you can't hide anything living in the projects. When Doris found out, she took a baseball bat to his beloved car in front of the entire neighborhood. And through winded breath, told him no son of hers was going to be a drug dealer! She also reminded him that his little brother who looked up to him was watching. A week later, he had a new car. A Mercedes Benz. And his baby brother was making deliveries for a dealer named Trig.

As he pulled off, Moola kept his eyes on his mother in the rearview mirror as she dealt with her pain alone.

* * *

"Happy Halloween!" Bria yelled, bursting through her parent's door and leaping into bed with them. Bryann and Rita groggily awakened and momentarily played with their daughter, before getting up to prepare for work. "Daddy, is you still gonna take me twick-or-tweatin'?"

"*Are* you still *going to* take me *trick-or-treating?*" Bryann said, correcting his daughter.

"Are you still going to take me twick-or-tweatin' after you get home from work, Daddy?" Bria asked again with a huge smile.

"Yes, I am, honey," Bryann replied with a kiss.

"Yay!" Bria cheered and chased Princess out of the room. Bryann was still half asleep and shuffled into the bathroom. Rita watched her husband rejuvenate as he splashed cold water on his face and hoped that taking their daughter trick-or-treating would change the dreary mood he'd been in since returning from Darrius's funeral. She was grateful he kept his word about not taking his anger out on his family, but she didn't like him moping around feeling responsible for the boy's death. She stopped him in the doorway and stared at her husband smiling.

"What?" he asked.

"You remember us back in the day… sneaking on the phone, 'You hang up. No you hang up.'"

"Bryann nodded smiling at the memory. "Then we'd agree on three to both hang up and your moms would come on the line and say both of ya'll hang up!"

She giggled and moved in close to touch his face, feeling and seeing the weight of the world in his eyes, "You are too perfect. You're that rare man that all women dream about, except you actually exist. I could kiss you. What am I saying? I can kiss you because you are mine." Rita said wrapping her arms around Bryann while planting a long passionate kiss on his lips. "And tonight, when you get home, we should try on our tricks-n-treats costumes."

"Oooo, tricks-n-treats…I see what you did there. Well, it just so happens that tricks-n-treats are two of my favorite things."

"I know all your favorite tricks-n-treats." Rita giggled.

He looked back at his wife, "If you live to be a hundred, I want to live to be a hundred minus one day, so I never have to live without you."

"Deal." Rita smiled.

* * *

When Bryann entered Home Sweet Home, he was greeted

159

by a fearsome-looking, life-sized killer scarecrow, complete with a bloody pitchfork.

"Wow! Great job with the decorations. The kids are going to have a ball at the party." Bryann said, complimenting Roxy on the job she did turning the lobby of Home Sweet Home into a house of horror. In addition to the scarecrow, there were spiderwebs all over the walls, some real, some not. Papier-mâché ghosts hanging from the ceiling, skeletons, jack-o-lanterns and rubber body parts lying about. Some co-workers even dressed in costumes.

"Thanks, Mista B. We got, apples for bobbing. Cookies, cake, candy, and for the adults I got a cheese platter. And it ain't from the government."

"Fancy." Bryann snickered shaking his head.

"I know right." Roxy said, adding plastic eyeballs to a bowl of fruit punch to make it a witch's brew. She was dressed in tight-fitting black spandex with a black leotard top. On her head she wore a small pair of black cat ears. Long whiskers were drawn on her face with an eyebrow pencil. "So ju like my costume?"

"Um—a black cat, right?"

"No. I'm what a hardworking man comes home to at the end of the day." she said, modeling her curviness for him. "What's wrong, cat got your tongue?"

Bryann was tongue-tied. He didn't like where this was going, and if someone walked in, they could get the wrong impression. Then, in walked Markeith dressed in a blue t-shirt with a big red S and H over his chest, a long flowing cape and a big brim hat tilted to the side.

"Goddamn, girl—your mama must've been a terrorist cause that cat suit got you lookin' like the bomb!"

"Thank you, Mista Greene, I'm glad somebody noticed," Roxy said, grinning at Bryann as he and Markeith boarded the elevator.

"Yo man, you need to cut back with the comments before Roxy brings you up on sexual harassment," Bryann warned as they stepped onto the elevator.

"Negro, please! And what do you call all that posing and flirting she was doing with you?" Markeith asked, laughing. "That was for your benefit. Anybody with eyes can see she wants you to be her *Aye Papi!*"

"Please stop."

Markeith threw an arm around Bryann's neck and moved in close. "So, tell me something, between you and me, if you wasn't with Rita, would you tap that ass?"

"I can't answer that," Bryann said in a serious tone. "Because I'd never replace a period with a question mark."

"Uh-huh. Whatever, Dudley Do Right. Bryann, you're my man fifty grand, but sometimes you can be so damn corny. I mean it's just a hypothetical question, dang. Now spill." Markeith said, trying his best to get his friend to admit there was at least a drop of dog's blood running through his veins.

Bryann hunched his shoulders. "There's nothing to spill." he said.

"Yeah, you probably right about staying away from that. The brothers in the mail room told me she's looser than my grandma's teeth after a taffy apple," Markeith said with a wink as they stepped off the elevator.

Bryann shook his head feeling guilty for laughing, then noticed his friend's costume for the first time. "So, what are you supposed to be? Superman?"

"Naw, I'm his cousin. Captain Save-A-Ho." Markeith said flapping his cape behind him. "And lemme' guess, you're a mild-mannered social worker?"

"Nope. I'm your future boss." Bryann said laughing and headed into his office to start a long day of work.

* * *

"Mommy? Mommy?" Bria whined.

"I changed my name," Rita said, absorbed by her computer.

"When is Daddy coming home?"

"I've told you, little girl. Your father will be home at six o'clock," Rita said, moving her fingers all over the keyboard of her laptop as she unsuccessfully tried to transcribe her notes from the day's court case.

"When is six o'clock?"

Rita sighed, then removed the extra-large headphones from her stomach and tore a blank page from the legal pad she had written her notes on and boldly drew the number six, a colon, and two zeroes, then handed it to her daughter.

"Here. When this pops up on the clock it will be six o'clock, okay?"

The intercom rang and Bria jumped up screaming, "Yay! Daddy's home!"

"It's not your daddy I just told you… Oh, never mind," Rita said, frustrated as she got up and went to the intercom. "Who is it?" she asked.

"It's Dee-Dee and Gainer," Dee-Dee's voice cheerfully replied, and Rita buzzed them in.

A few minutes later the doorbell rang, and she opened the front door, receiving hugs and kisses from her sister-in-law and Gainer. "What a surprise," Rita said, wondering how she was

161

supposed to get any work done.

"Look at you, I can't believe you and Bryann are going to have another baby! You weren't busy, were you?" Dee-Dee said excitedly, coming in with Gainer right behind her.

"No just catching up on some work before our trip." Rita smiled receiving a kiss on the cheek from Gainer.

"I'm surprised you heard us knocking, with those giant headphones on." he said.

"Oh these? They're for the baby."

"Don't tell me you already have the kid hooked on the crap music." The older man who preferred the Temptations and Marvin Gaye over Public Enemy and Big Daddy Kane rolled his eyes.

"No, Bryann made me a tape of tranquil music for the baby to listen to through headphones on my belly." Rita laughed recalling where her husband got his fondness of Motown from.

"The baby's not even here yet and already he or she is getting spoiled." Dee-Dee smiled hugging Rita.

"Aunt Dee-Dee, I'm still a baby, too!" Bria jealously said with her hands on her hips, looking like the spitting image of her dad when he was her age and he felt left out.

"That's right. You are Auntie's baby," Dee-Dee said while lifting her niece and covering her with kisses.

"So, speaking of your trip Rita, are you two ready for Jamaica? My partner, Frank, and his wife vacationed at Negril last summer. He said the ocean is so clear the beach looks like one big glass of blue water," Gainer said.

"I know, and I can't wait. But who would have thought going on vacation could be so exhausting? We leave next week, and we haven't even started to pack. And what's worse, I still can't find the perfect bathing suit."

"Relax. It'll all work itself out," Dee-Dee promised.

"From your lips to God's ears. Well, at least I don't have to worry about a babysitter. My parents are going to keep her."

"But I wanna stay with Aunt Dee-Dee and Unca Gaina," Bria protested, climbing into Gainer's arms. She loved her grandparents but easily became bored at their house.

"Now we discussed this already Bria. Aunt Dee-Dee and Uncle Gainer have to work."

"Sorry, squirt," Gainer said.

Unable to resist her niece's pouting, Dee-Dee turned to her sister-in-law. "Rita, how about if your parents keep her for the week and I pick her up Friday and keep her until you come back?"

"Dee-Dee, you and Gainer don't need a hyper five-year-old running around after a hard day's work. My folks are retired. And—" Once she got a look at her daughter's face, she was in trouble. Besides, she remembered how boring her folks could be.

"Okay, I'll call my mother and work something out. Anyway, what brings you two by?"

"We were driving by, and Gainer suggested we check on Bryann. How has he been since that boy was killed?" Dee-Dee said in a hushed voice, so her niece didn't hear.

"Well, he's not freaking out like before, but it's like he blames himself for what happened, and I don't know what to do. I hope taking Bria trick-or-treating will put him in a better mood. So, while we are on the subject, has anyone been arrested?" Rita asked, pouring out soda for Dee-Dee and handing Gainer a beer.

"No, not yet. We've gotten a bunch of confidential calls at the station that Gang-Greene is responsible, but nothing came of it. We figured that it was probably kids from the Wolf Pack looking for new ways to mess with their enemies."

"Whoever did this will be caught, but I'm just glad you and Bryann worked things out and are back together. Cause, girl, that brother of mine is lost without you," Dee-Dee said relieved.

"And I without him. But enough talking about all this negativity and drama. So, what's going on with you two? How was your day?"

"Well, it was fine. Until this one here blasted the receptionist at her doctor's office earlier today." Gainer pointed a thumb at Dee-Dee.

"What happened Sis?" Rita asked.

"I'm just sick of these nosy heffas asking you your business! You're a receptionist, not a nurse. So, stay in your lane. We're in this cramped little waiting room no bigger than a broom closet and she wants to know why I'm here. Why, so I can share it with everybody in the room? No, I don't think so."

"But they have to ask so then can inform the Doctor." Rita rationalized.

"I can do that myself. What's the point of doctor, patient confidentiality if I'm gonna confide what ails me to a room full of strangers?" Dee-Dee snapped; Gainer shook his head smirking. Rita nodded thinking she had a point. "There's no way I should know some lady named Agatha Pinkney with a tilted blue wig has chronic diarrhea." She said and Bria immediately began laughing. "See, and that's what happened at the Doctor's office. When she asked me why I was here I said I'll tell the Doctor. You know the guy who went to Med school?"

"Well, is everything alright?" Rita asked concerned.

"Huh? Oh yeah gurl everything's fine, it's just a little cold, No big deal. The Doctor prescribed me some antibiotics. But she don't need to know that."

"He should'a prescribed you some crazy pills too." Gainer wisecracked and his lady waved at him.

"Diarrhea! Diarrhea! When you're climbing up a mountain and your butt becomes a fountain. Diarrhea! Diarrhea!" Rita began to sing cracking herself and Bria up.

"When you eat a lot of Snickers, and it trickles down your knickers. Diarrhea! Diarrhea!" Dee-Dee joined in singing to Bria as the trio laughed and danced around.

Rita shook her head and smiled then turned to Gainer and asked in a low voice. "You know I was thinking, should we be alarmed about this boy being killed? I mean, what if it was a revenge killing? Who's to say Bryann isn't in danger, too?"

"Yeah, I thought about that, but this kid was a real lowlife and had a few enemies. So, I don't think you have anything to be worried about."

"You really don't think there's anything to worry about?" Rita asked.

Gainer shook his head. "Nah. I've dealt with enough situations like this to know that those punks who offed that kid are somewhere not even thinking about your husband. Believe me everything is fine."

Directly outside, under the Halloween clouds on a grey October day, in a parked van across the street sat Pig, Slam, and four young hoods. Some were hyper, others anxious and all were nervous as they passed a smoking blunt back and forth to get themselves in the right frame of mind while awaiting to carry out Trig's next move.

Chapter 19

BRYANN GLANCED UP at the wall clock over the nineteen-year-old girl's shoulder seated before his desk. He remained courteous as she rattled on about how no one at Home Sweet Home was doing anything to help her and her kids get out of their jacked-up situation. The social worker was tired of explaining to her that since she was unemployed with no steady income her only option was an emergency-assistance service program. She was eligible for housing, but there was a waiting list. Until then, she either would have to live with relatives or stay in a shelter. What he really wanted to know was why she had three kids when she was still a child herself. And why she chose men she knew had no intentions of sticking around once she had their baby. But seeing as how those were considered demeaning questions by his supervisors, and if she complained he could get into trouble, he kept his questions on a professional level.

"So what do you want to do, Geneva?" Bryann asked, noticing it was now five forty-five and he had somewhere important to be.

"I got three kids and nowhere to live. I guess I ain't really got no choices, do I, Mr. Bonner?" the young mother asked in a disappointed voice while staring at her mischievous sons run around his office with runny noses. All three boys—ages five, three, and one and a half—looked nothing alike since they had different fathers who abandoned their mother shortly after they were born.

Her tired, gaunt face told that she knew her way through the bewildering labyrinth of welfare offices, mean streets, and criminal courts. Dressed in droopy, dull clothing, Geneva looked like she was tired of being a mother. Her youth was quickly being siphoned along with her energy by the three little men she was solely responsible for. Her once thick head of dark hair was thinning and pulled back in an unflattering ponytail. The color in her cheeks were flush and her eyes had bags under them.

"I can't stay with my mother. She ain't got no room for us there. Shit, she got kids of her own to take care of." Geneva said, sounding full of self-pity.

"Still no word from the boys' fathers?" Bryann asked.

"I'm their mother *and* their father, thank you!" she snapped.

"I'm sorry, I wasn't implying that you aren't doing a good job."

Geneva took out a cigarette to calm her nerves. Normally, Bryann did not allow smoking in his office, but he made an exception. "I know you didn't. To be honest, out of all the men in my life, you're the only one who seems to really care about me and my kids. I just get pissed when I think about them no-good niggas I allowed to ruin my life. I don't even know where Melquan's daddy is; if he's alive or dead. Last I heard he got body-bagged caught up in some mess with the Wolf Pack. Jayquan's daddy got four other kids by three different girls, is living with his new girlfriend who is pregnant, and ain't supporting not one of them babies. As for Dayquan's father, he's doing double life for shooting a cop."

"Then I guess you and your kids will have to stay in a shelter for a while." Bryann said, slightly dizzy from the ghetto soap opera that Geneva just laid on him.

"And then where… the projects?" she asked, and Bryann sighed slumping in his chair because they both knew the answer. "The projects supposed to be a steppingstone not a lifestyle for generation after generation." She frowned envisioning her future in a neighborhood where everyone is afraid. Urinating in the halls and elevators. Drugs, CAUTION tape and crime outside her door.

"I understand your angst and frustration. I do. But many have used the opportunities we provide here to educate themselves through trade and or college. And some prominent black and brown people have gone on to turn their lives around for the better. This can be the end of your story or the beginning."

"Mr. Bonner, can I ask you a question?" she asked, staring at her kids blankly.
He nodded yes. "Why do grownups think kids have it easy today?"

Bryann was at a loss and could only shake his head and sigh.

It was ten after six by the time he had finished counseling Geneva, filling out forms, and making sure that she got to the shelter in time for dinner and beds for her and her kids. He called home and apologized, then explained what happened and that he was on his way.

* * *

Dressed in her Nubiana Princess Power costume, complete with the purple tiara, matching cape and power saber, Bria insisted that her mother take her trick-or-treating. She was worried that her neighbor down the hall, LaDonna, would get all the good candy. Gainer had a brainstorm. He suggested that he and Dee-Dee take her, and Bryann could meet up with them along the way. Rita stared at all the unfinished work she still had waiting on her and was more than grateful for them to take her off her hands for a little while. It was settled, and Bria wiped her crocodile tears.

* * *

166

Bryann was speed walking, trying to get home as fast as he could and keep his promise to his daughter. Along the way, he spotted other fathers and their costumed children enjoying the holiday, so he picked up the pace. He ran into the street without looking and a black Escalade came to a screeching halt in front of him. He leapt back onto the sidewalk and narrowly escaped getting run over.

"Hey! Watch where you're going, idiot! You could've killed me!" Bryann yelled at the black tinted windows.

The door on the driver's side opened, and huge boots stepped onto the pavement. JackHammer smiled as he stepped out. Bryann swallowed hard. "Didn't mean to scare you."

"Please, the only place I am afraid of you is in your dreams!" Bryann snapped.

JackHammer raised his eyebrows and a grin pulled at the corners of his mouth, impressed.

The passenger door opened, and Biggie Smalls' song, 'What's Beef?' mockingly blasted as Trig stepped out onto the curb.

"What'd I tell you Hammer? My cousin's heart don't pump Kool-Aid!"

"Well somebody needs to tell him there's a fine line between courage and stupidity!"

"Easy-easy, fellas. So wusup Bryann, how are you doing?" he asked with a sinister grin.

"Fine, and you?" Bryann answered suspiciously, never taking his eyes off JackHammer.

"Can't complain. But I am complaining about Al Roker. Fat boy said it was gonna be a brisk sixty-five and it's in the mid-fifties. Now see if I did take the college route like you did, I would have become a weatherman. Motherfuckers making big bank for lying. That's an honest job even I can do. Professional liar." Trig laughed like he hadn't a care in the world as he rubbed his hands together.

"So what do you want?"

"Damn cousin! You don't seem too happy to see a nigga." Trig said.

"Whatever. Look, Trig. I don't have time for you and ghetto Popeye right now." Bryann hissed causing JackHammer to lift an eyebrow at the snap.

"Hold on there, partner. You gonna make time cause we need to talk," Trig said, placing his hand on Bryann's shoulder.

"About?" Bryann asked, shrugging his hand away.

"About you trying to play 21 Jump Street and set me up."

"Look, Trig—it's no secret you have kids selling your

drugs and that you killed Darrius. Just be thankful that I can't prove it!"

Trig cut an eye at JackHammer who was awaiting the signal to tear Bryann's head off.

* * *

Slam turned up a bottle of beer and through it he could see Gainer and Dee-Dee exiting the building with Bria. Rita waved good-bye then went back into the building, alone.

"Yo! The pig is finally leaving!" he announced to everyone in the van, waking up the dozing thugs. When he realized what he'd said, he turned to the fat man. "No pun intended."

"It's all good," Pig said, removing a cell phone and mashing numbers.

* * *

The pager on Trig's hip began vibrating and he checked it, then glanced at JackHammer with a nod. "Now, why you gotta go and say shit like that, man? I swear, people who don't know my business tend to make up my business. And that's bad for business." He said and flashed his gun then smiled down at it like a proud Papa. "You know how our oppressors enslaved us? They got to the gun first, the great equalizer unfortunately."

"Wrong. Historically it wasn't their strength, nor their weapons, nor their numbers. It was because tribes were fighting each other and trapping and enslaving their brothers. Debilitating their piers and with that, themselves. It's never been the division outside what screwed us, but the one inside our community that made a pact with the enemy, and everybody ended up paying for it. Sound familiar?" Bryann asked looking him the eye with an accusing stare.

"So is this the part in your history lesson where you tell me how we are our own worst enemy?" Trig smirked.

"No. This is the part where I tell you it's pointless to explain logic to the illogical." Bryann shook his head repulsed they were related.

"A smarter man would've said that running motherfuc-" JackHammer snarled.

Bryann shook his head and silenced him holding up his hand, "I can't with people who think you're arguing every time you express how you feel. I used to think conversation was the key until I realized comprehension is. Because if a person can't comprehend what you're saying in a conversation, everything's going to be an argument because they have a lot of growing to do."

JackHammer stood there with a confused expression, not sure what to say in response.

Trig snickered, "Whoa-shit! Damn cousin. That's the first time I ever saw somebody get knocked the fuck out with words. I guess words are weapons. Hammer, pick up your bottom jaw off the floor. Look Bryann, seeing as I don't want to waste your time, I just have one question. Why'd you go to such great lengths to take me out? And don't say it was only for Darrius. I know it was deeper than that!"

"I have my reasons. They're myriad, valid and none-ya." Bryann replied.

"Bryann, seriously…why?"

"After what you did to me you can honestly stand there and boldly ask me that?"

"Do you have some particular problem with me?" Trig asked cluelessly.

Bryann's face almost slid off, he gasped so hard. "Remember when we were kids and my conscience started getting the best of me about all the things we were doing? Crimes we were committing?"

"Vaguely."

"Well I remember! It was around the time I met Rita and wanted out, but you wouldn't let me! You said we were making too much money to stop. And when I told you I was going to walk regardless, you said you'd place a call to social services. Tell them that my sister was doing an insufficient job of raising me by herself and that they would take me away and put me in a group home."

"Aha. So that's the Pepsi twist." Trig almost laughed in Bryann's face and had to cover his mouth and apologize. "Is that what all this is about? You pining away over some old shit? Somebody's suffering from selective amnesia. Instead of trying to crucify me, your ungrateful ass ought to be thanking me. You was a stoop kid until your corner hugging cousin came along. And it was me who instilled confidence in your bitch ass."

"No—Gainer did that! What you did was take advantage of a kid all messed up over losing his folks and made him into you!"

"Fam, you could never be me."

"That's the only thing we will ever agree on. You're the Devil reincarnated!"

"Ouch! I'm guessing time has not healed these wounds?" Trig grinned. Bryann found nothing amusing. "While we're on the subject of Rita. You ever worry that something could happen to that fine-ass dark roasted cup of coffee of yours simmering all alone, when you're not around?"

Bryann froze in his tracks. "What'd you just say?" He glared.

"Oh, nothing. But it sure would be a shame if something bad happened to her, all alone in that big ol' empty apartment with no one to *protect* her."

"Trig, this is between you and me," Bryann said.

"Maybe," Trig said, then tapped the side of his nose just like he used to do when they were kids, signaling him of impending danger without saying a word. "Maybe not. I always say, if you're gonna risk it all make sure she's worth it. And I get it. Rita was worth it, which is why I want to apologize in advance."

"Apologize for what?"

"What's about to happen."

A look of horror flashed over Bryann's face and he ran off home.

"Hey, wait up!" Trig called, but Bryann was already gone.

* * *

Slam stood in the middle of the street and polished off the beer. With a deafening belch he sent the empty bottle smashing to the ground. He dug his hand into his jacket pocket and pulled out the keys Darrius forged, to Bryann and Rita's apartment.

"Okay, y'all, before we forget put on your gloves," Slam reminded the group.

The thuggish posse pulled out rubber gloves and pulled them over scarred knuckles, then followed Pig and Slam toward the best-kept building on the block.

* * *

Bryann raced down the street, pushing costumed kids and their parents out of his way, yelling apologies over his shoulder. He sprinted blindly into the street and a car had to slam on its brakes to keep from running him over. As the driver cursed him for his actions, Bryann was already gone.

* * *

Rita decided to take a long, relaxing hot shower before returning to work. She had brought home some assignments so that she could work double time on them and finish up before her cruise. She was looking forward to it because she knew that once she gave birth to Ryann they weren't going to have an opportunity to get away again for a long time. She placed a Cranberries CD into the stereo. Put her favorite song, Dream on repeat. Then turned the volume all the way up. Afterwards she began to disrobe, dancing and singing along, on her way to the bathroom, leaving a trail of clothes behind.

With the Cranberries in the backdrop and the hot water

running full blast, she didn't hear the front door unlock. Princess stopped grooming herself and trotted to the door to receive her nightly scratch behind the ears from Bryann. When the door opened, she hissed at the unfamiliar faces. In a flash, a strong kick shot through the door and lifted the family pet into the air. Princess cried out in pain and landed on her side in a twisted pose, silenced for good.

"What the hell's the matter with you, Pig? You ain't have to kill the cat, man!" Slam said, staring down at the lifeless animal and shaking his head with pity. "That was some real sick shit."

"Nigga if you got a problem with it, call Ace Ventura." Pig said, enjoying the repulsed looks on everyone's face. He knew many of them felt he was as soft as his body, so he wanted to prove he was as unpredictable as the next man.

"So, where's this bitch at?" he asked, looking around the living room.

Slam pointed at the trail of clothes lining the hall. "I'll give you one guess."

* * *

Bryann stood fidgety on the corner of the busy intersection, only a few blocks from his home and Rita. He frantically looked left and right, ready to dart into the traffic. In the distance he could hear the wail of an ambulance. When he looked back he could see the bright noisy truck with its flashing lights approaching his way. All the cars came to a halt so it could pass and Bryann spotted his opportunity. Without a second thought, he ran into the street, trying to keep up along the side the four-wheeled shield.

* * *

As Rita showered, Slam, Pig and the hoods tried not to giggle as they tiptoed along her trail of clothes.

* * *

Love and determination forced Bryann's aching legs to keep moving—it was a race between man and machine. It appeared as if the man was going to win until his weight, lack of stamina and legs double-crossed him and cramped up. Bryann slowed as a burning feeling shot up and down his long limbs. The ambulance sped by and left him standing doe-eyed directly in the lane of a sports car flying at top speed toward him. From behind the wheel, a woman screamed and put on the breaks the moment she saw Bryann. She hit the horn and yanked the wheel hard to the right. The tires grinded skid marks into the street as she tried desperately to avoid him. But it was too late and Bryann was struck hard and launched several feet in the air. He came crashing down hard on the asphalt, tumbling to a bloody stop.

* * *

Rita lip-sang, along with Delores O'Riordan of the Cranberries into her loofa back scrubber, under the warm pulsing water of the shower. After dealing with her energetic daughter and a ton of work, the heated water against her tense muscles was invigorating, almost therapeutic. Suddenly, the curtain was snatched back. She screamed at the presence of the five intruders as they gawked at her. Pig stepped forward ogling her nude, wet body and dropped his vision to her crotch with a perverted grin that made his hog-like features all the more frightening.

Rita swung the loofah at him and the disgusting slob caught it in mid-swing then said, "Mmm-mmm-mmm! Damn! If we are what we eat pretty lady, I could be *you* by the morning."

* * *

The driver of the car that hit Bryann jumped out to help him up. When his weight fell on his injured leg, he screamed out in pain.

"Oh, my God! I'm so sorry, but you appeared out of nowhere!" she sympathized, while making it clear she wasn't liable. "You sure you're okay? I could take you to the hospital," she said.

"I'm fine!" Bryann growled and quickly hobbled off.

* * *

Rita sat on the edge of her bed wrapped in a white kimono robe. Dripping wet, the silk material allowed the men in room to see through it and view perfectly an outline of her curvy buttocks and breasts. She folded her arms to cover herself. Pig stood over her, salivating. Her curly, wet hair covered her face partially. And it aroused him even more.

"So, are you going to tell me what's going on?" she asked sternly, while concealing her fear.

"I told you when your hubby arrives, y'all will be informed together," Slam replied.

Rita sucked her teeth and rolled her eyes at the uninvited guests in her home. Her mind wandered to her beloved pet Princess, somewhere safe, hiding, she hoped her cat was ok. She felt a pair of eyes fixed on her and looked up at Pig, who wiped the drool from the corner of his crusty lips.

"What are you staring at?" she asked with a repulsed look.

172

"Damn, you sure is pretty," Pig said shyly. He spotted a pair of red thongs on the floor with and picked them up. "Will you look at that. It says, finger licking good. So, is it?" he asked, then brought the undergarments to his nose and inhaled deeply. "Umm, I bet that pussy is nice and sweet."

Rita could no longer conceal her fear, and the look on her face showed it.

"Chill out, Pig. You're freaking her out…and me as well." Slam said.

"Nah, you're wrong, bro. Look at how nervous she is—she must be excited."

Pig moved in close. Rita was trembling as he put his pudgy hand on her breast and inserted it into her robe. The sight of the fat pervert molesting her before his friends suddenly filled her with rage and she leaped forward, smacking him across his chubby face so hard it jiggled like a bowl of gelatin. The room filled with laughter as Pig jumped back, holding his stinging cheek.

"Yeah, baby! Kick his fat ass!" Slam said laughing and holding his stomach.

"Crazy-ass bitch!" Pig growled and balled his fist and knocked her backward over the bed. Her head struck the corner of the nightstand and a gash opened over her eye. As Rita lay on the floor bleeding she wondered where her husband was.

* * *

The pain shooting from Bryann's left leg was unbearable as he burst into the lobby of his building and toward the elevator. He hit the button and rested against the elevator door, swallowing gulps of air. After a minute, he noticed from the elevator's display that it was stuck. On his floor. He turned toward the steps then looked down at his swollen leg. It was definitely dislocated. He gritted his teeth and began the climb. With each step he flinched from pain. It was harder than anything he had ever attempted before. But he refused to stop. Rita needed him.

* * *

Rita picked herself off the floor. Her right eye was throbbing, and blood ran down her face.

"This shit is getting boring fast," Slam said over a yawn. "Say, where's your old man at anyway?" he asked Rita, who glared in his direction.

Pig grabbed the collar of her robe and yanked her forward causing her breast to spill out. He stole a peek as she quickly covered herself back up. "Bitch, you heard my boy talking to you!

Why ain't he here?"

Tears of anger flowed down Rita's cheeks, and she raked her nails across his face. "Go to hell you fat, disgusting bastard!" she screamed as she began punching and kicking him all over his head and body. Pig shouted to "Get this crazy hoe off me!" as he tried unsuccessfully to block her blows. Slam and the others didn't lift a finger to help because they were too busy laughing and cheering her on.

"Damn, Pig, she's really kicking your ass! You should like, take a self-defense class at the Y, or something! This shit is pitiful," one thug said.

Pig snarled and backhanded Rita across the cheek so hard her head rocked on her shoulders and she crumpled up like a rag doll on the floor. "You guys are a fucking riot!" he said and stuck his finger in his mouth, then spit blood. "Bitch loosened my tooth!"

* * *

By the time Bryann reached his floor his leg had swollen to twice its normal size, and he could barely walk. He worked through the pain and opted to slide against the wall.

"Rita," he called her name, over and over. The suffering was unbearable, and he felt like quitting, then managed to call up an image of her. When he got to his apartment he turned the knob and was not shocked to find it unlocked. He pushed open the door and entered. The first thing he saw was Princess lying dead on the floor. Over the loud music playing, he could make out the sound of angry voices trailing off down the hall brought him out of his trance, and he inched forward.

In the kitchen, a thug with two tattoo tears running down his right eye who was supposed to be a lookout had his head stuck in the refrigerator looking for milk to go along with the slice of cherry cheesecake he cut for himself and sat on the counter. Bryann snuck up on him and accidentally knocked a fork off the counter. The thug yanked his head out the refrigerator and spun around. He was about to alert his comrades, when he noticed Bryann having difficulty standing on his leg. He smiled sinisterly and decided to take advantage of the situation. Cracking his knuckles, the dark, muscular man came forward with fists raised. Thinking quickly, Bryann snatched a frying pan off the stove. The thug swung and missed, leaving himself exposed for Bryann to crack the frying pan over his skull and put him on the floor bleeding from the ear. With one down and uncertain of how many more to go, Bryann continued on for the love of his woman.

Rita was half conscious as Pig held her up by her robe smacking her repeatedly. "Wake up, bitch! It seems like your old man don't give a damn about you," he said, then pushed her on the bed. When she landed, her short robe spread around her thighs exposing herself.

"Now, will you look at that?" Pig asked the room, licking his greasy lips. "It's times like this that I really do love my job."

The sight of Rita's naked body gave everyone in the room an instant hard-on with the exception of Slam, who kept his preferences a secret but pretended to be aroused. Pig began unbuckling his pants and walking toward her.

"Yo, Pig. I know you ain't about to do what I think you about to do?" Slam asked.

"Why not? Shit, as fine as this bitch is I don't know why you ain't over here with me! Besides, we gonna kill her anyway, and I can't see wasting a good lay." Pig reasoned, dropping his pants and a dingy pair of tent-sized boxers. He stood on the side of the bed, mooning his boys with his wide ass that looked like chewed bubble gum. His four-inch penis was erect and throbbing. "Gather around, gentlemen," he said with a hand gesture like a side show leader residing over a freak show. "And maybe you'll learn something."

"Yo, Pig, you think I should get Todd from up front?" A short, homely thug asked of his cousin who was guarding the front door.

"Fuck Todd," Pig replied.

"Don't fuck Todd, fuck *her,*" the ugly thug said, pointing at Rita.

Everyone began laughing as they huddled behind Pig, hoping he would go first to give them the courage to follow. Pig untied Rita's belt then opened her robe, and his eyes bulged at her beautiful body. She couldn't put up a fight since she was still groggy from the pummeling he'd given her.

"Now this is gonna be good," the fat man said, climbing onto the bed.

Rita turned to him frowning and softly said, "Bryann."

"Sorry, baby, but Bryann ain't here right now. But if you'll spread your legs at the beep, I'll make sure he gets the message." Pig snickered. "Now listen to the music and relax baby. You're gonna enjoy this."

Focused on the show and the loud stereo playing the Cranberries in constant rotation, no one in the room realized someone entered. Someone furious. Someone with murder in their eyes! Pig was about to enter Rita by force when suddenly the drooling punk on his right was cracked in the face by a frying pan. He hit the ground screaming that his nose was broken as blood spurted out like a broken faucet. A hand reached through the crowd and grabbed Pig by the collar and snatched him off Rita slamming him to the floor. Everyone spun around and was taken by surprise as Bryann busted his way through the mob swinging the frying pan wildly over his head. He cracked another scumbag upside the dome causing the others to duck for cover. When Bryann saw his wife on the bed, naked and bleeding, his heart turned to stone. A spasm of pain came over him as he felt her anguish.

"Rita, baby, speak to me. Jesus, what did they do to you?" he whispered, disregarding the gathering posse behind him.

"Nothing yet, but if you move out my way I can finish what I was about to start!" Pig called out, feeling brave with an army to back him up.

Bryann was about to respond when Rita moaned and half-opened her eyes. "Bryann?" she called, managing a half-smile on seeing her husband. "You came. I knew you would," she said, holding out her hand.

Bryann kissed her hand, fighting back tears. For less than a second they stared into one another's eyes listening to the beautiful music, sharing a moment in a private world of their own. "Yes, baby, I'm here."

"They hurt me—they hurt me so bad," she whispered with a grimace and coughed.

"I know, and I promise you they'll pay! Baby, where's Bria at? *Where's our daughter?*" Bryann asked, horrified when he didn't see her.

"Dee-Dee took her," she whispered.

Was his sister able to escape with Bria? Was she going to get help? All that mattered was his daughter would not have to bear witness to what was about to go down. Bryann began breathing heavily like he was having an asthmatic attack as rage filled him. Pig and the others traded baffled looks and hunched shoulders, unsure of what to make out of the angry man's reaction.

Bryann's eyes went from slits to balls of pure fire and with each passing second his fury grew like an inferno. Rita was his first love. His only love! His soulmate! To see her like this. In this condition. Bloody. Beaten. Bruised. About to be raped, was unbearable! Inexcusable! Unforgivable! He felt like a caged animal was inside of him fighting to strike out! The magnitude of what those pitiful excuses for men did to his beloved, sent a cold deadliness, fury through him that only their bloodshed could vanquish. Someone had to pay! And he was going to collect!

"Yo, homes," Slam said, stepping behind Bryann. "Nothing personal, but we got orders to do you in."

Bryann delicately closed his wife's robe, planted a tender kiss on her bruised lips and tied the belt into a neat bow. He then squeezed his eyes tightly as a tear rolled down his cheek and exhaled loudly, allowing the adrenaline to kick in. When he opened his eyes, the pain in his leg vanished.

"Is that right?" he asked calmly while standing. Then, without warning, he spun around unleashing a right hook to Slam's jaw that painted the far wall with blood and put the bigger man onto his back.

Instantly, the room came alive as Bryann and the five men did battle! "Dammit, pin his arms!" someone yelled, as the men scrambled around trying to take him down. A bulky thug grabbed Bryann from behind in a bear hug and lifted him in an attempt to restrain him so the rest could overpower him. Bryann kicked a man running at him in the chest then swung the frying pan hard over his shoulder, banging the man holding him in the middle of his forehead smashing his eye socket. He then grabbed the dazed man and tossed him through the same standing mirror he used to stand in front of with his wife, cutting the lowlife to bloody shreds. Pig cowered near the dresser watching and praying someone would take the wild man out.

Slam used the exercise bike to pull himself up, then rubbed his jaw and spat a wad of blood on the floor. "You got a nasty right," he complimented.

Bryann glared at the man. Slam returned his own look and swung a chopping right. At the same time, Bryann swung the frying pan and flesh and steel met with a loud crunch. Slam screamed in agony as his knuckles were pushed back two inches into the center of his hand, squishing it into a pulp of deformity. Even the nails on two of his fingers swelled up and peeled off leaving gory rawness. Bryann showed no mercy, head-butting then planting his leg in Slam's groin and that was the end of him.

The two remaining hoods traded concerned looks and moved in circling Bryann like vultures. Without warning, the homely one charged and caught a frying pan across the face. He bounced off the floor, holding his mouth as teeth scattered. The second thug spun around with a roundhouse kick across Bryann's temple then followed up with an uppercut. Neither shot seemed to have any effect on him—it was as if he had been programmed to do something and nothing could stop him. The thug on the floor with bloody gums grabbed Bryann's leg and squeezed. That did have an effect, making Bryann scream and collapse and drop his frying pan. Before he hit the floor, the first thug was on top of him, trying to stab him with a shard of broken mirror. Bryann grabbed his wrist, stopping the pointed tip inches from his chest. He bent his good knee and maneuvered his leg in between him and the man on top of him then kicked hard, propelling him across the room. Beyond exhaustion, he still rose to his feet and managed to kick the bloody gummed thug in the face.

Before Bryann could take another breath, the man he sent across the room was back on his feet and coming at him. Bryann wished there were another way as he raised his fists. The thug threw a right cross and Bryann weaved and bobbed out of harm's way. The years he spent on the streets under his cousin Trig's guidance as angry young man taking on any and everyone, came back to him as if he had been in a life-or-death struggle only yesterday. He came back with a double straight jab and snapped back his opponent's head. Before he could recover Bryann moved in, unleashing a flurry of wild punches that left him bloody and disfigured.

Bryann spun around ready for whoever was next, sucking air. But no one was left except for Pig, still trembling by the dresser. He limped over to the coward and looked down at him with contempt. Never in his life had he ever thought of ending someone's life, but it would have been easy at that moment.

"Please don't kill me!" Pig begged.

"Your coward ass ain't even worth it!" Bryann said with a sneer, then spit on him and turned his back.

Something inside Pig snapped. He was tired of being a joke, a coward, a punk. He looked around and spotted a broken shard of mirror on the floor. As Bryann went over to tend to his wife, he felt a sudden burning pain in his calf and was tackled to his floor. He hollered from the pain and crawled away from Pig. But Pig liked this, he was now in command. He had already concocted a magnificent battle in his head between Bryann and himself, and how he was the only one who could take him. Trig and the others would have no choice but to respect him now.

"Now who's the punk?" Pig demanded, kicking Bryann hard in the ribs as he tried to crawl away.

Bryann ignored him, focusing on his frying pan lying off to the side. By the time Pig realized what he was after there was nothing he could do. Bryann rolled over and brought it down on Pig's foot, then quickly smashed his knees. Pig fell and they were both on the same level. Pig tried to scramble away but Bryann pulled him back. He climbed on top of him as Pig raised his hands to his face attempting to block the blows he knew were coming, he knew he deserved. Bryann raised the frying pan high over his head and paused. He sat there, staring at Pig beneath him trembling with sheer terror in his eyes. He could not do this. He was not like them.

He dropped the skillet and climbed off him then studied his leg. It wasn't pretty. He got a firm grip on the piece of mirror sticking out his calf, gritted his teeth, and yanked it out, wetting the

floor with a disgusting slurp noise and more blood. A loud scream
followed, and the pain was so bad he wanted to curl up and cry but
there was no time, he had to get Rita and himself out of there.
Reaching deep down within himself and finding leftover strength,
he hobbled to Rita's side leaving Pig lying on the floor, baffled.
Everything was so intense no one realized the music shut off.

"Baby! Baby! Get up! We've got to get out of here!" he
said frantically, shaking her by her arms. "Come on, Rita! They'll
be here any minute!" It was no use, she was too out of it to walk.
He realized he'd have to carry her. Bryann leaned forward and
scooped his hands under her limp body and lifted her up. He turned
around to leave and bumped into JackHammer's wide chest,
almost dropping his wife.

"Damn I hate that song! Mary plays that shit all the time
too. Yo cousin, why'd you run off like that? You could have gotten
a ride with us," Trig said from the doorway.

"Jesus, this place looks like a butcher's market! Wait! You
did all of this? No fucking way!" JackHammer said surveying all
the men sprawled out on the floor.

"Told you my cousin is the truth!" Trig bragged.

Disgust was written all over Trig's face as he glanced at his
men. Bryann was feeling weak from all the blood he lost. He was
also having difficulty holding his wife in his arms. He gently
placed her back on the bed and whispered in her ear, "No matter
what happens, I love you." As he let up, Rita stopped him with a
weak grip and shook her head. He planted a gentle kiss on her lips,
then turned to JackHammer and raised his fists in a defensive
stance.

JackHammer looked directly into Bryann's eyes and found
no trace of fear, only a man ready to die fighting to protect his
woman. Bryann swung with his last bit of strength and hit
JackHammer on the chin. The big man barley moved and envied
his courage, wishing he could defend his own woman the same
way. He turned back at Trig who nodded an order to hurt him. He
sighed and regrettably sunk his huge fist into Bryann's stomach.
Bryann dropped, spitting up bile as his ribs were crushed.

Trig picked up a picture of Bryann smiling and cradling his
wife, then walked over to his cousin who was on all fours heaving,
struggling to breathe, coughing up blood. He smiled down at him
lasciviously.

"Let some people tell it, you're this perfect black dude.
Beautiful wife. Cute kid. Matching pajama Christmas pics.
Incapable of doing the wrong thing, puts others interests before his
own. But we both know that's a lie or you wouldn't be
experiencing this karmic punishment. Look at yourself. I mean you
could have had it all: money, a top-ranking position in my crew.

But you threw it back in my face. And I get it. You had nobler ambitions. Hell…you got my vote for mayor. The problem was you had to come and fuck with my shit! I never came to where you work and made problems for you did I?" he demanded, kicking Bryann hard in his side. "No! But you insisted on doing that shit to me! That's why your little friend Darrius is taking a dirt nap and that's why you and your wife are all fucked up! Yesterday's choices reveal today's results. So, thinking back on all this, I got one fucking question to ask your stupid ass. Was it worth it?"

Bryann grimaced and clutched his stomach as if he was trying to keep its contents from spilling onto the floor. His lips moved but no sound came out.

"What? Speak up, motherfucker!" Trig ordered.

Bryann coughed and motioned him to come closer. Trig moved in close to hear him and Bryann lunged forward, head-butting him in the face, splitting open his nose.

"Fuck you!" Bryann yelled to the top of his lungs.

"Motherfucker!" Trig held his face as blood ran down. "Happiness is fleeting. It's all on borrowed time. And so is yours. JackHammer, do what you do best!"

Bryann was lifted off the ground then felt a fist strike his body. When he hollered in pain, Rita's eyes flashed opened.

"Now hold this punk ass bitch up so I can make him extinct," Trig said nasally. Rita saw the telephone next to her, and her hand inched towards it. JackHammer held up Bryann as Trig reached in his shoulder holster and withdrew his weapon then smiled at the piece of steel. "My very first gun. It's been with me through a lotta shit. And saved my black ass from even more. You too if I recall. Stick ups, business deals gone sour, street beefs and betrayals. It's not a gat. It's family. It's loyal. Which is more than I can say for you cousin. You know I broke my number one rule and trusted you? Let you walk into my place of business, and you betrayed me. And after all we've been through. I never would have done that to you."

"You betrayed me first getting me involved with your bullshit as a kid. On top of that you're poisoning our community. Profiting from people's pain. Murdering kids. You left me no choice."

"Nah. We all have choices. And yours landed you here. The road to hell is paved with good intentions. And you've come to the end of yours." Trig said pointing the gun at his cousin. "I'll give your sister my condolences!"

"Get away from my man!" Rita screamed, jumping up with the telephone cord wrapped tightly around her fist and swung. Trig turned in time to catch the base of the phone across the side of his face. With a thump and dull sounding ring, he rolled against the far wall.

Trig grabbed his face in pain. His palm was red and sticky. He looked at Rita through blurred vision and murder in his eyes, then cocked his gun with her in his sights. "Fucking bitch!"

"No! Don't do it Trig! Kill me instead!" Bryann begged, wiggling frantically, trying to break JackHammer's mighty hold.

With his face contorted, arms extended, two hands; strong hand on top, Trig took aim and then turned to his cousin and smiled. "Remember when you compared me to the Devil? Well, witness hell!" he snarled and squeezed one off. The gun discharged like rolling thunder, bright as lightning.

The bullet left its chamber and the room became as quiet as a mausoleum. Bryann could hear himself screaming out his wife's name, but no other sound. Then everything stopped and was frozen in time, as a tiny red dot appeared over Rita's chest. She gasped, then instantly the wall behind her was splattered with blood as the bullet exited, ripping her chest cavity to shreds and tearing a gaping hole in her back. She turned to Bryann and held out her hands with a horrified expression, unable to scream. Trig squeezed the trigger again and again and again, tearing into her body and knocking her backward onto the bed.

"Rita! Noooooooooo!" Bryann screamed but she didn't answer. Bryann reached behind himself and grabbed JackHammer's scrotum and violently twisted it. JackHammer let go of Bryann and hit the floor squealing in agony.

Bryann rushed to Rita's side. There was blood everywhere, all over the walls, the bed, floor, him. "No-no-no-no, please, God, no! Don't let her be dead!" Bryann begged.

But it was too late. She was gone.

He took her in his arms and began crying violently. As he rocked her lifeless body her head slumped forward. "It's okay, baby, I'm here," he said, stroking her sticky wet hair.

Trig saw the perfect opportunity to kill his cousin and lifted his gun, squeezing the trigger. But it was out of bullets.

As Bryann held his wife, something shiny caught his eye, and he glanced over. It was a shard of broken mirror, and through it he could see Trig going for a gun on the floor. Bryann gently laid Rita down and kissed her, the whole while keeping his eyes glued on the piece of mirror. Trig got the thug's gun and was about to shoot when Bryann threw a sharp sidekick, knocking the gun out of his hands. The move caught Trig by surprise, and he froze as Bryann lunged forward and tackled him like a linebacker. Trig tried to gain control of the situation and delivered a combination of punches to Bryann's head and face. But his cousin was blinded by rage and felt nothing.

"Murderer!" Bryann screamed seething with anger, as he

pounded away on Trig's face with fists of fury trying to put his fist through the back of Trig's skull. Trig could not block the barrage of punches and began to feel numb and was blacking out. Bryann showed no signs of letting up. He screamed over and over, "You killed her! You murderer! Coward! Why'd you take her from me? Why?" he cried.

Trig coughed on his own blood and looked at his cousin through swollen eyes, then he fixed his stare on a hanging picture of Bryann, Rita, and Bria. His bruised lips parted, and he whispered. "I trusted you. You betrayed me."

"Who...betrayed...whom?" Bryann replied, then screamed to the top of his lungs and cocked back a raw fist about to deliver yet another devastating blow and remove Trig's loose teeth. Suddenly a hulking hand circled around his neck, and he gasped for air as his feet left the floor.

"Trig, you okay?" JackHammer asked, holding Bryann like a pillow.

Trig nodded his head and struggled to his feet, then placed a gun against Bryann's temple. "You're a dead man!" he mumbled, tasting his own blood.

"This ain't over!" Bryann said with hatred in his eyes.

"Come again?" Trig asked, careful not to get to close.

"As God is my witness in this life, or another. You will pay for what you did to her!"

Trig laughed. Nothing scared him but he found himself nervous and secretly bothered by how Bryann still had the courage to make such a bold threat. He returned the barrel of his revolver between his eyes.

"Uh-uh! After what this prick did to me, a bullet is too good for him!" JackHammer said, stopping Trig in mid-squeeze and slightly stooped as his groin still throbbed.

"Well, what do you suggest?" Trig asked.

"This!" JackHammer shouted, running toward the window with Bryann flailing in his arms like a rag doll. JackHammer rammed Bryann face first through the window. Bryann's eyes widened as he saw the floor of the alley rush at him top speed, then everything went black.

Trig looked out the window at Bryann far below, motionless on the concrete. "I warned you. Empathy will get you killed." he frowned.

"We better bounce!" JackHammer said.

"Yeah," Trig said looking at his watch.

"What about these worthless idiots?" JackHammer asked, pointing at the men on the floor.

"Try and wake them. If they're too fucked up to walk, shoot 'em in the head. I ain't leaving behind nobody to snitch!"

Immediately, Pig sprang up.

After getting everyone to their feet, Trig and his army left Bryann's apartment. He glanced down the hall at the elevator and saw a stick wedged in the door, holding it open. "Which one of you geniuses put this stick in the door?" he demanded.

Pig looked nervous. "I thought if he had to take the stairs up, he'd be tired and we'd have no problem taking him out," he mumbled.

"By the look of your nose, I see your brilliant plan worked."

Pig wanted to ask Trig about his own nose that looked like a squashed tomato but knew it would be suicide.

Trig ordered Pig to remove the stick, and they took the stairs down. As they were nearing the lobby, Trig heard people entering the building downstairs and held a finger to his lips. He heard the elevator open and people get in. "Okay, come on," he whispered. When they entered the empty lobby, the elevator door was closing and between the narrow three-inch space of the door and door entrance, Bria and Trig made full on eye contact. The three-and-a-half-foot tall child innocently smiled and waved at the stranger in what she believed was a nasty Halloween costume. Trig stared back, shocked.

"Aw, shit!" Trig said in JackHammer's truck as they were speeding away with Pig and Slam following in the van.

"What?" JackHammer asked.

"A kid saw me from in the elevator."

"You sure?"

Trig nodded vigorously. "She waved at me."

JackHammer let out a sigh. "Fuck."

"Yo! What's worse? I'm almost certain it was Bryann's brat."

"Trig, she could make a material witness if you ever had to stand trial!"

"No shit, Sherlock!"

"Fuck! It, keeps getting worse."

The vehicles continued driving, putting as much distance between them and the crime scene as possible.

(TO BE CONTINUED)

Alley Katt Volume 2, FAITH; is now available in paperback and for download on all mobile devices. Visit www.chaosonthewrittenpage.com or Amazon.com

HAVOC & MAYHEM

by Derrick A. Bonner

HAVOC AND MAYHEM

The Trouble Consultant Chronicles Volume I

(Excerpt)

Chapter 1

"What's up? You're listening to the super rocking sounds of pure hip hop on 98.7 Kiss WRKS FM - New York City's number one radio station. I'm your host, Kool DJ Red Alert going berserk spinning the phattest jams you wanna hear on the ones and twos. And as we bid a fond farewell to nineteen eight-seven and welcome everybody into eighty-eight, I'm gonna play a new joint by my main man, Brooklyn's own, Big Daddy Kane to kick it off right. It's called Ain't No Half Steppin!"

The Trouble Consultant muted his car stereo then leaned back comfortably behind the wheel of his cherry red '57 Chevy Bel Air with a Sony Watchman on his lap and a sizzling fat blunt between his thumb and trigger finger, stone cold lampin'. Thanks to the dark tinted windows, the car's interior was pitch black and the only sources of light came from the fiery orange glow of the burning blunt and the bluish haze that the watchman gave off. On the miniature screen the ageless avatar of American Bandstand Dick Clark, was dressed warmly on the streets of New York. In the background, countless vibrant screaming people wearing party hats and plastic glasses that blinked 'Happy New Year' shook noisemakers and blew into plastic horns for the camera.

"Welcome back to Times Square! It is now less than 3 minutes 'til midnight when the ball will drop and this crowd will go wild. For this very moment they have all gathered. They are ready, they are anxious and they've all got their eyes on that lighted ball atop a seventy-foot flagpole hoisted twenty-two stories up in the air. We are just moments away from the count down to the year nineteen-eighty-eight. The ball is in place and I have just gotten word that it's ready to drop!"

The Trouble Consultant watched through tight eyes as he took a long deep toke, powerful enough to make a Rastafarian pass out. After exhaling he counted along as the famous apple shaped red ball of lights began its traditional year-end descent down the long pole to ring in the New Year. "Ten-nine-eight-seven-six-five-four-three-two-one-HAPPY NEW YEAR! Different year, same bullshit!" he said in a voice of pure gravel made rougher from an endless stream of blunts and Newports. He switched off the miniature television then laid his head back on the headrest enjoying his buzz as the night came alive with drunken shouting and gunfire on the mean streets of East New York. It was New

Years, Brooklyn style; top of the motherfucking food chain! The blunt had The Trouble Consultant feeling no pain, but he didn't want to get too lifted because he had a job to do. So, he put it out in the ash tray for later, then tilted back and put a couple of drops of Visine in each eye to get the red out. Now he was in the right frame of mind to work. He studied the intimidating-looking guard across the street standing outside of the dilapidated brownstone then cracked open a strawberry Calvin Cooler from the six pack on the floor. After emptying the bottle with one huge gulp to get rid of the dry mouth, he then fixed his stare into the rearview mirror and focused his attention on the passenger in the back seat.

"Aight partner, listen up back there. This is a simple job. I'ma go in, get the goods, come back out. Piece of cake. I don't anticipate needing any back up. So keep your overzealous ass in the car. If I need you, I'll call you. Are we clear?" The Trouble Consultant asked, and a deep throaty grunt was heard indicating that while the message was received, it wasn't appreciated. "Cool!" he said, then got out. The Trouble Consultant paused, snapped his fingers and removed twin Glocks with pearl handles from behind his back before tossing them under the seat. He slid a pair of leather gloves over his sharp-scarred knuckles, a bell Kangol hat on his head and covered his eyes with a pair of expensive Cazal frames. Taking one last look in the mirror, he checked the pulse on his neck. It was beating like a racehorse. He exhaled. No matter how many consulting gigs he performed in the past, the minutes right before it went down were always a little stressful. "Time to make the doughnuts," he said to himself. The frosty temperature didn't faze him at all as a gust of wind escorted him across the street. The Trouble Consultant pulled his collar up just beneath his dark eyes and went to the pay phone on the corner. He fed it some coins and after the third ring, someone picked up. "Hello…Yes, it's taken care of. I'll stop by your restaurant around closing time to collect the other half of my fee," he assured the person on the other end. After hanging up, he made a second call, turning his frown upside down when a familiar voice answered.

"Hello…" he began. "Hey brat. What are you still doing up?…Oh she did, huh…And Happy New Year to you too…Yeah, I saw it drop…On that little TV set you and Mommy got me for Christmas…No you don't get any New Year gifts…Because…Just because…Wasn't Christmas last week?…And isn't your birthday next week?…Well okay then, stop being so greedy begging Billy…Okay we'll talk about it tomorrow. Now put mommy on the phone…I love you too…Mmmwwaa kiss-kiss…Okay bye…" The Trouble Consultant rolled his eyes at his kid sister's antics. "Tee-Tee stop playing around and put Mommy on the phone before my money runs out…C'mon Tee-Tee. Quit play-heyyy

Mommy-O, how're you doing?…Fine, I'm just calling to say Happy New Year. You know I can't start off the new year without speaking to you and the brat…So you're still coming over tomorrow?…Cool…No Ma I didn't forget…I'm headed over to see him as soon as I leave this party…Of course I'm in a safe neighborhood," he said surveying the area smack dab in the middle of a bad place to be even in the daytime. "Nothing major," he continued as he noticed the tough looking guard outside the brownstone frisking a shyste looking man. "Just kicking it with some decent people to celebrate…. Yes, I promise to be careful…No, I won't be out too late. Stop worrying, I'll be fine. Listen, I'm about to head inside so I gotta go. See you mañana…I love you too Ma, bye."

Feeling like a first–class heel for lying to his mother, the Trouble Consultant hung up the phone. But he knew she would sleep much easier thinking the worse that could happen to her precious baby boy was he'd wake up with a killer hangover from too much celebrating. He pushed the guilt out of his head as he approached the screw-faced guard eyeing him, while mumbling into a walkie-talkie and trying to keep warm in a red and black Lumberjack jacket, with the hat to match.

"The Hawk's out tonight huh Big Man?" The Trouble Consultant greeted cheerfully.

"Fuck you want?" the Lumberjack growled sizing him up and down. He was so black the Vaseline on his face had him looking like a patent leather Easter shoe.

"Any action going on inside?"

"It's a hoe house. There's always action going on inside."

"True dat!"

"So, you wastin' my time or what?"

"Neither yours, nor mines," The Trouble Consultant said then held out his arms to be frisked.

The Lumberjack started at his wrists and worked his way down to his ankles checking for weapons. "Aight Money-grip, you straight."

The Trouble Consultant nodded and swung the open door open, then entered the house of ill repute. Making his way down the narrow hall, he could hear loud music coming from up ahead. Exiting through hanging beads in the doorway he paused and muttered, "Never judge a book by its cover."

The brothel's interior was nothing like its exterior. It was an exotic refuge from the outside world. Luxurious, warm and clean, decorated nicely with hanging plants, colorful throw rugs, matching curtains, leather furniture and glass tables. A live Christmas tree patiently awaiting to be tossed in the garbage stood in the corner and a few blinking decorations adorned the walls.

Bikini and hot-pants-clad women were lounging on couches, laughing, smoking weed and sipping champagne as pioneer rap group, Funky Four plus One's song 'That's the Joint' played in the background courtesy of a huge ghetto blaster boom box.

With stubble on his face and caution in his eyes, the Trouble Consultant flirted back with the bevy of beautiful women as he made his way towards a woman hairier than a Wookie and the size of Jabba the Hut, furiously twisting on a Rubik's Cube. Frustrated she couldn't solve the puzzle, she began peeling off the colored squares and putting them back on in the correct sequence. The Trouble Consultant pegged Jabba for the resident Madam and approached the disgusting example of womanhood gone wrong.

"Hello," he said.

The Madam glared at him as she practically sucked the filing out of her left rear molar. "So what chu want?" she inquired with an attitude.

"Well, it's New Years, and I can't think of a better way to ring it in than with a woman who will, fuck for a buck, holler for a dollar, do something strange for a lil bit of change, Miss um?" he pried for her name.

"Bitsy. As in itsy," she informed him. The Trouble Consultant's amused expression asked, *'are you serious?'* as he eyed the woman who was so ugly if she went into a haunted house, she'd come out with a job application.

"Look," she snapped. "Just go on over there and choose one of dem hoes. When you're ready come back to me for your room key. Rooms are twenty bucks an hour and whatever y'all do is between y'all. Oh and before I forget here, you get a free bottle of Asti Spumante compliments of Diamond Ken. Happy New Year."

Bitsy unenthusiastically handed him a bottle of bottom shelf champagne from the milk crate at her feet. The Trouble Consultant nodded thanks then glanced over his shoulder at the noisy ladies partying in the back. There was every type of woman for every type of preference. Thin, thick, short, tall, long hair, short hair, black, white, Latina and Asian. Basically, the United Nation of hoes. The effects of the cheap champagne were beginning to take control as two of the friendlier girls began dancing seductively under the mistletoe, kissing and groping one another. Drunk and caught up in the moment, one of them snatched the mistletoe down and held it just below her navel as her giggling partner puckered up and buried her face beneath it. The lewd act started a quick trend that spread throughout the room like a venereal disease and it wasn't long before the other prostitutes were wiggling out of their clothes with no shame oblivious to the rest of the room.

The Trouble Consultant watched the rising orgy for a hot second then looked over at Bitsy and frowned. The chunky Madam was becoming aroused and licked her lips while rubbing on her cellulite marked thighs.

"Hey Bitsy, wanna chill out with the self-love? You're gonna make me throw up everything I've ever ate," he said before blocking her view with a picture. "This here is the girl I want," he said with an all-business intensity.

Bitsy rolled her eyes at him, then snatched the picture and stared at the pretty black girl with long braids covered in white beads, Stevie Wonder style. Her eyes widened as she quickly regained her composure with an uninterested pout. "Where'd you get the snapshot?" she asked with a raised brow.

"I'm a huge fan," he said unconvincingly.

"Is that right? Well sorry. She ain't here," she shrugged.

"You sure about that?"

"Yeah I'm sure! What I gots ta lie to you fo'?" she snapped defensively. The Trouble Consultant could see the word 'LIAR' practically rise out of her forehead. He had been staking out the whorehouse for the past couple of hours and saw the girl in the picture come and go constantly with different men. He was about to cancel the job and settle for only half his consulting fee, because she obviously wanted to be there. Then ten minutes prior to Dick Clark's countdown, things switched up when he saw her try to leave and get dragged back inside kicking and screaming by a large fat man. She hadn't come back out since.

"Hmm, now that's funny because I heard from a very reliable source that I could find her here," The Trouble Consultant said, referring to himself.

"Well, they can't be all that reliable, cause ya heard wrong. Now like I said either choose one of them or breakout," Bitsy huffed.

"Nah. I gotta better idea. How about I chill out just in case she decides to come back," he said, ignoring her attitude and got comfortable on the black leather sofa across the room.
Bitsy sucked her teeth at The Trouble Consultant then gave him her back and snatched the phone off the hook. From his past experience in dealing with situations of this type he knew she was calling whoever it was she answered to. No doubt Mister complimentary champagne himself, Diamond Ken. "Hello, Faye? Put Diamond on the phone…Hello Diamond? There's some guy down here asking a whole bunch of questions about Mercedes. I think he's Five-O, cause he has a picture of her," Bitsy whispered into the receiver.

"Well, whoever the fuck he is he ain't a cop. That's for damn sure. I paid them crooked bastards off yesterday. He's more than likely just some lonely trick that heard about her vertical skills. You tell his stalker ass she's not here and if he doesn't want one of them hoes you got down there, then he can take his business elsewhere," a stern voice said on the opposite end.

Bitsy glanced over at the man in question as he turned down a big-breasted woman's advances who playfully removed his Kangol.

"I already told him that, but his bald-headed ass won't leave."

There was a long pregnant pause on the other end. "…Did you say bald?"

"Yeah he's bald. Why?" Bitsy asked.

"…Describe this guy to me," Diamond Ken asked with sudden concern in his voice.
Bitsy clocked the Trouble Consultant as he placed his Kangol back on his head,

"Well, he's a big guy, solid as a brick wall. Over six feet tall with a chest wide enough to play handball on. He looks to be in his late twenties or early thirties. And his voice is crazy deep. Kinda like a cross between Barry White and Tone Loc."

"What else?" the voice on the opposite end asked.

"Um I dunno, he's brown skinned. He's got a moustache and a goatee anything else you want to know?"

"Just one more thing. And this is very-very-VERY important….is he dressed in all red?"

Bitsy inconspicuously glanced back over at the mystery man who in the blink of an eye graduated from a random John, to a person of interest and studied his sharp style of dress. Just as Diamond Ken feared, everything he wore was the same crimson complexion. He was cloaked in a ruby red leather trench coat, wine colored leather gloves, an open collared magenta silk shirt, sharply creased cinnamon slacks, a copper snakeskin belt and tomato red Clarks Wallabee suede shoes. Even his argyle socks were maroon. Atop his dome sat a rose colored Kangol same as the Cazal frames hiding his eyes.

"Hey how'd you know that?" she asked cautiously.

"Fuck me! I hope I'm wrong, but I think that's Havoc," Diamond Ken said nervously.

"Havoc? As in Havoc and Mayhem? I thought they was just some corny ass ghetto rumor."

"Yeah, well that so-called rumor knocked the gold fronts down my homeboy Roc's throat so deep, dat fool has to stick his toothbrush up his ass just so he can brush them. Buss it, keep him there, I'll handle this."

"No problem Dee. I got your back," Bitsy said picking up on the reverence and fear in Diamond Ken's voice. In all the years she had known the evil natured cold as ice drug-pushing pimp, she had never witnessed anyone or anything take him off of his game. Until now. Which led her to believe that the mysterious man dripping in red might very well be Satan himself, here to personally escort the diabolical pimp to Hell for his life of sin. Bitsy hung up the phone and approached The Trouble Consultant with a three-dollar bill smile. "So, how are we doing?" she asked cheerfully.

"Chillin' like Bob Dylan," he replied while mindlessly spinning a thin gold whistle on a medium sized rope chain around his finger. By the sudden metamorphosis in her attitude he anticipated something was about to go down.

A second later, it did. The Lumberjack came in out of the cold and locked the door. "Roaches check in, but they don't check out!" The man hissed with an evil grin. At the same time another scary man larger than life came down the stairs shaking the structure with his weight and jingling from the Mr. T starter kit around his neck.

"This oughta be fun!" Bitsy smirked anticipating a good show as she pumped up the volume on the boom box then tore into a bag of Doritos.

'Another One Bites the Dust' by Queen began to play. Rising from his seat, The Trouble Consultant felt like he was in the middle of an action movie complete with soundtrack. He placed his chain and whistle back over his head and calmly removed his gloves with his teeth shaking his head with a sigh. The questions, the lies, the big tough guys. It had all become so boringly routine.

"Hey, little red riding hood. Diamond Ken wants to see you," The Lumberjack said while walking up on the Trouble Consultant from behind. As he put his hand on his shoulder, The Trouble Consultant growled at the hand like a junkyard dog.

"Yo Money-grip. I should warn you that my patience is about as long as the hair on the top of my head," he stated.

"Ooh I'm shitting in my pants. Now move it tough guy! Let's go!" The Lumberjack hissed unimpressed with a sharp shove.

Suddenly in a one handed move the Trouble Consultant removed the Lumberjack's hand from his shoulder, twisting his arm behind his back, bending it at an unnatural angle forcing him to drop to one knee.

"You're an eggshell," The Trouble Consultant said.

"Ow-shit! Fuck! Huh-a what?" the Lumberjack asked cringing in pain.

"An eggshell my friend."

"What the hell are you talking about?"

"Oh, it's quite simple. A few pounds of applied pressure anywhere on the body and-snap!" The Trouble Consultant said and with a gruesome popping sound, he dislocated the Lumberjack's arm like a bread stick. "See, what'd I tell you? An eggshell," he affirmed. The Lumberjack's shrieks blended with the prostitutes as a grotesque lump strained from his sleeve. The Trouble Consultant could no longer take his screaming and clubbed him over the head with his bottle of Asti Spumante before rolling his frustrated eyes. "I hate it when heads be frontin' like they're from Rikers Island, knowing good and damn well they're from Fantasy Island." he snapped.

Everything was happening so fast that Mr. T never had time to act. The Trouble Consultant walked up on him with eyes so mean they had no room for fear in them whatsoever and said, "Either I'm going past you or through you. But I am going up those stairs. Make a decision."

The hired muscle paused for a second thinking over his options. He then went for his gun but before he could pull out, an overhand right stretched him out like a throw rug.

"Too late!" The Trouble Consultant growled.

"Rasheed!" Bitsy screamed when she saw her baby brother go down, then clambered out of her seat and stared down the man responsible with murder in her eyes. "Ooh you done fucked up now!" she barked.

"That so? Well, come on Big Momma! Toro!" he goaded her flapping the tail of his coat like a matador. With a snarl and grunt Bitsy, charged forward like a runaway bull. The Trouble Consultant coolly waited for her to get closer then at the last possible second, stepped to the side, yanked open the closet door behind him and slammed her inside. He then braced a chair up against the doorknob, barricading the hefty woman inside. His adrenaline went from zero to one hundred in three seconds when a third man with dreadlocks appeared at the top clutching a Choo-Choo automatic and reminded him that this shit was real. Deadly real! Mechanically he reached behind his back for his own burners and swore loudly remembering that they were under his car seat.

The dreadlocked gunman shouted, "Bon Fi-yah!" at the top of his lungs.

"Oh shit!" the Trouble Consultant yelled and dove over the banister as the Jamaican opened fire with a shower of hot steel. Meanwhile, below the staircase amidst the panicked prostitutes running out the door screaming for their lives, Mr. T was regaining consciousness when a pair of red size thirteen Wallabees dropped out of the sky and lullabied him back to sleep. Relieving the pitiful fool of his weapon, the Trouble Consultant scrambled to his feet and fired up from below into the shooter's legs then stepped over him as he tumbled down the stairs. Once he reached the top of the stairs, he faced down two more of Diamond Ken's goons. The bigger of the two grabbed him in a bear hug, lifting him off the ground and squeezing until the Trouble Consultant, could hardly breathe before dropping his gun over the banister. The second rushed forward wildly swinging, burying his fists in his ribs and kidneys. Ignoring the pain, the Trouble Consultant kicked him in the chest, knocking him down before slamming his head back breaking the nose of the man holding him. With the fight taken out of him, he was tossed over the banister. The second man climbed to his feet and tossed a few misguided punches that were no match for the Trouble Consultant's vicious street-fighter moves as he 52 blocked them and sent him flying over the banister as well.

After taking out the trash, the Trouble Consultant brushed his hands together then rolled his eyes as four more huge goons appeared.

"Aw geez fellas for crying out loud! Didn't you Bro-tards see what I just did to Kid and Play back there? I mean honestly, why would you wanna put yourselves through that?" he asked earnestly. Unfazed, the leering crew advanced forward. "All right. But for your sake, I hope you have good medical and dental," he said raising his hands defensively and switched to a South-Paw fighting stance. "Let's do this!" Then, using good footwork, sharp jabs, elbows, knees, clenches, his opponents as barriers against each other, all the while sticking and moving, he proceeded to tear through the motley crew like a tornado. Once they were down for the count he called out for Mercedes down the long brown-carpeted hall. Muffled cries and the sounds of someone being abused came from behind the first door on his right. He violently kicked the door off its hinges only to discover an androgynous pale-faced man on all fours getting spanked by a shapely dominatrix in a leather corset, nipple rings, 6-inch spikes and panties to hide her modesty. "Oops my bad. Carry on," the Trouble Consultant frowned. A woman's sudden screams for help snatched his head alert and he took off. He burst into the room where the screams came from and discovered a naked woman with her back facing him. She wore her hair in long braids with white beads, Stevie Wonder style. "Mercedes?" he asked unsure. She shook her braids as if to say "yes" but he was suspicious. A 'trouble consulting' gig was never this easy. But then again, there's a first time for everything. "Throw something on, time to leave!" The Trouble Consultant instructed.

"Maybe it's you who should leave," the naked woman said and turned around in slow motion with her hands wrapped around a shiny silver nickel-plated 22. and a wide smile across her face. "In a pine box!"

"Shit!" it was the right hairstyle, but the wrong girl.

"Hands behind your head handsome. Now! Do it!" the naked imposter barked. With no other choice, the Trouble Consultant reluctantly obeyed.

"Diamond, I found him. He's out here baby," she yelled.

The door snatched open and a gaudy figure stepped out holding a double-barreled shotgun. Covered in sparkling jewelry, Diamond Ken was as clichéd as the cocked fedora he sported. In his left ear he wore a large diamond stud. All the fingers of both hands were covered in sparkling rings. On one wrist was a diamond bracelet and on the other a glistening diamond faced nugget watch. Even the Cazal shades he sported were diamond laden along the top of the frames. For a brief second, the Trouble Consultant's riveting appearance left the iced-out pimp frozen though he quickly shook it off and cocked the loaded shotgun. "Motherfucking Havoc!" Diamond Ken exclaimed.

Spinning around when he heard his street moniker called, the Trouble Consultant, better known as Havoc, brazenly seized Diamond Ken's wrist. As the two struggled over the shotgun, a misdirected shot fired blowing the naked woman back into the room.

"Faye!" Diamond Ken called out visibly upset over all the revenue he saw flying out of the window. In the blink of an eye Havoc head-butted the pimp to the floor then spun on his heels and zig-zagged down the opposite end of the hall as shotgun blasts chased after him tearing huge chunks into the walls. He came upon another flight of stairs and looked back to see Diamond Ken, gun in tow, coming for him as he bolted up another flight of steps. The third floor was dimly lit and every door he tried was locked. He put his hand on the last doorknob at the end of the hall when Diamond Ken entered the floor.

"You ain't gonna MacGuyver your way outta this one!" Diamond Ken said with a bead on Havoc. Havoc clenched his teeth and twisted the knob. To his surprise it opened, and he burst inside as the pimp fired another missed shot and cursed up a storm. Once inside, he caught his breath and locked the door behind himself. There was a large dresser in the corner and he pushed it in front of the door as a barricade, then backed away awaiting the pimp's forced entry when something moved behind him. He spun around with his fists raised to find a girl in bra and panties gagged with duct tape and handcuffed to an iron ring bolted to the wall. She too had white beaded braids like the girl from the picture but the room was dimly lit and her face was swollen, so Havoc still was not one hundred percent certain if it was her or not. He checked for the picture before remembering that Bitsy never returned it.

"Mercedes?" he asked still unsure. Shaking uncontrollably with fear, the girl managed a nod but that wasn't good enough for

Havoc. Moments ago, Faye claimed to be Mercedes too. He removed the tape from her mouth and asked in a stern voice, "What's your mother's middle name?"

"Huh?" she asked not sure if she heard him correctly.

Havoc clamped his hand around her chin, "Young lady, if you're planning something sneaky, we ain't the two and I ain't the one. Now tell me your mother's middle name!" he demanded.

"It's Jean. Barbara Jean Holiday," she replied meekly.

Havoc glared at the girl then let go of her face hoping that an impostor wouldn't know something as personal as the middle name for the mother of the person they were impersonating. Now that he located the goods, all he had to do was figure out a way to get them both out alive. Piece of cake. Then a toilet flushed.

"Somebody in there?" Havoc asked gesturing towards the bathroom door.

Mercedes nodded with wide frightened eyes and whispered, "Big Fella."

Havoc shook his head and sucked his teeth. "I swear this place is like Christmas, full of surprises."

The bathroom door creaked open and the room instantly became infected with a funky combination of shit and Lysol. Standing in the doorway naked and stretching was a horribly fat black man twice the size of Mount Fuji with thighs the size of infants. The obese man fanned the air and grimaced rubbing his stretch marked belly that hung so low it hid his dick.

"Coming out feeling 'bout ten pounds lighter. Okay baby let's do this," Big Fella suggested then realized he had company. "Nigga, where in da fuck did you come from?" he demanded.

"What did you just call me?" Havoc asked through clenched teeth.

Big Fella waddled over shaking the room with each step.

"What iz you deaf?" The obese man snarled but Havoc did not answer. "I said nigga where…hold up…wait a second. It's you!" A choke gurgled in his throat as his eyes locked on Havoc and traveled over his signature red attire. Nervously, he took a step back as if he'd just seen his own death. "The one who whipped Roc's ass," Big Fella mumbled.

Havoc pushed his Cazals back on his nose and smiled. It was always nice to be recognized for his work. Outside the door Diamond Ken listened with a confident grin, certain that his huge friend would make quick work of his problem. Havoc set it off and hit Big Fella in his large belly that jiggled like jello with no real effect. Big Fella looked down at his sloppy gut, unphased by the punch, then wiggled his eyebrows at Havoc. With a smirk he put Havoc on his back across the room with a hard uppercut punch. The nude obese man waddled over and stood above Havoc smiling victoriously. Havoc, repulsed by the view, climbed to one knee eyeing Big Fella through dark slits, with absolute rage. Then, without warning he planted his fist hard in the center of the fat man's crotch. The pain forced Big Fella's eyes to roll up in his head as he doubled over in pain holding himself. Havoc rose to his feet and dug into his coat pocket and pulled out a massive four-fingered ring that spelled out '**HAVOC**' in big bold block letters which doubled as a pair of brass knuckles and slid it on his left hand.

"A-yo fat ass, wanna know why I wear all red?" Havoc asked in a voice that sounded like boulders crashing. Unable to answer, Big Fella meekly shook his head. "Well aside from the fact I look flyy as hell, it's because it hides the bloodstains on my work clothes!" he explained before twisting back and landing a tremendous blow that exploded Big Fella's face and sent blood spraying like a broken water main.

With one hand protecting his face, Big Fella tried to fight back, while Havoc went to work hitting his torso like a punching bag and landing solid blows until his legs gave out from under him. A final devastating punch sent him crashing to the ground like a ton of bricks.

Once Big Fella was down for the count, Havoc immediately began searching for a way to free Mercedes. On the nightstand next to a hot plate keeping Big Fella's pot of chili steaming was a set of keys. He scooped them up and smiled when they fit Mercedes' shackles. As he prepared to set her free, the doorknob twisted back and forth wildly.

"Hey what the hell's going on in there? Yo Big Fella is everything aight?... Big? Nigga you good?" Diamond Ken called out. After no response it was obvious what had happened to his fat homeboy. "Havoc listen up!" he angrily shouted from the opposite side of the door. "I don't know how the fuck you managed to take out Big Fella, but the only way out of here is past me so open up and make it easier on yourself."

"Yeah, picture that!" Havoc retorted then looked around the room for something to defend himself with. Unable to find anything suitable, he ripped the newspaper from the window and looked before getting a very bright idea.

"I wanna go home!" Mercedes begged frantically.

"Chill. I got this," Havoc said as he forced the window open and let in a surge of freezing air. Suddenly a loud shotgun blast ripped through the door and removed a chunk of the dresser. Mercedes screamed when she saw Diamond Ken's angry face peek through the hole. After blowing off the lock he still could not push open the door because of the heavy dresser and Big Fella's unconscious torso in the way.

"Big Fella… get yo family-sized ass up. Mercedes get over here and help me," Diamond Ken ordered.

"Time to go! Out the window!" Havoc said sharply.

Mercedes looked up from sliding into her clothes, "Out the window?" she asked, nauseous with fear.

Havoc grabbed her by the hand and pointed out the window. "Look, down there. See? Try to aim yourself right there," he said referring to a huge pile of garbage mixed with, snow, clothes and a discarded mattress below the window. "I know it's not much, but if you land on it it'll absorb some of the impact from the fall."

Mercedes was scared and didn't know what to do. "But-but, um I don't -" she stuttered.

"Bitch I know you ain't thinking 'bout leaving with that chump cause if you is, word to my momma you'll be even sorrier than he's gonna be once I get in there!" Diamond Ken threatened.

"Charming guy. I can see why you're having such a hard time debating if you should leave him or not. Here, let me help you decide." Havoc said and grabbed Big Fella's pot of chili that was still bubbling on the hot pot and flung it at the hole in the door Diamond Ken had his face poking through. As the pimp screamed in pain and shouted profanity laced threats Havoc turned to Mercedes. "So, you stayin' or what?" The teenage runaway pictured her face on the side of a milk carton then nodded and nervously climbed out the window. "As soon as you land, head for the red car across the street. But do not open the door! Wait for me I'll be right behind," Havoc instructed.

"Ok." Mercedes meekly said, wondering why he didn't want her to open his car door. She hung for a moment, said a quick prayer then let go screaming and landed on her plump behind. She was sore and would most definitely wake up with bruises tomorrow, but just like Havoc assured her, the combination of snow and trash absorbed the blunt of her fall.

It was now Havoc's turn and as he lowered himself out, he noticed Diamond Ken was no longer at the door. 'Shit!' It was definitely time to leave! He dropped out and when he landed, he was staring up at the business end of the pimp's shotgun.

"Leaving so soon?" Diamond Ken asked with a red scorch mark over his greasy face and winded from galloping down three flights of stairs. "The party's just starting!" he said and kneed Havoc hard in the face. "That's for throwing that hot shit on me!" Havoc tasted his blood and angrily went to stand. "Ah-ah-ah don't even think about it! Not unless you trying to win first prize in a wet t-shirt contest!" the pimp warned holding his gun threateningly. Havoc cut his eyes at Mercedes trembling with fear then eyed his Chevy across the street. Taking hold of the whistle around his neck, he blew into it, but it made no sound. "Yo homeboy I think your whistle's busted. But if you trying to call the neighborhood watch you're wasting your time. Cause I'm it!" Diamond Ken laughed.

Havoc ignored the pimp and waited for something to happen. Inside of his car a pair of yellow eyes blinked open followed by a deep growl that sounded like a monster. The Chevy's back door opened, and everyone was mesmerized as a huge paw stepped into the street making a crunching noise when it's razor-sharp nails dug into the ice. Havoc turned back to Diamond Ken with a devilish grin.

"Nah, my dog whistle works just fine," Havoc smirked. The fearless pimp was paralyzed with terror from what had stepped out of the car. Havoc stood, brushing the snow from his legs and smiled devilishly. "Oh, I see you haven't met my partner. Diamond Ken…meet Mayhem."

The pimp was speechless. As soon as he laid eyes on the tan and reddish canine that stood at an imposing twenty-seven inches high and easily weighed one hundred and thirty pounds with its large, wrinkled head, short black muzzle and big drooling jowls, sporting an intimidating spiked red leather collar, he knew he was not dealing with an ordinary dog.

Sixty percent Mastiff and forty percent Bull dog. Bullmastiffs were bred to be one of the most powerful dogs on the planet and have had many jobs throughout history. Romans used them as war dogs due to their aggressive nature. They were used as fighting dogs in the gladiator pits. In England they guarded livestock and were English gatekeeper's night watch dog and primary source of defense against poachers during the 19th century. And in the 20th century, the Trouble Consultant's primary aid against killer psycho pimps and other deviants.

Diamond Ken's face was tight with anticipation over what the freak of nature was plotting on doing to him. Prior to Mayhem the biggest, meanest looking dog he had ever come across was Terminator, the one-eyed ferocious rottweiler that guarded the auto body mechanic shop on Pitkin Avenue, where he had his car phone and Alpine speakers installed. But compared to Mayhem that mutt was a poodle. Mayhem stretched with a yawn displaying sharp teeth that looked like a shark's grin and caused a tidal wave of muscles to ripple from nose to tail. With shaky hands, Diamond Ken swallowed hard and aimed his shotgun at the large beast.

"NO!" Havoc shouted and kicked the gun from the pimp's hands as a shot fired and snow exploded around Mayhem. Havoc then landed seven lightning-quick punches to his face and stomach until he folded up like lawn furniture.

Holding his ribs and sucking oxygen, Diamond Ken struggled to his feet and whipped out a Rambo knife then held it out menacingly. Mayhem jumped into protective mode. Terrified, the pimp took off running. Havoc cut his eyes at his dog anxiously awaiting his next command.

"Handle that!" Havoc instructed.

In a flash Mayhem took off after the pimp and using the knock and pin method like its ancestors were trained to do against poachers, the powerful dog pounced on top of Diamond Ken causing him to lose his knife and pinned his shoulders with overwhelming strength. A menacing growl drilled a hole in Diamond Ken's ears but to his surprise it didn't come from Mayhem, it came from Havoc.

"Cu-cu-call off your dog man. Please!" Diamond Ken begged as the snow between his crotch turned bright yellow. Havoc was so furious with the pimp for almost shooting his best friend that he was tempted to give the command that would prompt the dog to tear out his throat.

"Mayhem, come." Havoc called deciding against it and threw a kiss in the air while patting his thigh. Mayhem ignored Havoc and stayed put, inhaling the sweet fragrance of fear emitting from Diamond Ken's pores causing the hound to drool all over his face. "Mayhem I said, come!" the dog's master called again this time with authority in his voice and with a salty grunt, Mayhem trotted over to his side. "Good girl. That's my precious girl." Havoc said bowing to kiss her on the head and she wagged her tail then playfully pounced around excitedly like an overgrown puppy pleased she made her master happy. Havoc picked up Diamond Ken's shotgun and placed it to the side of his head like he was about to make a hole in one.

The pimp squeezed his eyes shut and screamed out, "Please don't kill me!" as more urine escaped from his bladder. Havoc pumped the shotgun spilling blue shells all over Diamond Ken.

"You know, I was planning on beating the piss out of you, but I'll fall back. Seeing as how you've already done that for me," Havoc said and chucked the emptied gun then exited without another word with Mercedes trailing behind.

Happy to still be alive, Diamond Ken breathed a sigh of relief, that is until he noticed all the women whose flaws, weaknesses and addictions that he constantly used against them to keep them under his thumb were watching him with Poetic Justice etched across their lips.

Realizing how weak he must look in his stable's eyes the pimp sprang to his feet worried that if he did not do something right now to regain his power over them, he would lose them as well.

"G'wan! Take her junkie ass! After the work she put in tonight she could use the vacation. But mark my words, she'll be back. I mean shit, where the fuck else is a twenty-four seven, super-duper freaky hoe gonna go?" Diamond Ken snickered in a voice as cold as ice chips. Mercedes stopped dead in her tracks and spun around then marched back over to Diamond Ken. "What… back so soon? That didn't take long. Come on hoe. Come back to Daddy," the vile pimp smiled with his arms open wide. Mercedes stopped before him and eyed the man who took advantage of her then without warning, hauled off and slapped him hard across the face and began sobbing uncontrollably.

"How dare you! Who the hell do you think you are?" Diamond Ken snarled and raised his arm to backhand her. Havoc cleared his throat then shook his head as Mayhem growled, warning him that he was about to make a huge mistake. The pimp's arm wisely swung to his side.

Havoc eyed him like he was trash then turned to Mercedes. "Let's get out of here."

With a sniffle and nod, Mercedes marched past the sad faces of fellow streetwalkers. Some were hating, others desperately wished someone loved them enough to hire a Brooklyn-Knight to rescue them. As soon as Havoc slid behind the wheel of his ride, he removed his heavy four-fingered ring because it felt uncomfortable when driving and stuffed it back in his pocket. He then reached under his seat, grabbed his Glocks, then put them back in their holsters. Now he felt whole again. He glanced over at Mercedes. She was staring straight ahead with a blank look and rocking in her seat with her eyes fixed on Diamond Ken still talking like he was the man. Havoc shook his head with a sigh. Deep down he pitied her. She had borne witness to so many loveless acts of sex and violence, yet she wasn't even old enough to sit at a bar and order a drink.

"Hey, don't trip over the people who aren't happy for you. They aren't happy for themselves either. You dig?" Havoc said to her and Mercedes smiled with an understanding nod. He then eyed his dog in the rear-view mirror. "Gimme some," he said reaching an open palm over his shoulder and Mayhem placed her wide paw inside his hand to shake it. Then with a proud papa smile, he twisted the key in the ignition and popped in an eight-track tape. With 'Ooh Child' by the Five Stairsteps playing in the background, he was about to pull off when he heard a loud commotion and looked out the window. "Well will you look at that?" Havoc said as Diamond Ken went from demanding to begging on his hands

and knees that his stable not abandon him. It was painfully clear that he had collected his last pimp's commission off of them. In the game of macking and stacking, a Pimp's job is to dress, rest, finesse and let his hoes take care of the rest. And any self-respecting flesh-peddler who can't keep his shit together, much less his bladder intact might as well turn in his playa' card and fill out an application at some square-ass job because he was done in this field. "Damn, I guess it's true what they say. Pimping ain't easy," Havoc said ruefully then disappeared into the night.
He went in, got the goods and came out. Piece of cake.

HAVOC and MAYHEM; The Trouble Consultant Chronicles Volume 1, is available in paperback and for download on all mobile devices. Visit www.chaosonthewrittenpage.com or Amazon.com